Jack Vance

The Palace of Love

Jack Vance

THE DEMON PRINCES
Book III

The Palace of Love

Jack Vance

Spatterlight Press Signature Series, Volume 40

Published by Spatterlight Press

Cover art by David Russell

ISBN 978-1-61947-111-5

Spatterlight Press LLC
340 S. Lemon Ave #1916
Walnut, CA 91789

www.jackvance.com

Jack Vance

The Palace of Love

CHAPTER I

From *Popular Handbook to the Planets*, 348th edition, 1525:

SARKOVY: Single planet of Phi Ophiuchi.
Planetary constants:

Diameter.....9,600 miles
Sidereal day.....37.2 hours
Mass.....1.40
G......0.98

Sarkovy is moist and cloudy; with an axis normal to the orbital plane it knows no seasons.

The surface lacks physiographical contrast; the characteristic features of the landscape are the steppes: Hopman Steppe, Gorobundur Steppe, the Great Black Steppe, and others... From the abundant flora the notorious Sarkoy venefices leach and distill the poisons for which they are famous.

The population is largely nomadic, though certain tribes, generically known as Night Hobs, live among the forests. (For detailed information regarding the rather appalling customs of the Sarkoy, consult the *Encyclopedia of Sociology* and *The Sexual Habits of the Sarkoy*, by B.A. Egar.)

The Sarkoy pantheon is ruled by Godogma, who carries a flower and a flail and walks on wheels. Everywhere along the Sarkoy steppes may be found tall poles with wheels on high, in praise of Godogma, the striding wheeling God of Fate.

News feature in *Rigellian Journal,* Avente, Alphanor:
Paing, Godoland, Sarkovy: July 12:

> As if Claris Adam were to be destroyed for beguiling William Wales:
>
> As if the Abbatram of Pamfile were to be liquefied for smelling too strongly:
>
> As if Deacon Fitzbah of Shaker City were to be immolated for an excess of zeal:
>
> Today from Sarkovy comes news that Master Venefice Kakarsis Asm must 'cooperate with the guild' for selling poison.
>
> Circumstances of course are not all that simple. Asm's customer, no ordinary murderer, was Viole Falushe, one of the 'Demon Princes'. The essence of the crime was neither 'trafficking with a notorious criminal' nor 'betrayal of guild secrets', but rather 'selling fixed-price poisons at a discount.'
>
> Kakarsis Asm must die.
>
> How? How else?

—~—

THE LONGER ALUSZ IPHIGENIA traveled in the company of Kirth Gersen, the less certain she became that she understood his personality. His moods perplexed her; his behavior was a source of misgiving. His modesty and self-effacement — were they inversion, brooding cynicism? His careful politeness — could it be no more than a sinister camouflage? Such questions entered her mind with increasing frequency, no matter how staunchly she rejected them.

On one occasion — the date was July 22nd, 1526; they sat on the Avente Esplanade in front of the Grand Rotunda — Gersen sought to explain the seeming contradictions of his character. "There's really no mystery. I've been trained to a certain function. It's all I know. To justify the training, to fulfill my life, I exercise the function. It's as simple as that."

Alusz Iphigenia knew the general outlines of Gersen's past. The five 'Demon Princes' joining for the historic raid on Mount Pleasant had destroyed or enslaved five thousand men and women. Among the handful of survivors were Rolf Gersen and his young grandson. Alusz Iphigenia realized that such an experience must alter anyone's life; still she herself had known tragedy and terror. "I am not changed," she told Gersen earnestly. "I feel neither rage nor hate."

"My grandfather felt the rage and hate," said Gersen in rather a flippant tone of voice. "So far as I'm concerned the hate is abstract."

Alusz Iphigenia became even more disturbed. "Are you then just a mechanism? This is mindlessness, to be the instrument of someone else's hate!"

Gersen grinned. "That's not quite accurate. My grandfather trained me, or rather, had me trained, and I am grateful to him. Without the training, I would be dead."

"He must have been a terrible man so to warp a child's mind!"

"He was a dedicated man," said Gersen. "He loved me and assumed I shared his dedication. I did and I do."

"But what of the future? Is revenge all you want from life?"

"'Revenge'? ... I don't think so. I have only one life to live and I know what I hope to achieve."

"But why not try to achieve the same goals through a lawful agency? Isn't this a better way?"

"There isn't any lawful agency. Only the IPCC*, which isn't altogether effective."

"Then why not bring the issues before the people of the Concourse, and the other important worlds? You have the energy, you have more than enough money. Isn't this better than killing men with your own hands?"

Gersen had no rational counter-arguments. "These aren't my talents," he told her. "I work alone, at what I do best."

"But you could learn!"

Gersen shook his head. "If I involve myself with words and harangues, I trap myself; I become futile."

---

* IPCC: Interworld Police Coordination Company — in theory, a private organization providing the local police systems of the Oikumene specialized consultation, a central information file, criminological laboratories; in practice, a supergovernmental agency occasionally functioning as law in itself. The company stock is widely disseminated, and though yielding no great financial return is much in demand.

Alusz Iphigenia rose to her feet. She walked to the balustrade, looked out across the Thaumaturge Ocean. Gersen studied the clear profile, the proud stance, as if he had never seen them before. The time was approaching when he must lose her, and everything that was easy and fresh and uncomplicated would leave his life. The breeze shifted her bright hair; she was looking down into the blue water, watching the shifting glints and planes of Rigel light... Gersen sighed, picked up a newspaper, morosely scanned the front page.

COSMOLOGIST KILLED
Hyrcan Major Attacks Camping Party

Gersen glanced at the text:

> Trovenei, Phrygia: July 21:
>
> Johan Strub, advocate of the star-capture theory, which assigns the original parentage of the Concourse Worlds to Blue Companion, yesterday was set upon by an adult hyrcan major, and almost instantly killed. Dr. Strub and several members of his family were exploring the Midas Mountains of upper Phrygia and unwittingly crossed the elving-platform of a king beast. Before others in his party were able to destroy the eight-foot ogre, Dr. Strub had suffered fatal blows.
>
> Dr. Strub is chiefly noted for his efforts to prove that Blue Companion and the twenty-six worlds of the Concourse were originally an independent system which wandered into the gravitational domain of Rigel. Such a circumstance would explain the disparity in the ages of the Concourse worlds and Rigel, a comparatively young star...

Gersen looked up. Alusz Iphigenia had not moved. He read on:

COSMOPOLIS MAGAZINE ABOUT TO BE SOLD?
Famous Old Journal Faces Extinction;
Directors Make Last-ditch Efforts at Salvage

London, England, Earth: June 25:

The ancient firm of Radian Publishing Company today sought a stop-gap loan to meet the chronic annual deficit incurred in the publication of *Cosmopolis,* the 792-year-old magazine devoted to the life and affairs of the civilized universe. Sherman Zugweil, Chairman of Radian's Board of Directors, admitted a crisis to be at hand, but announced himself confident of coping with it and keeping the doughty old journal in circulation another eight hundred years...

Alusz Iphigenia had shifted her position. Elbows on the balustrade, chin resting in her hands, she studied the horizon. Contemplating the soft contours, Gersen felt himself softening. He now was a man of almost unlimited wealth; they could live a life of wonderful ease and pleasure... Gersen considered a long minute, then shrugged and looked back to the newspaper.

SARKOVY POISON-MASTER TO DIE;
GUILD RULES VIOLATED

Paing, Godoland, Sarkovy: July 12:

As if Claris Adam were to be destroyed...

Alusz Iphigenia turned a glance over her shoulder. Gersen was reading the newspaper in complete absorption. She swung around in outrage. Here was sang-froid indeed! While she wrestled with doubts and conflicts, Gersen read a newspaper: an act of conspicuous insensitivity!

Gersen looked up, smiled. His mood had changed. He had come alive. Alusz Iphigenia's fury ebbed. Gersen was a man beyond her understanding; whether he were vastly more subtle than she or vastly more elemental she would never know.

Gersen had risen to his feet. "We're going on a trip. Across space, toward Ophiuchus. Are you ready?"

"'Ready?' You mean now?"

"Yes. Now. Why not?"

"No reason... Yes, I'm ready. In two hours."

"I'll call the spaceport."

Chapter II

The Distis Spaceship Corporation produced nineteen models, ranging from a version of the 9B to the splendid Distis Imperatrix, with a black and gold hull. With funds derived from his epic looting of Interchange* Gersen had purchased a Pharaon, a spacious craft equipped with such niceties as an automatic atmospheric control which during the course of a voyage gradually altered air pressure and composition to match that of the destination.

Rigel and the Concourse receded. Ahead lay star-spangled darkness. Alusz Iphigenia studied the *Star Directory* with a puzzled frown. "Ophiuchus isn't a star. It's a sector. Where are we going?"

"The sun is Phi Ophiuchi," said Gersen, and, after a barely perceptible pause: "the planet is Sarkovy."

" 'Sarkovy'?" Alusz Iphigenia looked up quickly. "Isn't that where the poisons come from?"

Gersen gave a curt nod. "The Sarkoy are poisoners, no doubt about it."

Alusz Iphigenia looked dubiously out the forward port. Gersen's haste to leave Alphanor had puzzled her. She had credited a sudden determination to alter his way of life; now she was not so sure. She opened *Handbook to the Planets,* read the article on Sarkovy. Gersen stood by the pharmaceutical cabinet, compounding a conditioner against possibly noxious serums, proteins, viruses and bacilli of Sarkovy.

---

* Interchange: an institution of the planet Sasani in the near-Beyond, functioning as a detention depot and broker between kidnappers and those who sought to pay ransom. Gersen had swindled Interchange of ten billion SVU (Standard Value Units).

Alusz Iphigenia asked, "Why are you going to this planet? It seems an evil place."

"I want to talk to someone," said Gersen in a measured voice. He handed her a cup. "Drink this; you'll avoid itches and scabs."

Wordlessly Alusz Iphigenia drank the mixture.

There were no formalities at Sarkovy; Gersen landed at Paing Spaceport, as close as possible to the depot, a timber structure roofed with varnished reeds. A clerk registered them as visitors, and they were immediately set upon by a dozen men wearing dark brown gowns with bristling fur collars and cuffs. Each protested himself the foremost guide and sponsor of the region: "What do you wish, my sir, my lady? A visit to the village? I am a hetman —"

"If it's the sport of *harbite* you seek, I know of three excellent beasts in furious condition."

"Poisons by the dram or pound; I guarantee freshness and precision. Trust me for your poisons!"

Gersen looked from face to face. Several of the men were tattooed on the cheek with a dark blue Maltese cross; one wore two such tattoos. "Your name?"

"I am Edelrod. I know the lore of Sarkovy, marvellous tales. I can make your visit a joy, a period of edification —"

Gersen said, "I see you are a Venefice of the Undermaster category."

"True." Edelrod seemed a trifle crestfallen. "You have visited our world before?"

"For a brief period."

"You come to replenish your chest? Rest assured, sir, I can guide you to fascinating bargains, absolute novelties."

Gersen took Edelrod aside. "You are acquainted with Master Kakarsis Asm?"

"I know him. He is condemned to cooperation."

"He is not dead then?"

"He dies tomorrow night."

"Good," said Gersen. "I will hire you then, provided that your rates are not exorbitant."

"I lend my knowledge, my friendship, my protection: all for fifty SVU per day."

"Agreed. Well then, our first need is conveyance to the inn."

"At once." Edelrod summoned a dilapidated carryall; they bumped and jounced through Paing to the Poison Inn, a three-storied structure with walls of poles, a twelve-cone roof sheathed with green glass tiles. There was a barbaric grandeur to the great lobby. Rugs woven in bold patterns of black, white and scarlet covered the floor; along the wall were pilasters carved to represent attenuated harikap with gaunt sagging faces; vines with green leaves and purple flowers hung from the roof beams. Windows thirty feet high overlooked Gorobundur Steppe, with a black-green swamp to the west, a dark forest to the east. Meals were to be taken in a vast dining room furnished with tables, chairs and buffets of a dense black wood. To Alusz Iphigenia's relief, the kitchen appeared to be operated by outworlders, and they were offered a choice of six cuisines. Alusz Iphigenia nevertheless distrusted the food. "For all we know it's seasoned with some horrid drug."

Gersen made light of her qualms. "They wouldn't waste good poison on us. I can't guarantee much else. This is nomad-style bread, the little black things are reed-berries, and this is some sort of stew or goulash." He tasted it. "I've eaten worse."

Alusz Iphigenia glumly ate the reed-berries, which had a dank smoky flavor. "How long do you plan to remain here?" she asked politely.

"Two days or so, provided all goes well."

"Your business of course is your own affair; but I feel a certain curiosity—"

"There's no mystery. I want information from a man who may not live long."

"I see." But it was plain that Alusz Iphigenia felt no great interest in Gersen's plans, and she remained in the lobby while Gersen sought out Edelrod.

"I would like to speak with Kakarsis Asm. Can this be arranged?"

Edelrod pulled thoughtfully at his long nose. "A ticklish matter. He must 'cooperate with the guild'; such men are guarded carefully, for obvious reasons. Of course I can try to make arrangements. Is expense a critical factor?"

"Naturally. I expect to pay no more than fifty SVU into the guild treasury, another fifty to the Guild-master and perhaps twenty or thirty to you."

Edelrod pursed his lips. He was a plump man of uncertain age, with a pelt of soft heavy black hair. "Your largesse is not of the 'regal' variety. The people of Sarkovy respect reckless liberality above all other virtues."

"If I understand the signs correctly," said Gersen, "I have surprised you by the money I seem willing to spend. The amounts I mentioned are the top limit. If you can't arrange matters at these rates I will inquire of someone else."

"I can only do my best," said Edelrod despondently. "Please wait in the lobby; I will make inquiries."

Gersen went to sit beside Alusz Iphigenia, who pointedly asked no questions... Edelrod presently returned with a jubilant expression. "I have set affairs in motion. The cost will be very little more than the figures you suggested." And he snapped his fingers exultantly.

"I have had second thoughts," said Gersen. "I don't care to speak to Master Asm."

Edelrod became agitated. "But it is feasible! I have approached the Guild-master!"

"Perhaps on another occasion."

Edelrod made a sour grimace. "Foregoing all personal gain, I might arrange matters for some trifling sum—two hundred SVU or thereabout."

"The information is of no great value. I am leaving tomorrow for Kadaing, where my old friend Master Venefice Coudirou can settle everything for me."

Edelrod raised his eyebrows and allowed his eyes to bulge. "Why then! this alters all! You should have mentioned your connection with Coudirou! I believe the Guild-master will accept substantially less than his previous demands."

"You know my top figure," said Gersen.

"Very well," sighed Edelrod. "The interview may be conducted later this afternoon... In the meantime, what are your wishes? Would you care to explore the countryside? The weather is fine; the woods are ablaze with flowers, sultrys, pop-barks; there is a well-drained path."

Alusz Iphigenia, who had been restless, rose to her feet. Edelrod led them along a path which crossed a brackish river and plunged into the forest.

The vegetation was a typical Sarkovy mélange: trees, shrubs, cycads, bubble-shells, grasses of a hundred varieties. The high foliage was for the most part black and brown with occasional splotches of red; below were purples, greens, pale blues. Edelrod enlivened the stroll with a discussion of various plants beside the way. He indicated a small gray fungus. "Here is the source of twitus, an excellent selective poison, fatal only if ingested twice within a week. It ranks in this respect with mervan, which migrates harmlessly to the skin, and becomes a lethal principle only upon exposure to direct sunlight. I have known persons who fearing mervan kept to their tents for days on end."

They came to a little clearing. Edelrod looked sharply in all directions. "I have no overt enemies, but several people have died here recently... Today all seems well. Notice this tree growing to the side." He pointed to a slender white-barked sapling with round yellow leaves. "Some call it the coin-tree, others the good-for-nought. It is completely inoffensive, either as a primary or an operative. You might ingest the whole of it: leaves, bark, pith, roots, and note nothing other than a sluggishness of digestion. Recently one of our venefices became irritated at such insipidity. He made an intensive study of the coin-tree, and after several years finally derived a substance of unusual potency. To be useful it must be dissolved in methycin and wafted into the air as a fog or a mist, whence it enters the corpus through the eyes, causing first blindness, then numbness, then complete paralysis. Think of it! From waste, a useful and effective poison! Is this not a tribute to human persistence and ingenuity?"

"An impressive accomplishment," said Gersen. Alusz Iphigenia remained silent.

Edelrod went on: "We are frequently asked why we persist in deriving our poisons from natural sources. Why do we not immure ourselves in laboratories and synthesize? The answer is of course that natural poisons, being initially associated with living tissue, are the more effective."

"I would suspect the presence of catalyzing impurities in the natural poisons," Gersen suggested, "rather than metaphysical association."

Edelrod held up a minatory finger. "Never scoff at the role of the mind! For instance—let me see...there should be one somewhere near...Yes. See there: the little reptile."

Under a mottled white and blue leaf rested a small lizard-like creature.

"This is the meng. From one of his organs comes a substance which can be distributed either as ulgar or as furux. The same substance, mind you! But when sold as ulgar and used as such, the symptoms are spasms, biting off of the tongue and a frothing madness. When sold and used as furux, the interskeletal cartilage is dissolved so that the frame goes limp. What do you say to that? Is that not metaphysics of the most exalted sort?"

"Interesting, certainly...Hm...What occurs when the substance is sold and used as, say for the sake of argument, water?"

Edelrod pulled at his nose. "An interesting experiment. I wonder... But the proposal encases a fallacy. Who would buy and administer an expensive vial of water?"

"The suggestion was poorly thought out," admitted Gersen.

Edelrod made an indulgent gesture. "Not at all, not at all. From just such apparent folly come notable variations. The graybloom, for instance. Who would have ever suspected the virtue to be derived from its perfume, until Grand Master Strubal turned it upside down and left it in the dark for a month, whereupon it became tox meratis? One waft will kill; the venefice need merely walk past his subject."

Alusz Iphigenia stooped to pick up a small rounded pebble of quartz. "What horrible substance do you produce from this stone?"

Edelrod looked away, half-embarrassed. "None whatever. At least none to my knowledge. Though we use such pebbles in ball-mills to crush photis seed to a flour. Never fear; your pebble is not so useless as it seems!"

Alusz Iphigenia tossed it away in disgust. "Unbelievable," she muttered, "that people should dedicate themselves to such activity."

Edelrod shrugged. "We serve a useful purpose; everyone occasionally needs poison. We are capable of this excellence and we feel duty-bound to pursue it." He inspected Alusz Iphigenia with curiosity. "Have you no skills of your own?"

"No."

"At the hotel you may buy a booklet entitled *Primer to the Art of Preparing and Using Poisons,* and I believe it includes a small kit of some basic alkaloids. If you are interested in developing a skill —"

"Thank you. I have no such inclination."

Edelrod made a polite gesture, as if to acknowledge that each must steer his own course through life.

They continued; in due course the forest thinned, the path turned out upon the steppe. At the edge of town stood a long eight-coned structure of iron-bound timber with ten iron doors facing to the steppe. Across an area of packed clay were hundreds of small booths and shops. "The caravanserai," explained Edelrod. "This is the seat of the Convenance, from which the judgments come." He pointed to a platform at the top of the caravanserai, where four caged men gazed disconsolately down into the square. "To the far right stands Kakarsis Asm."

"Can I speak to him now?" Gersen asked.

"I will go to inquire. Wait, if you please, at this booth, where my grandmother will prepare you a fine tea."

Alusz Iphigenia looked dubiously at the appurtenances of the booth. On a plank a brass urn bubbled furiously, flanked by brass drinking pots. Shelves displayed a hundred glass jars containing herbs, roots and substances impossible to identify.

"All clean and salubrious," Edelrod declared cheerfully. "Rest and invigorate yourselves; I will return with good news."

Alusz Iphigenia wordlessly seated herself at a bench. After consultation with Edelrod's grandmother Gersen procured pots of mildly stimulating verbena tea. They watched a caravan trundling in from the steppe: first an eight-wheeled wagon carrying the shrine, the cabin of the hetman and brass tanks of water. Behind were several dozen other wagons, some large, some small, motors rumbling, clacking, whining. All carried astounding super-structures at the very peak of which were tented living quarters, with goods and bales loaded below. Some men rode motorcycles, others lounged on the wagons, which were driven by old women or slaves of the tribe. Children ran behind, rode bicycles or dangled perilously from the understructure.

The caravan halted; women, children arranged tripods, hung up cauldrons and began to prepare a meal, while slaves unloaded goods from the wagons: furs, rare woods, bundles of herbs, chunks of agate and opal, caged birds, tubs of raw gums and poisons, and two captive harikap, the near-intelligent creature which furnished the sport at the Sarkoy sport known as *harbite*. Meanwhile the men of the tribe gathered in a quiet suspicious cluster to drink tea and glower toward the bazaar where they expected to be cheated.

Edelrod stepped briskly forth from the caravanserai. Gersen grumbled to Alusz Iphigenia, "Here he comes with six reasons why the business will cost more money."

Edelrod procured an infusion of scorched ajol from his grandmother. He sat down and silently began to sip.

"Well?" asked Gersen.

Edelrod sighed, shook his head. "My arrangements have been for naught. The Chief Monitor declares the interview impossible."

"Just as well," said Gersen. "I only wished to bring him the condolences of Viole Falushe. It will make small difference one way or another. Where will he 'cooperate'?"

"At the Poison Inn, as diversion for the Convenance, which currently is in residence at Paing."

"Perhaps I will have a chance to utter a few words there, or at least make a reassuring signal," said Gersen. "Well, then, let us look through the bazaar."

Subdued and depressed, Edelrod took them through the bazaar. Only in the Poison Quarter did he recover his animation, and pointed here and there to bargains and especially noteworthy preparations. He seized a ball of gray wax. "Observe this deadly material! I handle it without fear: I am immunized! But if you were to rub it on an article belonging to your enemy — his comb, his ear-scraper — he is as good as gone. Another application is to spread a film over your identification papers. Then, should an over-officious administrator hector you, he is contaminated and pays for his insolence."

Alusz Iphigenia took a deep breath. "How does a Sarkoy survive to become an adult?"

"Two words," Edelrod replied, holding two fingers didactically high. "Caution, immunity. I am immune to thirty poisons. I carry indicators and alarms to warn of cluthe, meratis, black-tox and vole. I observe the most punctilious caution in eating, smelling, donning garments, bedding with a strange female—ha! ha! Here is a favorite trick, and the over-impulsive lecher finds himself in difficulties. But to go on. I am cautious in these situations and also in passing downwind of a covert, even though I have no fear of meratis. Caution has become second nature. If I suspect that I have or am about to have an enemy, I cultivate his friendship and poison him, to diminish the risk."

"You will live to become an old man," said Gersen.

Edelrod reverently made a circular motion with his two hands, moving in opposite directions, to symbolize a halting of Godogma's wheel. "Let us hope so. And here—" he pointed to a bulb containing white powder "—cluthe. Useful, versatile, effective. If you need poison, buy here."

"I have cluthe," said Gersen. "Though it may be somewhat stale."

"Discard it, or you will be disappointed," Edelrod told him earnestly. "It will merely provoke suppurating sores and gangrene." He turned to the dealer. "Your stock is fresh?"

"Fresh indeed, fresh as the morning dew."

After a bout of heated bargaining Gersen bought a small casket of cluthe. Alusz Iphigenia stood with her back turned, her head at an angle of angry disapproval.

"Now then," said Gersen, "back to the hotel."

Edelrod said tentatively, "A thought occurs to me. Were I to bring the monitors a cask of high-quality tea, at a cost of perhaps twenty or thirty SVU, they might well allow your visit."

"By all means. Make them such a gift."

"You will naturally reimburse me?"

"What? When you already have been conceded a lavish hundred and twenty SVU?"

Edelrod made an impatient gesture. "You do not realize the difficulties!" He snapped his fingers petulantly. "Very well. So be it. My friendship for you impels me to sacrifice. Where is the money?"

"Here is fifty. The remainder after the interview."

"What of the lady? Where will she wait?"

"Not here in the bazaar. The nomads might consider her part of the merchandise."

Edelrod chuckled. "Such events have been known. But have no apprehension! She is under the aegis of Submaster Iddel Edelrod. She is as safe as a two-hundred-ton statue of a dead dog."

But Gersen insisted on hiring a conveyance and sending Alusz Iphigenia back to the Poison Inn. Edelrod then conducted Gersen into the caravanserai, through a set of halls, up to the roof. Six monitors hulked on stools beside a bubbling cauldron. Hitching fur collars up around their necks, they glanced incuriously at Edelrod, then turning back to their tea, muttered among themselves: evidently a satiric observation for they all gave hoarse caws of amusement.

Gersen approached the cage of Kakarsis Asm, one-time Master Venefice, now condemned to 'cooperation'. Asm was somewhat taller than the average Sarkoy, though still bulky through chest and belly. His head was long, narrow in the forehead, broad at the cheekbones, heavy at the mouth. A thick black pelt grew low down his forehead; his lank black mustache drooped dispiritedly. In keeping with his criminal status, he wore no shoes, and his feet, tattooed with wheels in the traditional fashion, were mottled pink and blue with cold.

Edelrod addressed Asm in a peremptory voice: "Villainous dog, here is a nobleman from off-world who deigns to inspect you. Be on your best behavior."

Asm raised his hand as if he were casting poison; Edelrod jumped back with a startled oath, and Asm laughed. Gersen turned to Edelrod: "Wait to the side. I wish to speak privately to Master Asm."

Edelrod grudgingly withdrew. Asm, seating himself on a stool, inspected Gersen with eyes like flints. "I have paid to speak to you," said Gersen. "In fact I come from Alphanor for this purpose."

Asm made no response.

"Has Viole Falushe made representations on your behalf?" asked Gersen.

A gleam shone behind the near-opacity of the eyes. "You come from Viole Falushe?"

"No."

The gleam died.

"It would seem," said Gersen, "that having involved you in wrongdoing, he should likewise be here, sentenced to 'cooperation'."

"There's an agreeable thought," said Asm.

"I don't fully understand the crime. You were caged and sentenced because you sold to a notorious criminal?"

Asm snorted, spat into a corner of the cage. "How should I recognize him as Viole Falushe? I knew him long ago under a different name. He has changed; he is unrecognizable."

"Why then should you be sentenced to 'cooperation'?"

"The decretal was clear enough. The Guild-master had prepared a special price schedule for Viole Falushe. All unaware I sold him two drams of patziglop and a dram of vole; little enough, but there can be no remission. The Guild-master has long been my enemy, though he has never dared to test my poisons." He spat again, glanced reflectively sidewise at Gersen. "Why should I talk with you?"

"Because I will undertake that you die by alpha or beta, rather than 'cooperation'."

Asm gave a sad sardonic snort of regret. "With Guild-master Petrus on the scene? Small chance. He wishes to test his new pyrong."

"Guild-master Petrus can be persuaded. By money if no other means."

Asm shrugged. "I expect little, but what then? I lose nothing by talk. What do you wish to know?"

"I take it Viole Falushe has departed the planet?"

"Long ago."

"Where and when did you know him previously?"

"Long ago. How many years? Twenty? Thirty? A long time. He was then a slaver, but very young. No more than a boy. Indeed, he was the youngest slaver I had yet known. He arrived in a rickety old ship bulging with young girls, all fearful of his wrath. Would you believe it? They were happy to be sold to me!" Asm shook his head in wonder. "A terrible young man! He quaked and quivered with the force of his passions. Today he is different. The passion is still terrible, but Viole Falushe has grown to surround it. He is a different man."

"What was his name when you first knew him?"

Asm shook his head. "It escapes me. I do not know. Perhaps I never knew. He traded two fine girls for money and poison. They cried with relief to leave the ship. The others cried from their ill-fortune. Ah, what sobbing!" Asm gave his head a wry shake. "Inga and Dundine were their names. How they would chatter! They knew the lad well and never tired of reviling him."

"What became of them? Do they still live?"

"There I am ignorant." Asm jumped to his feet, strode back and forth, returned as abruptly to his stool. "I was called south to Sogmere. I sold the girls. There was little depreciation; I had only used them two years."

"Who bought them?"

"It was Gascoyne the Wholesaler, of Murchison's Star. I can tell no more, for this is all I know."

"And where was the first home of the girls?"

"Earth."

Gersen ruminated a moment. "And Viole Falushe as he is now: what is his description?"

"He is a tall man, well-favored. His hair is dark. He has no remarkable or distinguishing features. I knew him when his madness was rampant, when it altered the look of his face. Now — he is careful and polite. He speaks softly. He smiles. His condition might never be known, unless, like me, you had known him as a lad."

Gersen asked further questions: Asm was unable to augment his remarks. Gersen prepared to depart. Asm, feigning indifference, said, "You intend to speak to Guild-master Petrus on my behalf?"

"Yes."

Asm thought a moment. He opened his mouth and spoke, as if it were an effort: "Be careful. He is a positive man, and baleful. If you thrust at him over-strongly, he will poison you."

"Thank you," said Gersen. "I hope to be able to help you." He signaled Edelrod, who had watched in poorly disguised curiosity. "Take me to Guild-master Petrus."

Edelrod led Gersen down into the caravanserai, by one crooked hall after another, finally to a room hung with yellow silk. On a cushion sat a thin man with intricately tattooed cheeks examining a row of small flagons. "An outworld gentleman to speak to the Guild-master," said Edelrod.

The thin man hopped erect, approached Gersen, carefully smelled his hands, patted his garments, inspected his tongue and teeth. "One moment." He disappeared behind the silks. Presently he returned to signal Gersen. "This way, if you will."

Gersen entered a high windowless chamber — so high indeed the ceiling could not be seen. Four spherical lamps hanging low on long chains threw an oily yellow light. On the table the ubiquitous brass cauldron bubbled. The air was heavy with warmth and odor: must, fabric, leather, sweat, the sharp dry exhalation of herbs. Guild-master Petrus had been sleeping. Now he was awake, and leaning forward from his couch, tossed herbs into a pot and prepared an infusion. He was an old man with bright black eyes, a pallid skin. He greeted Gersen with a quick nod.

Gersen said, "You're an old man."

"I have one hundred and ninety-four Earth years."

"How much longer do you expect to live?"

"Six years at least, or so I hope. Many men wish me poisoned."

"On the roof four criminals await execution. Are all to 'cooperate'?"

"All. I have a dozen new poisons to test, as have other Masters of the Guild."

"I have assured Asm that he will die by alpha or beta."

"You must have the gift of perceiving miracles. I myself am a skeptic. The arrogance of Asm has long been a blemish upon the region. He now must cooperate with the Guild Standards Committee."

Gersen eventually paid SVU 425 that Asm might die by alpha.

Edelrod, somewhat sulky, met Gersen in the hall. They set off through Paing by streets lined with tall timber huts on stilts, the façade of each hut constructed to represent a visage doleful, saturnine or astounded; and so they returned to the Poison Inn.

Alusz Iphigenia was in her room; Gersen decided not to disturb her. He bathed in a wooden vat, went down to the lobby to look out across the steppe. Dusk blurred the landscape, the wheeled poles were black intricate silhouettes.

Gersen ordered a pot of tea and with nothing better to do reflected on the condition of his life… By ordinary standards he was a fortunate man, wealthy beyond the grasp of the mind. What of the future? Suppose that by some freak of fortune he were able to achieve his goal, with the five Demon Princes destroyed, what then? Could he integrate himself into the normal flow of existence? Or had he become so distorted that always, to the end of his days, he must seek out men to destroy? Gersen gave a grim chuckle. Unlikely that he would survive to confront the problem. In the meantime, what had he learned from Asm? Only that twenty or thirty years ago a young madman had sold a pair of girls, Dundine and Inga, to Asm, who later sold them to Gascoyne the Wholesaler of Murchison's Star. Next to nothing... Except that Dundine and Inga knew their kidnapper well and 'never ceased to revile him'.

Alusz Iphigenia appeared. She ignored Gersen and went to look out over the dark steppe, where now one or two far lights flickered. In the sky appeared a purple glow, a bank of white lights, and a packet of the Robarth–Hercules Line descended to the field. Alusz Iphigenia watched a few moments, then turned and came to sit by Gersen, holding herself stiffly erect. She shook her head at his offer of tea. "How long must you stay here?"

"Only until tomorrow night."

"Why may not we leave now? You have conferred with your friend, you have bought your poison."

As if in response to her question Edelrod appeared, bowing in absurd punctilio. Tonight he wore a long gown of green cloth, a tall fur cap. "Health and immunity!" he greeted them. "Do you attend the poisonings? They are scheduled for the hotel rotunda, for the education of gathered notables."

"Tonight? I thought they were tomorrow night."

"The date has been set forward, by a whirl of Godogma's wheel. Tonight the rogues must 'cooperate'."

"We will be there," said Gersen.

Alusz Iphigenia rose swiftly to her feet, departed the lobby.

Gersen found her in her room. "Are you angry with me?"

"Not angry. I am utterly bewildered. I can't understand your morbid fascination with these horrible people... Death..."

"This isn't a fair statement. The people live by a system different from ours. I am interested. I live by my ability to avoid death. I might learn something to help me survive."

"But you don't need this knowledge! You have a vast fortune, ten billion SVU in cash —"

"No longer."

"'No longer'? Have you lost it?"

"The 'vast fortune' is no longer cash. There now exists an anonymous corporation, of which I own the stock. The money yields a daily income, a million SVU more or less. Still a vast fortune, of course."

"With all this money you need not involve yourself. Hire murderers to do your work. Hire the disgusting Edelrod! For money he would poison his mother!"

"Any murderer I could hire could be hired to murder me. But there is another consideration. I don't care for notoriety, or publicity. To be effective I must be unknown: a nonentity. I fear I have already been noted by the Institute, and this would be a great misfortune."

Alusz Iphigenia spoke with great earnestness. "You are obsessed! You are a monomaniac! This concentration on lethality, effectiveness, masters you completely!"

Gersen forbore to point out that this same 'effectiveness' and 'lethality' had preserved her existence on several occasions.

"You have other capacities," Alusz Iphigenia went on. "You have sensibilities, even frivolities. You never indulge them. You are spiritually starved, crippled. You think only of power, death, poison, devious plots, revenge!"

Gersen was startled by her vehemence. The accusations were distorted far enough of the mark that they carried no sting; still if she believed them, what a monster he must appear in her eyes! Soothingly he replied, "What you say simply isn't true. Maybe some day you'll know this, maybe some day..." Gersen's voice dwindled, in the face of the angry shake Alusz Iphigenia gave her head which sent her gold-brown hair flying. Additionally, what he was about to say, now that he considered it, seemed somewhat improbable, even absurd: talk of relaxation, a home, a family.

Alusz Iphigenia spoke in a cold voice: "What then of me?"

"I have no right to rule your life, or disturb you," said Gersen. "You have only one life; you must make the best of it."

Alusz Iphigenia rose to her feet, calm and composed. Sadly Gersen went to his own room. Still, in a sense, the quarrel was welcome. Perhaps, motivated subconsciously, he had brought her to Sarkovy to indicate the direction his life must go, to give her the option of detaching herself.

Somewhat to his surprise she appeared for dinner, though grim and pale.

The dining room was crowded; everywhere were the fur collars and black-furred pates of Sarkoy notables. Tonight an unusual number of women were present, in their peculiar purple, brown and black gowns, weighed down with necklaces, bangles, hair-pieces of turquoise and jade. In one corner sat a large group of tourists from the excursion ship which had put into Paing earlier in the evening — the occasion, Gersen decided, for the advancement of the poisonings. By their costumes the tourists were from one of the Concourse planets: Alphanor, to judge by their beige and gray skin-toning. At Gersen's elbow appeared Edelrod. "Aha, Lord Gersen! A pleasure to see you here. May I join you and your lovely lady? I may be able to assist for the poisonings."

Taking Gersen's assent for granted he seated himself at the table. "Tonight a banquet of six courses, Sarkoy style. I recommend that you attempt it. You are here on our wonderful planet, you must enjoy it to the hilt. I am pleased to be present. All goes well tonight, I trust?"

"Quite well, thank you."

Edelrod spoke correctly: tonight only the Sarkoy cuisine was offered. The first course was served: a pale green broth of swamp produce, rather bitter, accompanied by stalks of deep-fried reed, a salad of celery root, whortleberry and shreds of pungent black bark. As they ate, porters carried four posts out upon the terrace, set them upright into sockets.

The second course appeared: a ragoût of pale meat in coral sauce, heavily seasoned, with side dishes of jellied plantain, crystallized jaoic, a local fruit.

Alusz Iphigenia ate without great appetite; Gersen felt no hunger whatever.

The third course was set before them: collops of perfumed paste on disks of chilled melon, accompanied by what appeared to be small molluscs in spiced oil. As the platters were being removed in preparation for the fourth course, the criminals were led out on the terrace, where they stood blinking into the lights. They were naked except for heavy padded collars, bulky mattress-like gloves, a tight girdle around the waist. Each was attached to a post by six feet of chain.

Alusz Iphigenia looked them over with seeming indifference. "These are the criminals? What are their offenses?"

Edelrod looked up from the battery of bowls which had just been set before him, containing a hash of crushed insects and cereal, pickles, a plum-colored conserve and pellets of fried meat. Apprehending the question he glanced at the criminals. "There is Asm, who betrayed the guild. Next is a nomad who committed a sexual offense."

Alusz Iphigenia laughed incredulously. "On Sarkovy is this possible?"

Edelrod gave her a look of pained reproach. "The third threw sour milk on his grandmother. The fourth dishonored a fetish."

Alusz Iphigenia wore a puzzled expression. She glanced at Gersen to learn whether or not Edelrod were serious.

Gersen said, "The offenses seem arbitrary, but some of our restraints seem strange to the folk of Sarkovy."

"Precisely the case," stated Edelrod. "Every planet has its own rules. I am appalled at the insensitivity of certain folk who come here from other worlds. Avarice is a typical offense. On Sarkovy one man's property is the property of all. Money? It is distributed without a second thought! Unstinting generosity excites approval!" And he looked expectantly toward Gersen, who only smiled.

Alusz Iphigenia had let the fourth course go untasted. The fifth course was served: a wafer of baked pastry on which were arranged three large steamed centipedes, with a garnish of a chopped blue vegetable, and a dish of glossy-black paste, which gave off an acrid aromatic odor. Alusz Iphigenia rose to her feet, departed the dining room. Edelrod looked after her solicitously. "She is not well?"

"I fear not."

"A pity." Edelrod attacked his food with gusto. "The meal is by no means at its end."

To the terrace came four undermasters from the guild and a Master Venefice, to direct proceedings and make analytic comments.

All seemed in readiness for the poisonings. The undermasters set a tabouret in front of each of the criminals, with the poisons arranged in white saucers.

"The first subject," called forth the Master Venefice, "is one Kakarsis Asm. In requital for manipulations deleterious to the guild, he has agreed to test a variation of that activant known as 'alpha'. When ingested orally, alpha almost instantly shocks the main spinal ganglion. Tonight we test alpha in a new solvent, which may well result in the most rapid lethality yet discovered by man. Criminal Asm, cooperate, if you please."

Kakarsis Asm rolled his eyes to right and left. The undermaster stepped forward; Kakarsis Asm opened his mouth, gulped the dose and a second or two later was dead.

"Amazing!" declared Edelrod. "Something new every week!"

The executions proceeded, the Master Venefice supplying informative details. The sexual offender tried to kick poison into the undermaster's face and was reprimanded; otherwise the poisonings proceeded smoothly. The sixth course, an elaborate salad, was followed by teas, infusions and trays of sweetmeats, and the banquet was at an end.

Gersen slowly went up to the suite. Alusz Iphigenia had packed her belongings. Gersen stood by the door, puzzled by a sudden gleam of panic in Alusz Iphigenia's eyes, unaware that against the white woodwork he appeared a dark sinister shape.

Alusz Iphigenia spoke in a breathless rush, "The excursion ship is returning to Alphanor. I have booked passage. We must go our own ways."

Gersen was silent for a moment. Then he said: "There is money in your bank account. I'll see that more is paid into it, as much as you'll ever need... If emergency arises, if there are inadequate funds, notify the bank manager. He'll make the necessary arrangements."

Alusz Iphigenia said nothing. Gersen went to the door. "Should you ever need help..."

Alusz Iphigenia gave a short nod. "I'll remember."

"Goodby then."

"Goodby."

*

Gersen went to his own room, where he lay on his bed, hands behind his head. So ended a pleasant passage in his life. Never again, he told himself, never would he involve a woman with the dark necessities of his life: especially one so honorable and generous and kind...

Early in the morning the Robarth–Hercules packet departed, with Alusz Iphigenia aboard. Gersen went to the spaceport, signed the exit register, paid a departure tax, pressed a gratuity upon Edelrod and departed Sarkovy.

Chapter III

From *Popular Handbook to the Planets*, 348th edition, 1525:

ALOYSIUS: Sixth planet to Vega.
Planetary constants:

Diameter. . . . .7,340 miles
Sidereal day. . . . .19.8 hours
Mass. 0.86
etc.

Aloysius with its sister planets, Boniface and Cuthbert, were the first worlds to be intensively colonized from Earth. Aloysius hence presents aspects of considerable antiquity, the more so that the first settlers, a dynamic group of Conservationists, refused to build structures not in harmony with the landscape.

The Conservationists are gone, but their influence lingers. The pretentious glass towers of Alphanor and Earth, the concrete of Olliphane, the unbridled confusion which has overtaken the Markab system: these are nowhere to be seen.

The axis of Aloysius is inclined at an angle of 31.7 degrees to its plane of orbit, hence there are seasonal fluctuations of notable severity, mollified somewhat by a dense atmosphere. There are nine continents: Dorgan is the largest, with New Wexford its chief city. Owing to a calculated policy of low taxes and favorable regulations, New Wexford has long functioned as an important financial center, with an influence far in excess of its population.

The autochthonous flora and fauna are not particularly noteworthy. Through intensive effort by the original settlers, terrestrial trees and shrubs are widespread, the conifers especially finding a hospitable environment.

—⁂—

LANDING FORMALITIES AT ALOYSIUS were as rigorous as those of Sarkovy were lax. At a distance of a million miles, the 'first shell', Gersen announced his intention to land, identified himself and his ship, gave references, explained the reasons for his visit, and was allowed to approach the 'second shell' at a distance of a half-million miles. Here he waited while his application was studied, his references checked. He was then ordered down into the 'third shell', a hundred thousand miles above the planet, and here, after a brief delay he was given landing clearance. The formalities were irksome, but not to be avoided. Had Gersen neglected to halt at the first shell, weapons would have been trained on his ship. Had he failed to heed the 'second shell' a Thribolt gun would have fired a salvo of adhesive-paper disks at his ship. Had he then failed to halt, he and his ship would have been destroyed.*

* The Thribolt gun shoots a Jarnell-powered projectile toward its target. A quest-needle protrudes a hundred and sixty feet ahead of the projectile, at the so-called 'preliminary roil' section of the intersplit, and is in tenuous contact with undisturbed space. Upon encountering matter, the quest-needle disengages the intersplit and triggers its charge: either adhesive paper disks or high explosives. In effect the Thribolt gun is an instantaneous weapon over vast distances, its effectiveness limited only by the accuracy of the aiming and launching techniques, since, once in flight, the projectile cannot change direction.

On every technically competent world, methods of guiding the Thribolt projectile by automatic sensors are under intensive study, and have been since the development of the original weapon. The most promising system is to fix upon the distance of the target by conventional radar, drive the projectile by intersplit for a very brief period, in order to bring it into space near the target, upon which it then takes a new fix. Timers of great delicacy and dependability are necessary, together with the utmost discretion on the part of the launchers, for there is nothing to prevent the projectile, once it leaves the intersplit, from fixing upon a new target which inconveniently happens to be cruising close at hand. None of the secondary or tertiary systems are considered trustworthy and are used only under special circumstances.

Gersen complied with all necessary regulations, received clearance and landed at the Dorgan Central Spaceport.

New Wexford lay twenty miles north, a city of crooked streets, steep hills and old buildings of almost medieval aspect. The banks, brokerage houses, exchanges occupied the center of the city, with hotels, shops and agencies on the surrounding hills, and some of the finest private homes in the Oikumene scattered about the surrounding countryside.

Gersen checked into the vast Congreve Hotel, bought newspapers, ate a placid lunch. The life of the city flowed past him: mercantilists in their consciously archaic garb; aristocrats from Boniface, anxious only to return; occasionally a citizen of Cuthbert, conspicuous for the eccentric flair of his garments and his glossy depilated head. Earth-folk at the Congreve could be identified by somber garments and an indefinable self-assurance — a quality the citizens of the outer worlds found exasperating, no less than the geocentric term 'outer worlds' itself.

Gersen relaxed. The atmosphere of New Wexford was soothing; everywhere were reassuring evidences of solidity, good-living, law and order; he liked the steep streets; the stone and iron buildings, which now, after more than a thousand years, could no longer be denigrated as 'self-conscious quainterie', the Cuthbertian epithet.

Gersen had paid one previous visit to New Wexford. Two weeks of discreet investigation had then pointed to one Jehan Addels of Trans-Space Investment Corporation as an economist of extraordinary resource and acumen. Gersen had called Addels by public telephone, blanking his own image. Addels was a youngish man, slight of body, with a long quizzical face, a balding scalp which he had not troubled to have rehaired. "Addels here."

"I am someone you don't know; my name is irrelevant. I believe you are employed by Trans-Space?"

"Correct."

"How much do they pay you?"

"Sixty thousand, plus some fringe benefits," Addels replied without embarrassment, though he was talking to a stranger over a blank screen. "Why?"

"I'd like to hire you in a similar capacity at a hundred thousand, with a monthly raise of a thousand, and a bonus every five years of, say, a million SVU."

"The terms are appealing," Addels replied drily. "Who are you?"

"I prefer to remain anonymous," said Gersen. "If you insist, I'll meet you and explain as much as you like. Essentially, what you need to know is that I am not a criminal; the money I want you to handle has not been acquired contrary to the laws of New Wexford."

"Hm. How much is the sum in question? What securities are represented?"

"Ten billion SVU, in cash."

"Whisht!" breathed Jehan Addels. "Where —" a flicker of annoyance crossed his face and he broke off his sentence. Jehan Addels liked to think of himself as imperturbable. He continued. "This is an extraordinary amount of money. I can't believe it was accumulated by conventional means."

"I haven't said this. The money came from Beyond, where conventions don't exist."

Addels smiled thinly. "And no laws. Hence, no legality. And no criminals... Still, the source of your funds is no concern of mine. Exactly what do you wish done?"

"I want the money invested to yield income, but I want to call no attention to the money. I want no rumors, no publicity. I want the money invested without causing even a ripple of notice."

"Difficult." Addels reflected a moment. "Not impossible, however — if the program is properly planned."

"This is at your discretion. You will control the entire operation, subject to an occasional suggestion from me. Naturally you may hire a staff, though the staff is to be told nothing."

"Small problem there. I know nothing."

"You are agreeable to my terms?"

"Certainly, if the whole business is not a hoax. I can't avoid becoming an extremely wealthy man, both from my salary and from investments I can make collateral with yours. But I will believe it when I see the money. Presumably it is not counterfeit."

"Your own fake-meter will assure you of this."

"Ten billion SVU," mused Addels. "An enormous sum, which might well be expected to tempt even an honest man. How do you know I won't embezzle from you?"

"I understand that you are not only a cautious man, but a man of discipline. Also, you should have no inducement to embezzle. Otherwise I have no safeguards."

Jehan Addels gave his head a crisp nod. "Where is the money?"

"It will be delivered wherever you like. Or you can come to the Congreve Hotel and pick it up yourself."

"The situation is not all that simple. Suppose I should die overnight? How would you recover your money? If you should die, how would I learn of the fact? What disposition would I then make of this vast sum, presuming that it exists?"

"Come to Suite 650 at the Congreve Hotel. I'll give you the money and we'll make arrangements for any immediate contingencies."

Jehan Addels appeared in Gersen's suite half an hour later. He inspected the money, which was contained in two large cases, checked a few of the notes with his fake-meter, and shook his head in awe. "This is a tremendous responsibility. I could give you a receipt, but it would be a meaningless formality."

"Take the money," said Gersen. "Tomorrow, include in your will an instruction that in the event of your death the money is mine. If I die, or if I do not communicate with you within a year, use the income for charitable purposes. But I expect to be back in New Wexford within two or three months. Hereafter, I will communicate with you only by telephone, using the name Henry Lucas."

"Very well," said Addels, rather heavily. "I think this takes care of all contingencies."

"Remember, absolute discretion! Not even your family must know the details of your new occupation."

"As you wish."

The next morning Gersen departed Aloysius for Alphanor; now, three months later, he was back in New Wexford, again at the Congreve Hotel.

Going to a public telephone, blanking the screen as before, he tapped out Jehan Addels' call-number. The screen burst into a pattern of green leaves and pink briar roses. A female voice spoke: "Braemar Investment Company."

"Mr. Henry Lucas to speak to Mr. Addels."

"Thank you."

Addels' face appeared on the screen. "Addels."

"This is Henry Lucas."

Addels leaned back in his chair. "I am happy — and I may say, relieved — to hear from you."

"The line is clear?"

Addels checked his anti-eavesdrop meter and blinker light. "All clear."

"How are matters progressing?"

"Well enough." Addels proceeded to describe his arrangements. He had paid the cash into ten numbered accounts in as many banks, five in New Wexford, five on Earth, and was gradually converting the cash into income-producing investments, using enormous delicacy to avoid sending tremors along the sandpapered nerves of the financial world.

"I had not comprehended the magnitude of the job when I undertook it," said Addels. "It is simply staggering! Mind you, I am not complaining: I could not ask for a more interesting or more challenging job. But investing ten billion SVU discreetly is like jumping into water without getting wet. I am putting together a staff merely to handle details of investigation and management. Eventually, for maximum efficiency, I think we will be forced to become a bank, or perhaps several banks."

"Whatever is most appropriate," said Gersen. "In the meantime, I have a special job for you."

Addels instantly became wary. "And what is this job?"

"Recently I've been reading that the Radian Publishing Company, which publishes *Cosmopolis*, is in financial difficulties. I would like you to buy control."

Addels pursed his lips. "I can do this without difficulty, of course. In fact I can buy outright; Radian is on the verge of bankruptcy. But you should know that as an investment, this is not an attractive buy. They have been losing money steadily for years, which of course is why they can be had so easily."

"In this case we will buy as a speculation, and try to put things right. I have a particular reason in wishing to own *Cosmopolis*."

Addels hastily disavowed any intent to act counter to Gersen's wishes. "I merely want you to be under no misapprehensions. I will start acquiring Radian stock tomorrow."

Murchison's Star, Sagitta 203 in the *Star Directory*, lay out in the galactic plane behind Vega, thirty light-years beyond the Pale. It was one of a cluster of five varicolored suns: two red dwarfs, a blue-white dwarf, a peculiar unclassifiable blue-green star of medium size and a yellow-orange G6, which was Murchison's Star. Murchison, the single planet, was somewhat smaller than Earth, with a single huge continent cincturing the world. A searing wind blew dunes around the equatorial zone; mountainous highlands sloped gradually to the polar seas. In the mountains lived aborigines, black creatures of unpredictable characteristics: by turns murderously savage, torpid, hysterical, or cooperative. In the latter mood they served a useful purpose, supplying dyes and fibers for the tapestries which were one of Murchison's principal exports. The factories which produced the tapestries were concentrated about the city Sabra and employed thousands of female operatives. These were supplied by a dozen slaving concerns, chief among which was Gascoyne the Wholesaler. By virtue of efficient inventory control Gascoyne was able to give his customers efficient service at reasonable prices. He made no effort to compete with the specialty houses, dealt mainly in Industrial and Agricultural classifications. At Sabra his principal business was in Industrial F-2 Selecteds: women unprepossessing or past the first bloom of youth, but warranted to be of good health and agility, cooperative, diligent and amiable: such were the terms of Gascoyne's Ten-Point Guaranty.

Sabra, on the shore of the north polar sea, was a drab haphazard city with a heterogeneous population whose main goal was to earn sufficient money to go elsewhere. The coastal plain to the south was studded with hundreds of peculiar volcanic stubs, each crowned with a bristle of liver-colored vegetation. Sabra's single distinction was Orban Circus, an open area at the heart of the city centered on one of these volcanic stubs. The Grand Murchison Hotel occupied the crest of the stub; around the Circus were the most important establishments of the planet: Wilhelm's Trade Hotel, the Tapestry Mart; the depot of Gascoyne the Wholesaler; Odenour's Technical Academy; Cady's Tavern; the Blue Ape Hotel; the Hercules Import Company; warehouse and showroom of the Tapestry Producers' Cooperative; the Sportsman Supply and Trophy House; Gambel's Spaceship Sales; the District Victualling Company.

Sabra was a city large enough and wealthy enough to need protection from raiders and free-booters, even though, like Brinktown in another quarter of the Beyond, it fulfilled a service to the folk who lived beyond the Pale. Thribolt batteries were constantly manned by members of the City Militia, and ships coming in from space were regarded with intense suspicion.

Gersen, approaching with circumspection, radioed down to the spaceport, and was directed into a landing orbit. At the spaceport he was subjected to interrogation by members of the local Deweaseling Brigade*, who were reassured by Gersen's Pharaon. Weasels uniformly traveled space in Locater 9Bs; these were the only ships the IPCC chose to risk Beyond. Gersen for once could afford to be candid. He stated that he had come to Sabra to locate a woman brought here twenty or more years before by Gascoyne the Wholesaler. The Deweaselers, watching the pips and bulbs on their truth machine, exchanged sardonic glances, amused by this excess of quixotry, and waved Gersen forth to the freedom of the city.

The time was mid-morning; Gersen registered at the Grand Murchison Hotel on top of Orban Stub, which was crowded almost to capacity with tapestry buyers, commercial salesmen from the Oikumene, sportsmen intent on stalking the Bower Mountain aborigines.

Gersen bathed, changed into local costume: scarlet plush pantaloons and a black jacket. Descending to the dining room he ate a lunch of local sea produce: seaweed salad, a dish of local molluscs. Directly

---

* The single interworld organization of Beyond, existing to identify and destroy agents of the IPCC. The IPCC, accepting a contract to locate and destroy a malefactor who had fled the Oikumene, could implement its commitments only by sending one or more agents Beyond, where they were known as weasels and considered fair game.

below was the depot and offices of Gascoyne the Wholesaler: a rambling structure of three stories enclosing a central courtyard. An enormous pink and blue sign across the façade read:

GASCOYNE'S MART
SELECT SLAVES *for any* PURPOSE

A pair of handsome women and a stalwart man were depicted below. At the bottom of the sign a message read:

Gascoyne's 10-Point Warranty is Justly Famous!

Gersen finished his lunch, descended to the circus, crossed to Gascoyne's Mart. He was lucky enough to find Gascoyne himself available and was ushered into a private office. Gascoyne was a handsome well-built man of indeterminate age, with dark curly hair, a dashing black mustache, expressive eyebrows. His office was simple and informal, with a bare floor, an old wooden desk, an information screen showing evidence of much use. On one wall hung a plaque with Gascoyne's famous ten-point guaranty limned in gold leaf and surrounded by scarlet festoons. Gersen explained the purpose of his visit: "About twenty-five years ago, give or take five years, you visited Sarkovy, where you bought a pair of women from a certain Kakarsis Asm. Their names were Inga and Dundine. I am anxious to locate these women; perhaps you would be good enough to search them out in your records."

"Gladly," said Gascoyne. "I can't say as I recall the circumstances, but —" He went to the information bank, worked the knobs and dials a moment, evoking flashes of blue light and a sudden grinning visage which flickered away. Gascoyne shook his head despondently. "Might as well be a stone for all the use it gives me. I must have it repaired... Well, we shall see. This way, if you please." He took Gersen into a back room lined with ledgers. "Sarkovy. I go there seldom. A pestilent world, the home of a wicked race!" He searched his ledgers, one year after another. "This must be the trip. So long ago! Thirty years! Now, let us look. My, my, how this old ledger brings back the memories! 'Good old days' is not just a banality! ... What were the names again?"

"Inga, Dundine. I don't know their last names."

"No matter. Here they are." He copied numbers upon a slip of paper, went to another ledger, turned to the numbers in question. "They were both sold here on Murchison. Inga went to Qualag's Factory. You know where that is? Third along the right bank of the river. Dundine went to Juniper Factory, across the river from Qualag's. I trust these women were not friends or relatives? Like any other, my business has its disagreeable aspects. At Qualag's and Juniper the women live wholesome productive lives, but certainly they are not pampered. Still, who is in this life?" And raising his eyebrows, he made a deprecatory gesture around his austere office.

Gersen gave his head a wry shake of sympathy. He thanked Gascoyne and departed.

Qualag's Factory was a half-dozen four-story buildings around a compound. Gersen entered the lobby of the main office, which was hung with sample tapestries. A pallid male clerk with varnished blond hair came to inquire his business.

"Gascoyne tells me," said Gersen, "that thirty years ago Qualag's purchased a female named Inga, on your invoice 10V623. Can you tell me if this woman is still employed by you?"

The clerk shuffled off to search his records, then went to an intercom and spoke a few words. Gersen waited. Into the office came a tall placid-faced woman with heavy arms and legs.

The clerk said petulantly: "Gentleman here wants to know about Inga, B2-AG95. There's a yellow card on her with two white clips but I can't find the reference."

"You're looking under Dormitory F. The B2s are all Dorm A." The woman located the correct reference. "Inga. B2-AG95. Dead. I remember her very well. An Earth woman giving herself all style of airs. Complained constantly of this and that. She came to the dye-works while I was recreation counsellor. I remember her well. She worked in blues and greens, and it put her off; she finally threw herself into a vat of dusty-orange. That's long ago... My, how time flies."

Leaving Qualag's Gersen crossed the river by a bridge and walked to the Juniper Factory, which was somewhat larger than Qualag's. The office was similar, though with a brisker atmosphere.

Gersen again put his question, this time in connection with Dundine. But the clerk was not cooperative and refused to check the records. "We aren't allowed to give out such information," said the clerk, looking disdainfully at Gersen from the altitude afforded him by his position behind the counter.

"Let me discuss the matter with the manager," said Gersen.

"Mr. Plusse owns the factory. If you will be seated I will announce you." Gersen went to examine a tapestry ten feet wide by six feet high, representing a flowered field on which stood hundreds of fanciful birds.

"Mr. Plusse will see you, sir."

Mr. Plusse was a small surly man with a white top-knot and eyes of blue agate. Clearly he had no intention of obliging Gersen or anyone else. "Sorry, sir. We have our production to consider. Trouble enough with the women as it is. We do our best for them; we provide good food and recreational facilities, bathe them once a week. Still it's impossible to keep them satisfied."

"May I ask if the woman still works for you?"

"It makes no difference if she does or not; you would not be allowed to disturb her."

"If she is here, if she is the woman I am looking for, I'll be glad to recompense you for any inconvenience."

"Hmf. Just a moment." Mr. Plusse spoke into the intercom. "Is not there a Dundine in wicker-stitching? What's her current index?... Hmf... I see." He returned to Gersen, whom he now regarded in a thoughtful new light. "A valuable employee. I can't have her badgered. If you insist on speaking to her, you'll have to buy her. The price is three thousand SVU."

Without a word Gersen put down the money. Mr. Plusse licked his small pink mouth. "Hmf." He spoke into the intercom, "With a minimum of commotion, bring Dundine to this office."

Ten minutes passed, while Mr. Plusse ostentatiously made notations on a chart. The door opened; the clerk entered with a large-bodied woman in a white smock. Her features were big and moist; her hair was short, mouse-brown, crimped and tied with string. Wringing her hands apprehensively she stared from Mr. Plusse to Gersen and back again.

"You are leaving our service," said Mr. Plusse in a dry voice. "This gentleman has bought you."

Dundine looked at Gersen with bright fear. "Oh, what do you plan to do with me, sir? I'm useful and well here, I do my work; I don't want to go out on the back farms; I wouldn't want to do this, and I'm too old for barge work."

"Nothing like that, Dundine. I've paid Mr. Plusse off, you're a free woman now. You can go back to your home if you like."

Tears sprang into her eyes. "I don't believe it."

"It's true."

"But — why did you do this?" Dundine's face wavered between bewilderment, fear and doubt.

"I want to ask you a few questions."

Dundine turned her back, bent her head over her hands.

After a moment Gersen asked, "Is there anything you want to bring with you?"

"No. Nothing. If I was wealthy I'd take that little tapestry on the wall, the little girls dancing. I did the wickering on that tapestry and I was all that fond of the thing."

"What is the price?" Gersen asked Mr. Plusse.

"That is our Style 19, which is priced at 750 SVU."

Gersen paid 750 SVU and took the tapestry. "Come, Dundine," he said shortly. "Best that we start off."

"But my goodbyes! My dear friends!"

"Impossible," said Mr. Plusse. "Do you wish to disturb the other women?"

Dundine sniffed and rubbed her nose. "There's my bonuses I haven't taken. It's three recreation half-periods. I'd like to give them to Almerina."

"That can't be done, as you know. We never allow transfer or bartering of bonus units. If you wish, you may use them now, before your departure."

Dundine looked uncertainly toward Gersen. "Do we have time? It seems a shame to let them go to waste... But I suppose it makes no difference now..."

They walked along the river-road toward the center of town, with Dundine casting timid glances toward Gersen.

"I can't imagine what you want of me," she said tremulously. "I'm certain I've never known you in my life."

"I'm interested in what you can tell me of Viole Falushe."

"Viole Falushe? But I know no such person. I can tell you nothing." Dundine stopped short, her knees shaking. "Are you going to take me back to the factory?"

"No," said Gersen hollowly. "I won't take you back." He looked at her in deep discouragement. "Aren't you the Dundine who was kidnapped with Inga?"

"Oh yes. I'm Dundine. Poor Inga. I've never heard of her since she went to Qualag's. They say it's ever so dreary at Qualag's."

Gersen's mind raced back and forth. "You were kidnapped and brought to Sarkovy?"

"Yes, indeed, and oh, what a time we had! Riding the steppes on those bouncing old wagons!"

"But the man who kidnapped you and brought you to Sarkovy — that was Viole Falushe, or so I am told."

"Him!" Dundine's mouth twisted as if she had bit into something sour. "His name wasn't Viole Falushe!"

And Gersen belatedly recalled that Kakarsis Asm had told him the same. The man who had sold Inga and Dundine had not used the name 'Viole Falushe' at that time.

"No, no," said Dundine in a soft voice, looking far back down her life. "That wasn't any Viole Falushe. It was that nasty little Vogel Filschner."

All the way back into the Oikumene, in fragments and ejaculations, bits from here, oddments from there, Dundine told her story, and Gersen gave over trying to elicit a connected narrative.

Expansive, inflated with freedom, Dundine talked with enthusiasm. She knew Vogel Filschner, yes indeed! She knew him well! So he changed his name to Viole Falushe? Small wonder, after the shame his mother must feel! Though Madame Filschner had never enjoyed the best of reputations, and no one had ever known Vogel Filschner's father. He had attended school with Dundine, two classes ahead.

"Where was this?" asked Gersen.

"Why, at Ambeules!" declared Dundine, surprised that Gersen did not already know the story as well as herself. Though Gersen knew Rotterdam, Hamburg and Paris, he had never visited Ambeules, a suburb of Rolingshaven on the west coast of Europe.

Vogel Filschner had always been a strange brooding boy, according to Dundine. "Extremely sensitive," she confided. "Ripe always for a great rage or eyefuls of tears. One never knew what Vogel might do!" And for a space she fell silent, shaking her head in marvel at the deeds of Vogel Filschner. "Then when he was sixteen, and I but fourteen, a new girl came to school, and oh she was a pretty thing! Jheral Tinzy was her name, and who but Vogel Filschner should fall in love!"

But Vogel Filschner was grubby and unsavory; Jheral Tinzy, a girl of sensitivity, found him repulsive. "Who could blame her?" mused Dundine. "Vogel was an eery boy. I can see him yet: tall for his age, and somewhat thin, with a round belly and a round bottom, like a billiken. He walked with his head to the side, watching all with his dark burning eyes! They watched, they saw all, they never forgot a thing, did Vogel Filschner's eyes! I must say that Jheral Tinzy used him heartlessly, laughing and gay the while! She drove poor Vogel to desperation, this is my belief. And that man Vogel took up with — I can't recall his name! He wrote poetry, very strange and daring! He was thought ungodly, though he had patrons in the upper classes. Those days are so long ago, so tragic and so sweet! Ah if I could live them again, what changes there would be!"

At this point Dundine went into a nostalgic reminiscence: "— even now I can smell the air from the sea! Ambeules, our old district, is on the Gaas, and this is the loveliest part of the city, though by no means the richest. The flowers are unimaginable! To think that I have seen no flower for thirty years, except for those I myself have worked." And now nothing must do but that Dundine should examine her tapestry which she had draped upon the back bulkhead of the saloon.

Presently she returned to the subject of Vogel Filschner. "The most morbidly sensitive of youths! The poet egged him on. And truth to tell, Jheral Tinzy humiliated Vogel dreadfully. Whatever the cause, Vogel performed his terrible deed. There were twenty-nine girls in the choral society. Every Friday night we sang. Vogel had learned to operate a spaceship — it was a course all the boys took. So Vogel stole one of those little Locater ships, and when we came out from choral practice to the bus, it was Vogel who drove us away. He took us to the spaceship and made us all get aboard. But it was the one night Jheral Tinzy had not come to practice. Vogel had no knowledge of this until the last girl left the bus, and he was like a stone statue. Too late then! He had no choice but to flee." Dundine sighed. "Twenty-eight girls, pure and fresh as little flowers. How he dealt with us! We knew he was strange, but ferocious as a wild beast? No, never; how could we girls imagine such things? For reasons best known to himself he never used us in bed — Inga thought he was sulking because he had failed to capture Jheral. Godelia Parwitz and Rosamond — I can't think of her name — they tried to hit him with a metal implement, though it would have been the death of all had they succeeded, for none of us knew how to guide the ship. He punished them in a dreadful manner so that they cried and sobbed. Inga and I told him he was a wicked monster to act so. He only laughed, did Vogel Filschner. 'A wicked monster, am I? I'll show you a wicked monster!' And he took us to Sarkovy and sold us to Mr. Asm.

"But first he stopped at another world and sold ten girls who were the least well-favored. Then Inga and I and six others who hated him the most were sold on Sarkovy. Of the others, the most beautiful, I know nothing. Thanks to Kalzibah, I have been succored."

Dundine wanted to return to Earth. At New Wexford Gersen furnished her a wardrobe, a ticket to Earth and funds sufficient to keep her in comfort the rest of her life. At the spaceport she embarrassed him by falling on her knees and kissing his hands. "I thought to die and have my ashes scattered on a far planet! How was I so lucky? With so many other poor creatures, why did Kalzibah select me for his favor?"

The same question, in different terms, had been troubling Gersen himself. With his wealth, he might have bought the whole of Qualag and Juniper and every other factory in Sabra, and brought each of the wretched women to their homes... What then? he asked himself. Sabra tapestries were in demand. New factories would be established, new slaves imported. A year later all would be as before.

Still... Gersen heaved a sigh. The universe abounded with evils. No one man could defeat them all. Meanwhile Dundine was wiping her eyes, and apparently preparing to fall on her knees once more. Gersen said hastily, "One request I wish to make of you."

"Anything, anything!"

"You plan to return to Rolingshaven?"

"It is my home."

"You must not reveal how you were brought from Sabra. Tell no one! Invent any wild tale. But do not mention me. Do not mention that I asked you of Vogel Filschner."

"Trust me! The fiends of hell can tear forth my tongue, even then I will not speak!"

"Goodby then." Gersen departed hastily before Dundine could again demonstrate her gratitude.

At a public telephone he called Braemar Investment Company. "Henry Lucas to speak to Mr. Addels."

"A moment, Mr. Lucas."

Addels appeared on the screen. "Mr. Lucas?"

Gersen allowed his image to go forth. "All continues to go well?"

"As well as could be expected. My problems arise only from the sheer mass of our money. I should say, *your* money." Addels permitted himself to smile. "But gradually I am training an organization. Incidentally, Radian Publishing Company is ours. We had it cheaply, because of the circumstances I mentioned previously."

"No one has been inquisitive? There have been no questions, no rumors?"

"To the best of my knowledge: none. Zane Publishing Company bought Radian; Irwin and Jeddah own Zane, a numbered account at a Pontefract bank owns Irwin and Jeddah. Braemar Investment is the numbered account. Who is Braemar Investment? Ostensibly it is I."

"Well done!" said Gersen. "You could not have managed better."

Addels acknowledged the praise with a stiff nod. "I must say once more that Radian seems a poor investment, at least on the basis of past performance."

"Why has it been losing money? Everyone seems to read *Cosmopolis*. I see it everywhere."

"Perhaps this is so. Nevertheless circulation has slowly been declining. More significantly, the typical reader no longer is a decision-maker. The management has been trying to please everyone, including the advertisers; as a result the magazine has lost its flair."

"There would seem to be a remedy for the situation," said Gersen. "Hire a new editor, a man of imagination and intelligence. Instruct him to revitalize the magazine, without regard for advertisers or circulation, sparing no reasonable expense. When the magazine regains its prestige, circulation and advertisers will return fast enough."

"I am relieved that you preface the word 'expense' with 'reasonable'," said Addels in his driest voice. "I still am not accustomed to dealing with millions as if they were hundreds."

"No more am I," said Gersen. "The money means nothing to me — except that I find it uncommonly useful. One other matter. Instruct the *Cosmopolis* head office — I believe it is located in London — that a man named Henry Lucas will be sent to the editorial offices. Represent him as an employee of Zane Publishing if you like. He is to be put on the payroll as a special writer, who will work when and where he chooses, without interference."

"Very well, sir. I will do as you require."

Chapter IV

From *Introduction to Old Earth,* by Ferencz Szantho:

> *Erdenfreude*: a mysterious and intimate emotion which dilates blood vessels, slides chills along the subcutaneous nerves, arouses qualms of apprehension and excitement like those infecting a girl at her first ball. *Erdenfreude* typically attacks the outworld man approaching Earth for the first time. Only the dull, the insensitive, are immune. The excitable have been known to suffer near-fatal palpitations.
>
> The cause is the subject of learned dispute. Neurologists describe the condition as anticipatory adjustment of the organism to absolute normality of all the sensory modes: color recognition, sonic perception, coriolis force and gravitational equilibrium. The psychologists differ; *Erdenfreude,* they state, is the flux of a hundred thousand racial memories boiling up almost to the level of consciousness. Geneticists speak of RNA; metaphysicians refer to the soul; parapsychologists make the possibly irrelevant observation that haunted houses are to be found on Earth alone.

—᯾—

History is bunk.
—Henry Ford.

—᯾—

Gersen, who had lived nine years on Earth, nevertheless felt something of an outworlder's exhilaration as he hung above the great globe awaiting his clearance from Space Security. Finally it arrived, with precise landing instructions, and Gersen dropped down to the West Europe spaceport at Tarn. He passed through sanitation procedures and health inspection, the most stringent of the Oikumene, punched appropriate buttons at the Immigration Control console, and finally was allowed to proceed about his business.

He rode to London by tube, and registered at the Royal Oak Hotel, a block off the Strand. The season was early autumn; the sun shone through a high thin overcast. Old London, permeated with the vapors of antiquity, shone like a fine gray pearl.

Gersen's clothes were in the Alphanor style, fuller in cut and richer in color than the clothes of London. On the Strand he went into a gentleman's outfitter, where he selected a fabric, then stripped to his underwear and was measured by photonic scanners. Five minutes later he was delivered his new garments: black trousers, a jacket of dark brown and beige, a white blouse and black cravat. Inconspicuous now, Gersen continued along the Strand.

Dusk came to the sky. Every planet had its distinctive dusk, thought Gersen. The dusk of Alphanor, for instance, was an electric blue, gradually fading to the richest of ultramarines. Sarkovy dusk was a dead dismal gray, with a tawny overtone. Dusk at Sabra had been brown-gold, with domains of color around the other stars of the cluster. The dusk of Earth was dusk as it should be: soft, heather-grey, soothing, an ending and a beginning... Gersen dined at a restaurant which had maintained an unbroken tenancy of over seventeen hundred years. The old oak beams, fumed and waxed, were as stout as ever; the plaster recently had been scraped of twenty layers of white-wash and refinished: a process which occurred every hundred years or so... Gersen's thoughts reverted to his youth. He had visited London twice with his grandfather, though for the most part they had lived at Amsterdam. There never had been dinners such as this, never leisure or idleness. Gersen shook his head sadly as he recalled the exercises to which his merciless grandfather had put him. A wonder that he had stood up to the discipline.

Gersen bought a copy of *Cosmopolis* and returned to the hotel. He went into the bar, and sitting at a table ordered a pint of Worthington's Ale, brewed at Burton-on-Trent as had been the case for something less than two thousand years. He opened *Cosmopolis*. It was easy to understand why the magazine had become moribund. There were three long articles: *Have Earthmen Become Less Virile?...Patricia Poitrine: New Toast of the Smart Set...A Clergyman's Guide to Spiritual Renewal...* Gersen flicked through the pages, then laid the magazine aside. He drained the mug, and went up to his room.

In the morning he visited the editorial offices of *Cosmopolis*, and asked to speak to the Personnel Director. This was Mrs. Neutra, a brittle, black-haired woman wearing a great deal of preposterous jewellery. She showed no inclination to speak to Gersen. "Sorry, sorry, sorry. I can't consider anything or anyone at this moment. I'm in a flap. Everybody's in a flap. There's been a shake-up; no one's job is any good."

"Perhaps I had better speak to the Editor-in-Chief," said Gersen. "There was to have been a letter from Zane Publishing, and it should have arrived."

The Personnel Director made a gesture of irritation. "Who or what is Zane Publishing?"

"The new ownership," said Gersen politely.

"Oh." The woman pushed among the papers on her desk. "Maybe this is it." She read. "Oh you're Henry Lucas."

"Yes."

"Hmm...Piff puff...You're to be a special writer. Something we just don't need at the moment. But I'm only Personnel Director. Oh hell, fill out the application, make an appointment for your psychiatric tests. If you survive, and you probably won't, show up a week from tomorrow for your orientation course."

Gersen shook his head. "I don't have time for any of these formalities. I doubt if the new owners have much sympathy with them."

"Sorry, Mr. Lucas. This is our inflexible program."

"What does the letter say?"

"It says to put Mr. Henry Lucas on the payroll as special writer."

"Then please do so."

"Oh double bing-bang hell. If this is how things are going to go, why have a personnel director? Why have psychiatric tests and orientation courses? Why not just let janitors put out the rag?"

The woman seized a form, wrote with swift strokes of a flamboyant quill-pen. "Here you are. Take it into the managing editor, he'll arrange your assignment."

The managing editor was a portly gentleman with lips pursed in a worried pout. "Yes, Mr. Lucas. Mrs. Neutra just called me. I understand you have been sent in by the new ownership."

"I've been associated with them for a long time," said Gersen. "But all I want at this moment is whatever identification you supply your special correspondents, so that if necessary I can demonstrate that I'm an employee of *Cosmopolis*."

The managing editor spoke into an intercom. "On your way out, step into Department 2A and your card will be prepared." He leaned morosely back into his chair. "It seems that you are to be a roving reporter, responsible to no one. A very nice billet, if I may say so. What do you propose to write about?"

"One thing or another," said Gersen. "Whatever comes up."

The managing editor's face sagged with bewilderment. "You can't go out and write a *Cosmopolis* article like that! Our issues are programmed months ahead! We use public opinion polls to find what subjects people are interested in."

"How can they know what they're interested in if they haven't read it?" asked Gersen. "The new owners are throwing the public opinion polls away."

The managing editor shook his head sadly. "How will we know what to write about?"

"I have an idea or two. For instance, the Institute could stand an airing. What are its current aims? Who are the men of Degrees 101, 102, 103? What information have they suppressed? What of Tryon Russ and his anti-gravity machine? The Institute deserves a comprehensive study. You could easily devote an entire issue to the Institute."

The editor nodded curtly. "Don't you think it's a bit — well, intense? Are people really interested in these matters?"

"If not they should be."

"Easily said, but it's no way to run a magazine. People don't want to really understand anything; they want to think they have learned without the necessity of application. In our 'heavy' articles we try to supply keys and guides, so at least they'll have something to talk about at parties. But go on: what else do you have in mind?"

"I've been thinking of Viole Falushe and the Palace of Love. Exactly what goes on at this establishment? What face does Viole Falushe show, what name does he bear when he comes in from Beyond? Who are his guests at the Palace of Love? How have they fared? Would they care to return?"

"An interesting topic," the editor admitted. "A bit close to the knuckle perhaps. We prefer to sheer away from sensationalism and — shall we say — the grim facts of reality. Still I've often wondered about the Palace of Love. What in the world *does* go on? The usual, I suppose. But no one knows for sure. What else?"

"That's all for now." Gersen rose to his feet. "In fact I'll be working on this last story myself."

The managing editor shrugged his shoulders. "You seem to have been accorded a free hand."

Gersen immediately rode the sub-channel tube to Rolingshaven, arriving at the vast Zone Station a few minutes before noon. He crossed the white-tiled lobby, past slideways and escalators labeled WIEN, PARIS, TSARGRAD, BERLIN, BUDAPEST, KIEV, NEAPOLIS, a dozen other ancient cities. He paused at a kiosk to buy a map, then went to a café, settled himself at a table with a stein of beer and plate of sausages.

Gersen had lived long in Amsterdam and had passed through the Zone Station on several occasions, but of the city Rolingshaven he knew little. As he ate he studied the map.

Rolingshaven was a city of considerable extent, divided into four principal municipalities by two rivers, the Gaas and the Sluicht, and the great Evres Canal. At the north was Zummer, a rather grim district of apartment towers and careful malls laid out by some neat-minded city council of the far past. On the Heybau, a promontory hooking out into the sea, was the famous Handelhal Conservatory, the wonderful Galactic Zoo and the Kindergarten; Zummer otherwise was devoid of interest.

South across the Sluicht was the Old City, a teeming confusion of small shops, inns, hostels, restaurants, beer caverns, bookstalls, huddled offices, askew little houses of stone and timber, dating from the

Middle Ages: a district as chaotic and picturesque as Zummer was stark and dull; and here as well was the ancient University, overlooking the fish market along the banks of the Evres Canal.

Ambeules lay across the canal: a district of nine hills covered with homes and a periphery given to wharves, warehouses, shipyards, mud-flats from which were dredged the famous Flamande Oysters. The great Gaas estuary separated Ambeules from Dourrai, a district of somewhat lower hills again covered with small homes, with the great industries and fabrication plants straggling along the shore and southward.

This was the city where Viole Falushe, or more accurately, Vogel Filschner, had lived and where he had committed his first great crime. The exact locale was Ambeules, and Gersen decided to base himself in this area.

Finishing beer and sausages he rode an escalator to the third level above, where a local tube-car whisked him south under the Evres Canal to Ambeules Station. He rode to the surface, and looking right and left through the hazy radiance which characterized the region, approached the old woman who managed a newsstand. "Which is a good hotel nearby?"

The old woman pointed a brown finger. "Up Hoeblingasse to the Rembrandt Hotel: as good as any in Ambeules. Of course if it's elegance you require, then you must go to the Hotel Prince Franz Ludwig in Old Town, the finest of Europe with prices to match."

Gersen chose the Rembrandt Hotel, a pleasant old-fashioned structure with public rooms paneled in dark wood, and was taken to a suite of high-ceilinged rooms overlooking the great gray Gaas.

The day was still young. Gersen rode a cab to the Mairie, where he paid a small fee and was given access to the City Directory. He ran the record back to 1495. The screen spun to the letter F, Fi, and finally the name Filschner. At this time three Filschners were listed. Gersen made notes of the addresses. He likewise found two Tinzys, and made similar notes. Then he dialed to the current listings and found two Filschners and four Tinzys. One of the Filschners and one of the Tinzys had maintained the same address across the years.

Gersen next visited the office of the Ambeules *Helion,* and on the strength of his *Cosmopolis* card was given access to the morgue.

He brought the index to the screen, scanned it for the name Vogel Filschner, found a code number, coded and punched the *Show* button.

The tale was much as Dundine had told, though in condensed form. Vogel Filschner was described as "a boy given to spells of brooding and wandering alone by night". His mother, Hedwig Filschner, identified as a beautician, professed herself amazed at Vogel's outrageous deed. She described him as a "good boy, though very idealistic and moody".

Vogel Filschner had had no close friends. In the biology laboratory he had been teamed with a lad named Roman Haenigsen, the school chess champion. They had played an occasional game of chess during the lunch hour. Roman evinced no astonishment at Vogel's crime: "He was a fellow who hated to lose. Whenever I beat him, he would go savage and throw aside the pieces. Still, it amused me to play with him. I don't like people who take the game frivolously."

Vogel Filschner was not a frivolous boy, thought Gersen.

A photograph appeared: the kidnapped girls, grouped in a picture identified as the 'Philidor Bohus Choral Society'. In the front row stood a plump smiling girl in whom Gersen recognized Dundine. Among the girls would be Jheral Tinzy, and Gersen checked the faces against the caption. Jheral Tinzy was the third girl in the fourth row. Not only did a girl in the third row obscure her face; she also had turned her head aside at the time the photograph was taken, and what could be seen of her face was indistinct.

There was no photograph of Vogel Filschner.

The file ended. So much for that, thought Gersen. Vogel Filschner's identity with Viole Falushe was not widely apprehended in Ambeules, if at all. As verification, Gersen dialed for the file on Viole Falushe, the Demon Prince, but only a single reference excited his interest: 'Viole Falushe at various times has implied that his original home was Earth. On several occasions a rumor has reached us to the effect that Viole Falushe has been seen here in Ambeules. Why he should wish to haunt our unexciting district is a question which cannot be answered, and the rumors appear no more than an insane hoax.'

Gersen departed the newspaper offices and went to stand in the street. The Gendarmerie? Gersen decided against approaching them. Unlikely that they could tell him more than he already knew. Unlikely that they would if they could. Additionally, Gersen had no desire to arouse official curiosity.

Gersen checked the addresses he had noted, as well as the location of the Philidor Bohus Lyceum, against his map. The Lyceum was the nearest, at the far side of Lothar Parish. Gersen signaled a three-wheeled auto-cab, and was conveyed up one of the nine hills through a district of small detached houses. Some were constructed in the ancient fashion, of glazed dark red brick and a high pitched roof of milk-glass tiles; others in the new 'hollow trunk' style: narrow concrete cylinders two-thirds below the ground. There were houses of artificial sandstone compressed as a unit from molded soil; houses of pink or white panels surmounted by crimped metal domes; houses of laminated paper, with transparent roofs electrically charged to repel dust. The bulbs of uni-cast glass or glass-metal so common among the worlds of the Concourse had never won acceptance among the folk of western Europe, who compared them to pumpkins and paper lanterns, and called the people who lived in them 'non-human futurians'... The cab discharged Gersen before the Philidor Bohus Lyceum, a grim cube of synthetic black stone flanked by a pair of smaller cubes.

The director of the lyceum was Dr. Willem Ledinger, a bland large-bodied man with taffy-colored skin and a lank lock of yellow hair which wound around his scalp in a most peculiar manner. Gersen wondered at the man's audacity thus to present himself before several thousand adolescents. Ledinger was affable and unsuspicious, readily accepting Gersen's statement that *Cosmopolis* wished to present a survey of contemporary young people.

"I don't think there's much to write about," said Ledinger. "Our young people are, if I must say it, unexceptionable. We have many bright students and at least a fair quota of dullards..."

Gersen steered the conversation to students of the past and their careers; from here it was an easy connection to the subject of Vogel Filschner.

"Ah yes," mused Dr. Ledinger, patting his yellow top-knot. "Vogel Filschner. I haven't heard his name for years. Before my time, of course; I was a mere instructor across the city at Hulba Technical Academy. But the scandal reached us, never fear! Faculties have big ears! What a tragedy! To think of a lad like that going so far wrong!"

"He never returned to Ambeules, then?"

"He'd be a fool to do so. Or to advertise his presence, at any rate."

"Do you have the likeness of Vogel Filschner among your records? Perhaps I might do a separate piece upon this peculiar crime."

Grudgingly Dr. Ledinger admitted that photographs of Vogel Filschner were on file. "But why rake up the old nastiness? It is like breaking into graves."

"On the other hand, such an article might identify the rogue, and bring him to justice."

"'Justice'?" Dr. Ledinger curled his lip in disbelief. "After thirty years? He was a hysterical child. No matter what his crime, by this time he has made redemption and found peace. What could be gained by bringing him to what you call 'justice'?"

Gersen was somewhat startled by Dr. Ledinger's vehemence. "To dissuade others. Perhaps there is a potential Vogel Filschner among your students this very instant."

Dr. Ledinger smiled wistfully. "I don't doubt it an instant. Certain of these young rascals — well, I won't tell tales out of school. And I won't supply you with the photographs. I find the idea completely objectionable."

"Is there a yearbook for the year of the crime? Or better, the previous year?"

Dr. Ledinger looked at Gersen a moment, his affability slowly disappearing. Then he went to his wall, plucked a volume from the shelves. He watched quietly as Gersen turned the pages, and finally came upon the photograph of the Girls Choral Society he had already seen. Gersen pointed. "There is Jheral Tinzy, the girl who rebuffed Vogel, and drove him to his crime."

Dr. Ledinger examined the picture. "Think of it. Twenty-eight girls snatched away Beyond. Their lives blasted. I wonder how they fared. Some may still be alive, poor things."

"Whatever became of Jheral Tinzy? She was not among the group, if you recall."

Dr. Ledinger examined Gersen with suspicion. "You seem to know a great deal about the case. Have you been completely candid with me?"

Gersen grinned. "Not altogether. I am principally interested in Vogel

Filschner, but I don't want anyone to know I'm interested. If I can get the information I need discreetly, with no one the wiser, so much the better."

"You are a police officer? Or of the IPCC?"

Gersen displayed his identification. "Here is my sole claim to fame."

"Hmmf. *Cosmopolis* plans to publish an article on Vogel Filschner? It seems a waste of paper and ink. No wonder *Cosmopolis* has lost prestige."

"What of Jheral Tinzy? You have her photograph in your files?"

"Undoubtedly." Dr. Ledinger laid his hands upon the desk, to signal that the interview had reached its end. "But we cannot open our confidential files haphazardly. I am sorry."

Gersen rose to his feet. "Thank you, in any case."

"I have done nothing to help you," said Dr. Ledinger stonily.

Vogel Filschner had lived with his mother in a narrow little house at the eastern end of Ambeules, bordering on a dingy district of warehouses and transportation depots. Gersen climbed the embroidered iron steps, touched the button, faced the inspection eye. A woman's voice spoke. "Yes?"

Gersen spoke in his most confident voice: "I am trying to locate Madame Hedwig Filschner, who lived here many years ago."

"I know no one of that name. You must consult with Ewane Clodig, who owns the property. We only pay rent."

Ewane Clodig, whom Gersen found in the offices of Clodig Properties, consulted his records. "Madame Hedwig Filschner... The name is familiar... I don't see it on my list... Here it is. She moved, let me see, thirty years ago."

"You have her present address?"

"No sir. That is too much to ask. I have not even a forwarding address from thirty years ago... But it comes back! Is she not the mother of Vogel Filschner, the boy slaver?"

"Correct."

"Well then, I can tell you this. When the deed was known, she packed her belongings and disappeared and no one has heard of her since."

Jheral Tinzy's old home was a tall octagonal structure of the so-called Fourth Palladian style, situated halfway up Bailleul Hill. The address corresponded to one which Gersen had noted in the current directory; the family had not changed its residence.

A handsome woman of early middle-age answered the door. She wore a gay peasant smock, a flowered scarf around her head. Gersen appraised the woman before he spoke. She returned a gaze so direct as to be bold. "You're Jheral Tinzy?" Gersen asked tentatively.

"'Jheral'?" The woman's eyebrows arched high. "No. No indeed." She gave a sardonic bark of laughter. "What a strange thing to ask. Who are you?"

Gersen produced his identification. The woman read, returned the card. "What makes you think I am Jheral Tinzy?"

"She lived here at one time. She would be about your age."

"I'm her cousin." The woman considered Gersen more carefully than ever. "What did you want with Jheral?"

"May I come in? I'll explain."

The woman hesitated. As Gersen came forward she made a quick motion to restrain him. Then, after a dubious glance over her shoulder, she moved aside. Gersen entered a hall with a floor of immaculate white glass tiles. On one hand was the display wall characteristic of middle-class European homes; here hung a panel intricately inlaid with wood, bone and shell: Lenka workmanship from Nowhere, one of the Concourse planets; a set of perfume points from Pamfile; a rectangle of polished and perforated obsidian: one of the so-called supplication slabs* from Lupus 2311.

Gersen paused to examine a small tapestry of exquisite design and workmanship. "This is a beautiful piece. Do you know where it came from?"

"It's very rich," agreed the woman. "I believe it came from off-world."

---

* The non-human natives of Peninsula 4A, Lupus 2311, devote the greater part of their lives to the working of these slabs, which apparently have a religious significance. Twice each year, at the solstices, two hundred and twenty-four microscopically exact slabs are placed aboard a ceremonial barge, which is then allowed to drift out upon the ocean.

The Lupus Salvage Company maintains a ship just over the horizon from Peninsula 4A. As soon as the raft has drifted from sight of land, it is recovered, the slabs are removed, exported and sold as *objets d'art.*

"It looks to me like a Sabra piece," said Gersen.

From the upper floor came a harsh call: "Emma? Who is there?"

"Awake already," muttered the woman. She raised her voice. "A gentleman from *Cosmopolis,* Aunt."

"We wish no magazines!" cried the voice. "I am explicit!"

"Very well, Aunt. I'll tell him so." Emma signaled Gersen into a sitting room, jerked her head toward the source of the voice. "Jheral's mother. She is not well."

"A pity," said Gersen. "Where, incidentally, is Jheral?"

Emma turned her bold glance on Gersen. "Why do you want to know?"

"To be candid, I'm trying to locate a certain Vogel Filschner."

Emma laughed soundlessly and without mirth. "You've come to the wrong place to find Vogel Filschner. What a joke!"

"You knew him?"

"Oh yes. He was in the class under mine at the Lyceum."

"You haven't seen him since the kidnapping?"

"Oh no. Never. Still — it's strange that you should ask." Emma hesitated, smiling tremulously as if in embarrassment. "It's like a cloud passing over the sun. Sometimes I look around, sure that I've glimpsed Vogel Filschner — but he's never there."

"What happened to Jheral?"

Emma seated herself, looked far back down the years. "You must remember that there was much publicity and outcry. It was the greatest outrage in memory. Jheral became pointed at; there were unpleasant scenes. Several of the mothers actually slapped and abused Jheral; she had snubbed Vogel, driven him to crime, hence shared his guilt... I must admit," said Emma reflectively, "that Jheral was a heartless flirt. She was simply adorable, of course. She could bring the boys with one little side-look — like this..." Emma demonstrated. "Such a rascal. She even flirted with Vogel: pure sadism, because she couldn't bear the sight of him. Ah, the detestable Vogel! Every day Jheral would come home from school to tell us another of Vogel's enormities. How he dissected a frog, and then, after wiping his hands on a paper towel, ate his lunch! How badly he smelled, as if he never changed his clothes! How he would boast of his poetic mind, and try to impress her with his magnificence! It's true! Jheral with her tricks incited Vogel—and twenty-eight other girls paid the price."

"And then?"

"Great indignation. Everyone turned against Jheral, as perhaps they had always longed to do. Jheral finally ran away with an older man. She never returned to Ambeules. Not even her mother knows where she is."

Into the room rushed a blazing-eyed old woman with a mane of flying white hair. Gersen jumped behind a chair to avoid her charge. "What do you do, asking questions in this house? Be off with you; hasn't there been trouble enough? I don't trust your face; you are like all the rest! Out, never return! Scoundrel! The audacity, entering this house with your filthy questions..."

Gersen left the house as expeditiously as he was able. Emma started to accompany him to the door but her aunt, hobbling forward, shoved her aside.

The door closed; the near-hysterical ranting became muffled. Gersen heaved a deep breath. A virago! He had been lucky to escape without scratches.

At a nearby café Gersen drank a flask of wine and watched the sun sink toward the sea... An excellent possibility, of course, that the entire line of investigation, beginning with the notice in the Avente newspaper, was a wild goose chase. To date the only link between Viole Falushe and Vogel Filschner was the opinion of Kakarsis Asm. Emma Tinzy apparently believed that she had seen Vogel Filschner in Ambeules; Viole Falushe might well enjoy the dangerous pleasure of returning to the scenes of his childhood. If so, why had he not revealed himself to his old acquaintances? Although it seemed that Vogel Filschner had made precious few friends or acquaintances in any event. Jheral Tinzy perhaps had made the wisest of decisions when she took herself away from Ambeules: Viole Falushe had a notoriously long memory. His one friend had been Roman Haenigsen, the chess champion. Somewhere also had been mention of a poet who had incited Vogel Filschner to excess... Gersen called for a directory, and searched for the name Haenigsen. There it was; the book almost fell open to the name. Gersen copied the address and asked directions from a waiter. It appeared that Roman Haenigsen lived hardly five minutes' walk away. Finishing his wine, Gersen set off through the waning sunlight.

The house of Roman Haenigsen was the most elegant of the houses he had visited this day: a three-story structure of metal and meltstone panels, with electric windows to go transparent or opaque at a spoken word.

Haenigsen was only just arriving home when Gersen turned into the walkway: a small brisk man with a large head and prim meticulous features. He peered sharply at Gersen and asked his business. Candor in this case seemed more useful than indirection. Gersen said: "I am making inquiries in regard to your old classmate Vogel Filschner. I understand that you were almost his only friend."

"Hm," said Roman Haenigsen. He thought a moment. "Come, inside, if you will, and we will talk."

He took Gersen into a study decorated with all manner of chess memorabilia: portraits, busts, collections of chess-men, photographs. "Do you play chess?" he asked Gersen.

"I have played on occasion, though not often."

"Like anything else, one must practice to keep in fighting trim. Chess is an old game." He went to a board, disarranged the chess-men with affectionate contempt. "Every variation has been analyzed; there is a recorded game to illuminate the results of any reasonable move. If one had a sufficiently good memory, he would not need to think to win his games; he could merely play someone else's winning game. Luckily, no one owns such a memory but the robots. Still, you did not come here to talk of chess. Will you take a glass of liquor?"

"Thank you." Gersen accepted a crystal goblet containing an inch of spirits.

"Vogel Filschner! Strange to hear that name once more. Is his whereabouts known?"

"This is what I am attempting to learn."

Roman Haenigsen gave his head a wry shake. "You will learn nothing from me. I have neither seen him nor heard from him since 1494."

"I had hardly expected that he would return in his old identity. But it's possible —" Gersen paused as Roman Haenigsen snapped his fingers.

"Peculiar!" said Haenigsen. "Each Thursday night I play at the Chess

Club. Perhaps a year ago I noticed a man standing under the clock. I thought, surely that's not Vogel Filschner? He turned, I saw his face. It was a man somewhat like Vogel, but far different. A man of fine appearance and poise, a man who had nothing of Vogel's hangdog surliness. And yet — since you mention it — there was something to this man, perhaps his manner of holding his arms and hands, which reminded me of Vogel."

"You haven't seen this man since?"

"Not once."

"Did you speak to him?"

"No. In my surprise I must have halted to stare, but then I hurried on past."

"Can you think of anyone Vogel might wish to see? Did he have friends other than yourself?"

Roman Haenigsen pursed his lips wryly. "I was hardly his friend. We shared a laboratory table; I played him an occasional game of chess, which he often won. Had he applied himself he might have taken the championship. But he cared only for mooning over girls and writing bad poetry in imitation of a certain Navarth."

"Ah Navarth. This is the poet whom Vogel Filschner sought to emulate."

"Unfortunately. In my opinion Navarth was a charlatan, a bombast, a man of the most dubious attitudes."

"And what has become of Navarth?"

"I believe he still is about, though hardly the man he was thirty years ago. People have grown wise; studied decadence no longer shocks as it did when I was a lad. Vogel naturally was entranced, and went through the most ludicrous antics in order to identify with his idol. Yes indeed. If anyone is to blame for the crimes of Vogel Filschner it is the mad poet Navarth!"

Chapter V

Drinking whisky by the peg,
Singing songs of drunken glee,
I thought to swallow half a keg
But Tim R. Mortiss degurgled me.

Not precisely *comme il faut*
To practise frank polygamy;
I might have practised, even so,
But Tim R. Mortiss disturgled me.

Chorus:

Tim R. Mortiss, Tim R. Mortiss,
He's a loving friend.
He holds my hand while I'm asleep,
He guides me on my four-day creep,
He's with me to the end.

To woo a dainty Eskimo
I vowed to swim the Bering Sea.
No sooner had I wet a toe
When Tim R. Mortiss occurgled me.

A threat arcane, a fearful bane
Within an old phylactery.
I turned the rubbish down a drain,
Now Tim R. Mortiss perturgles me.

Chorus: (with a snapping of fingers and clicking of heels in mid-air)

Tim R. Mortiss, Tim R. Mortiss,
He's a loving friend.
He holds my hand while I'm asleep,
He guides me on my four-day creep,
He's with me to the end.

...Navarth

—~—

ON THE FOLLOWING DAY Gersen paid a second visit to the offices of the *Helion*. The dossier on Navarth was enthusiastic and ample, reporting scandals, improprieties, defiances and outrageous pronouncements across a period of forty years. The initial entry dealt with an opera presented by students of the university, with libretto by Navarth. The first performance was declared an infamy, and nine students were expelled from the university. Thereafter, Navarth's career soared and collapsed, re-surged, re-collapsed, at last with finality. For the past ten years he had resided aboard a houseboat on the Gaas estuary, near the Fitlingasse.

Gersen tubed to Station Hedrick on Boulevard Castel Vivence, surfaced into the commercial and shipping district of Ambeules, beside the Gaas estuary. The district roiled with the activity of agencies, warehouses, offices, wharves, buffets, restaurants, wine-shops, fruit-hawkers, news-kiosks, dispensaries. Barges nosed into docks to be unloaded by robots; drays rumbled along the boulevard; from below came the vibration of freight moving by tube. At a sweet-shop Gersen inquired for the Fitlingasse and was directed east along the boulevard.

Automatic open-sided passenger-wagons served the boulevard, with patrons riding on benches facing the street. Gersen rode a mile, two miles, with the Gaas on the right hand. The bustle diminished; the imposing blocks and masses of the commercial district gave way to three- and four-story structures of vast age: queer narrow-windowed buildings of melt-stone or terra-cotta panels, stained a hundred subtle colors by smoke and salt air. Occasionally the wagon passed vacant areas, where only weeds grew. Through these gaps could be seen the next street to the north, on a somewhat higher level than Boulevard Castel Vivence, with tall apartment buildings pressed tightly against each other.

The Fitlingasse was a narrow gray alley striking off up the hill. Gersen alighted and almost at once observed a hulking two-storied houseboat moored to a dilapidated dock. A wisp of smoke drifted up from the chimney: someone was aboard.

Gersen took stock of the surroundings. Hazy sunlight played on the estuary; on the far shore thousands of houses with brown tile roofs stood in ranks down to the water's edge. Elsewhere were unused wharves, rotting piles, a warehouse or two, a saloon with purple and green windows extending over the water. On the dock a girl of seventeen or eighteen sat tossing pebbles into the water. She gave Gersen a brief dispassionate stare, looked away. Gersen turned back to consider the houseboat. If this were Navarth's residence he enjoyed a very pleasant prospect — though the wan sunlight, the brown roofs of Dourrai, the rotting wharves, the lapping water, invested the scene with melancholy. Even the girl seemed somber beyond her years. She wore a short black skirt, a brown jacket. Her hair was dark and rumpled: whether from wind or neglect, it could not be known. Gersen approached and inquired, "Is Navarth aboard the houseboat?"

She nodded without change of expression, and watched with the detachment of a naturalist as Gersen descended the ladder to the landing then crossed an alarming gangplank to the foredeck of the houseboat.

Gersen knocked at the door. There was no response. Gersen knocked again. The door was flung violently open; a sleepy unshaven man peered forth. His age was indeterminate; he was thin, spindle-shanked, with a twisted beak of a nose, rumpled hair of no particular color, eyes which though perfectly set gave the impression of looking in two directions at once. His manner was wild and truculent. "Is there no privacy left in the world? Off the boat, at once. Whenever I settle for a moment's rest, some sheep-faced functionary, some importunate peddler of tracts insists on pounding me out of my couch. Will you not depart? Have I not made myself clear? I warn you, I have a trick or two up my sleeve..."

Gersen tried to speak to no avail. When Navarth reached within he hastily retreated to the dock. "A moment of your time!" he called. "I am no functionary, no salesman. I am named Henry Lucas, and I wish —"

Navarth shook his skinny fist. "Not now, not tomorrow, not in the total scope of the future, nor at any time thereafter, do I wish to make your acquaintance. Be off with you! You have the face of a man that brings ill news; a gnashing blacktooth grin. These matters are clear to me: you are fey! I want nothing of you. Go away." With a leer of evil triumph he swung the gangplank away from the landing, re-entered the houseboat.

Gersen returned to the dock. The girl sat as before. Gersen looked back down at the houseboat. He asked in a wondering voice: "Is he always like that?"

"He is Navarth," said the girl, as if this were all that need be said.

Gersen went to the saloon, drank a pint of beer. The bartender was a quiet watchful man of great height with an imposing stomach, and either knew nothing about Navarth or did not choose to reveal what he knew. Gersen gleaned no information.

He sat thinking. A half hour passed. Then going to the telephone directory, he looked in the classified section under 'Salvage'. An advertisement caught his eye:

▪ JOBAN SALVAGE AND TOW ▪

TUGS — CRANE BARGE — DIVING EQUIPMENT

No job too large or too small.

Gersen telephoned and made his needs known. He was assured that on the morrow the equipment he required would be at his service.

The following morning a heavy ocean-going tug drove up the estuary, turned, eased into the mooring next to Navarth's houseboat, with a bare three feet between. The mate bawled orders to the seamen; lines were flung up to the dock and dropped over bollards. The tug was moored.

Navarth came out on deck, dancing with fury. "Must you loom so close? Take that great hulk away; do you intend to thrust me into the dock?"

Leaning on the railing of the tug, Gersen looked down into Navarth's upturned face. "I believe I spoke a few words to you yesterday?"

"I recall very well; I requested your departure, and here you are again, more inconveniently than before."

"I wonder if you would give me the pleasure of a few minutes conversation? Perhaps there might be profit in it for you."

"Profit? Bah. I have poured more money out of my shoe than you have spent. I require only that you take your tug elsewhere."

"Certainly. We are here but for a few minutes."

Navarth gave a pettish nod. At the far side of the tug the diver Gersen had hired was climbing back aboard. Gersen turned to Navarth. "It's very important that I speak to you; if you would be so good as to —"

"This 'importance' exists from a single point of view. Be off with you and your mammoth tug!"

"At once," said Gersen. He nodded to the diver, who touched a button.

Under the houseboat sounded an explosion; the houseboat shuddered, began to list. Navarth ran back and forth in a frenzy. From the tug grapples were lowered and hooked to the houseboat's rub-rail. "Apparently there has been an explosion in your engine room," Gersen told Navarth.

"How can this be? There has never been an explosion before. There is not even an engine. I am about to sink!"

"Not so long as you are supported by the lines. But we are leaving in one minute and I must cast loose the grapples."

"What?" Navarth threw up his arms. "I will go to the bottom, together with the boat! Is this your desire?"

"If you recall, you yourself ordered me to leave," said Gersen in a reasonable voice. "Hence —" he turned to the crewmen. "Throw off the grapples! We depart!"

"No, no!" bellowed Navarth. "I'll sink!"

"If you invite me aboard your boat, if you talk to me and help me compose an article I'm writing, then that's a different matter," said Gersen. "I might be disposed to help you through this misfortune, even, perhaps, to the extent of repairing your hull."

"Why not?" stormed Navarth. "You are responsible for the explosion!"

"Careful, Navarth! That's at the very verge of slander! Remember, there are witnesses!"

"Bah! What you have done is piracy and extortion. Writing an article, indeed! Well, then — why didn't you say so in the first place? I too am a writer! Come aboard; we will talk. I am always grateful for some small diversion; a man without friends is a tree without leaves."

Gersen jumped down upon the houseboat; Navarth, now all amiability, arranged chairs where they caught the full play of the pallid sunlight. He brought forth a bottle of white wine. "Sit then; make yourself at ease!" He opened the bottle, poured, then leaning back in his chair drank with pleasure. His face was placid and guileless, as if all the racial wisdom had passed through leaving no perceptible traces. Like Earth, Navarth was old, irresponsible and melancholy, full of a dangerous mirth.

"You are a writer then? I may say you do not correspond to the usual image."

Gersen produced his *Cosmopolis* identification. "*Mr. Henry Lucas*," read Navarth. "*Special writer*. Why do you come to me? I am no longer heeded, my vogue is a memory. Discredited, penurious. Where was my offense? I sought to express truth in all its vehemence. This is a danger! A Meaning must be uttered idly, without emphasis. The listener is under no compulsion to react, his customary defenses are not in place, the Meaning enters his mind. I have much to say about the world, but every year the compulsion dwindles. Let them live and die; it is all one to me. What is the scope of your article?"

"Viole Falushe."

Navarth blinked. "An interesting topic, but why come to me?"

"Because you knew him as Vogel Filschner."

"Hm. Well, yes. This is a fact not generally known." With fingers suddenly limp Navarth poured more wine. "What specifically do you wish?"

"Knowledge."

"I suggest," said Navarth suddenly brisk, "that you seek the information at its source."

Gersen nodded agreement. "Well enough, if I knew where to look. But what if he is off Beyond? At his 'Palace of Love'."

"This is not the case; he is here on Earth." As soon as Navarth spoke he seemed to regret his ingenuousness and frowned in irritation.

Gersen leaned back, his doubts and misgivings dissolved. Vogel Filschner and Viole Falushe were one; here was a man who knew him in both identities.

Navarth had become uneasy and resentful. "A thousand topics more interesting than Viole Falushe."

"How do you know he's on Earth?"

Navarth made a sound of grand scorn. "How do I know anything? I am Navarth!" He pointed to a wisp of smoke on the sky. "I see that, I know." He pointed to a dead fish, floating belly upward. "I see that, I know." He raised the bottle of wine, held it up against the sunlight. "I see that, I know."

Gersen reflected a moment in silence. "I am in no position to criticize your epistemology," he said at last. "In the first place, I don't understand it… Have you no more explicit knowledge of Viole Falushe?"

Navarth attempted to lay his finger slyly alongside his nose, but miscalculating, prodded his eye. "There is a time for bravado and another for caution. I still do not know the point of your article."

"It is to be a judicious document, without exaggeration or apology. I intend that the facts shall speak for themselves."

Navarth pursed his lips. "A dangerous undertaking. Viole Falushe is the most sensitive of men. Do you recall the princess who detected a pea under forty mattresses? Viole Falushe can smell out a slur in a blind infant's morning invocation to Kalzibah… On the other hand, the world revolves; the carpet of knowledge unrolls. Viole Falushe has given me no cause for gratitude."

"Your appraisal of his character then is negative?" asked Gersen cautiously.

Navarth could control himself no longer. He drank wine with a grandiose gesture. "Negative indeed. Were I to give all orders, what a retribution I would create!" He slumped back in his chair, pointed a skinny finger toward the horizon, spoke in a hushed monotone: "A pyre tall as a mountain, and Viole Falushe at the top! Platforms surrounding for ten thousand musicians. With a single glance I strike the fire. The musicians play while their whisky boils and their instruments melt. Viole

Falushe sings soprano..." He poured more wine. "A wistful vision. It can never be. I would be content seeing Viole Falushe drowned or dismembered by lions..."

"You evidently are well acquainted."

Navarth nodded, his gaze fixed on the past. "Vogel Filschner read my poetry. An imaginative youth, but disoriented. How he changed, how he expanded! To his imagination he added control; he is now a great artist."

"Artist? What manner of artist?"

Navarth dismissed the question as irrelevant. "Never could he have arrived at his present stature without art, without style and proportion! Do not be deceived! Like myself he is a simple man, with the clearest of goals. Now you — you are the most complicated and opaque of men. I see a corner of your mind, then a black film shifts. Are you an Earthman? But tell me nothing." Navarth waved his hands as if to intercept any answer Gersen might feel called upon to make. "There is too much knowledge already in the world; we use facts as crutches, to the impoverishment of our senses. Facts are falsehoods, logic is deceit. I know a single system of communication: the declaiming of poetry."

"Viole Falushe is also a poet?"

"He has no great art with words," grumbled Navarth, unwilling to relinquish control of the conversation.

"When Viole Falushe visits Earth, where does he stay? Here with you?"

Navarth stared at Gersen unbelievingly. "This is a sorry thought."

"Where then does he stay?"

"Here, there, everywhere. He is as elusive as air."

"How do you seek him out?"

"That I never do. He occasionally visits me."

"And he has done so recently?"

"Yes, yes, yes. Have I not implied as much? Why are you so interested in Viole Falushe?"

"To answer this would be to inflict a fact upon you," said Gersen with a grin. "But it's no secret. I represent *Cosmopolis* magazine and I wish to write an article on his life and activities."

"Hmmf. A popinjay for vanity, is Viole Falushe. But why not put your questions to him directly?"

"I would like to do so. First I must make his acquaintance."

"Nothing is easier," declared Navarth, "provided you pay the fees."

"Why not? I am on a liberal expense account."

Navarth jumped to his feet, suddenly full of enthusiasm. "We will need a beautiful girl, young, unsullied. She must project a particular quality of scintillance, a susceptibility, a fervor, an urgency." He looked vaguely here and there, as if in search of something he had lost. Up on the dock he spied the girl whom Gersen had seen the day before. Navarth put fingers to his mouth, produced a shrill whistle, signaled the girl to approach. "She'll do very well."

"Is this an unsullied young scintillant?" asked Gersen. "She seems more of a guttersnipe."

"Ha ha!" cawed Navarth. "You will see! I am weak and cachectic, but I am Navarth: old as I am women bloom under my touch. You shall see."

The girl came aboard the houseboat, and listened to Navarth's program without comment. "We go forth to dine. Expense means nothing, we shall exalt ourselves with the finest. Prepare yourself then with silks, with jewels, with your most precious unguents. This is a wealthy gentleman, the finest of fellows. What is your name once more?"

"Henry Lucas."

"Henry Lucas. He is impatient to proceed. Go then, prepare yourself."

The girl shrugged. "I am prepared."

"You are the best judge of this," declared Navarth. "Inside then, while I consult my wardrobe." He glanced at the sky. "A yellow day, a yellow night. I will wear yellow."

He led the way into his saloon, which was furnished with a wooden table, two chairs of carved oak, shelves stuffed with books and oddments, a vase containing several stalks of pampas grass. Navarth reached into a cabinet for a second flagon of wine, which he opened and banged upon the table, along with glasses. "Drink." With this he disappeared into the next room.

Gersen and the girl were left alone. He examined her covertly. She wore the black skirt of yesterday, with a black short-sleeved blouse, sandals, no jewellery or skin-tone, which on Earth was not currently fashionable. The girl had good features, though her hair was a tangle.

She was either extremely poised or vastly indifferent. On impulse Gersen took a comb from Navarth's wash-stand and going to the girl, combed her hair. After a single startled glance she stood quiet and passive. Gersen wondered what went on in her mind. Was she as mad as Navarth?

"There," he said at last. "You look somewhat less of a ragamuffin."

Navarth returned, wearing a maroon jacket several sizes too large, a pair of yellow shoes. "You have not tasted the wine." He filled three glasses brimming. "A merry evening in prospect! Here, the three of us; three islands in the sea, on each island a castaway soul: we go forth together, and what shall we find?"

Gersen tasted the wine: a fine heady muscatel; he drank. Navarth poured the wine down his throat as if he were emptying a bucket into the estuary. The girl drank, without a tremor, without display of emotion. A strange girl! thought Gersen. Somewhere behind the grave face was flamboyance: what stimulus could bring it forth? What would cause her to laugh?

"Are we ready then?" Navarth looked inquiringly from the girl to Gersen, then threw open the door and ushered them graciously forth. "In search of Viole Falushe!"

Chapter VI

From 'Viole Falushe', Chapter III of *The Demon Princes*,
by Caril Carphen (Elucidarian Press, New Wexford, Aloysius, Vega):

Each of the Demon Princes must cope with the problem of notoriety. Each is sufficiently vain and flamboyant (Attel Malagate is the exception) to wish to flourish his personality, to impress his style upon as many lives as possible. Practical considerations, however, make anonymity and facelessness important, especially as each of the Demon Princes relishes his visits to the worlds of the Oikumene. Viole Falushe is no exception. Like Malagate, Kokor Hekkus, Lens Larque and Howard Alan Treesong, he jealously guards his identity, and not even guests at his 'Palace of Love' have seen his face.

In some respects Viole Falushe is the most human of the Demon Princes: which is to say his vices are on a scale of human understanding. The unimaginable cruelty, reptilian callousness, megalomania, weird mischief exemplified respectively by Kokor Hekkus, Malagate, Lens Larque and Howard Alan Treesong are totally absent. The evil in Viole Falushe can be characterized as arachnid vindictiveness, infantile sensitivity, monstrous self-indulgence.

His vices aside, there is an oddly appealing aspect to Viole Falushe, a warmth, an idealism: so much is conceded by the most uncompromising moralists. Listen to Viole Falushe himself, as he addresses the students of Cervantes University (by recording, naturally):

"I am an unhappy man. I am haunted by my inability to express the inexpressible, to come to terms with the unknown. The pursuit of beauty is, of course, a major psychological drive. In its various guises — which is to say, the urge to perfection, the yearning to merge with the eternal, the explorer's restlessness, the realization of an Absolute created by ourselves, yet larger than our totality — it is perhaps the most single important human thrust.

"I am tormented by this thrust; I strive, I build; yet paradoxically I suffer from the conviction that should I ever achieve my peculiar goals, I might find the results dissatisfying. In this case, the contest is worth more than the victory. I will not describe my own struggle, my griefs, my dark midnights, my heartbreaks. You might find them incomprehensible, or worse, ludicrous.

"I am often described as an evil man, and while I do not dispute the label, I have not taken the stricture to heart. Evil is a vector quality, operative only in the direction of the vector, and often the acts which incur the most censure do singularly small harm to and often benefit the people concerned.

"I am often asked regarding the Palace of Love, but I do not intend to gratify prurient curiosities in this connection. Suffice it to say that I espouse the augmentation of awareness, and find no fault with the gratification of the senses, though I myself practice an asceticism which might surprise you. The Palace of Love extends over a considerable area and is by no means a single structure, but rather a complex of gardens, pavilions, halls, domes, towers, promenades and scenic panoramas. The people of the Palace are all young and beautiful and know no other life; they are the happiest of mortals!"

So speaks Viole Falushe. Rumors are not so kind to him. He is said to be fascinated with erotic variations and culminations. One of his favorite games (reputedly) is to rear a beautiful maiden with great care in an isolated cloister. She is trained to the knowledge that some day she will meet a miraculous creature who will love her and then kill her... And one day she is liberated upon a small island where Viole Falushe awaits.

THE HOTEL PRINCE FRANZ LUDWIG was the most elegant rendezvous of Rolingshaven. The main foyer was enormous: it measured two hundred feet on a side, a hundred feet to the ceiling. Golden light exuded from twelve chandeliers; a deep golden-brown carpet enriched with subtle patterns covered the floor. The walls were covered with silk of pale blue and yellow; the ceiling depicted scenes from a medieval court. The furnishings were of an intricate antique style, solid yet graceful, with cushions of rose or yellow satin, the woodwork lacquered a muted gold. On marble tables stood eight-foot urns from which a profusion of flowers overflowed; beside each table stood a smartly uniformed page-boy. Here: a sumptuous intricacy which could be found nowhere but on old Earth. Never before had Gersen entered a place so grand.

Navarth selected a couch near an alcove where a quartet of musicians played a set of capriccios. Navarth summoned a page and ordered champagne.

"Is this where we seek Viole Falushe?" asked Gersen.

"I have seen him here on several occasions," said Navarth. "We shall be on the alert."

Sitting in the murmurous golden room they drank champagne. The girl's black skirt and blouse, her bare brown legs and sandals, through paradox or improbable juxtaposition, seemed neither tawdry nor unsuitable; and Gersen was somewhat puzzled. How had she managed the transformation?

Navarth spoke of this and that; the girl said little or nothing; Gersen was content to let events go at their own pace: indeed, he found himself enjoying the outing. The girl had put down considerable wine, but showed no effects. She seemed interested in the people who moved through the great foyer, but in a spirit of detachment. At last Gersen asked, "What is your name? I don't know how to speak to you."

The girl did not respond immediately. Navarth said, "Call her what you like. This is my custom. Tonight she is Zan Zu from Eridu."

The girl smiled, a brief flicker of amusement. Gersen decided that she was not, after all, a lackwit.

"Zan Zu, eh? Is this your name?"

"It's as good as any other."

"The champagne is finished, an excellent vintage. We go to dine!"

Navarth rose to his feet, and gave his arm to the girl. Crossing the foyer, they descended four broad stairs into the dining room, which was no less magnificent than the foyer.

Navarth ordered dinner with enthusiasm and finesse; never had Gersen enjoyed a finer meal: one which made him regret the limits imposed by the capacity of his stomach. Navarth ate with voracious enjoyment. Zan Zu of Eridu, as Gersen now thought of the girl, ate delicately, without interest. Gersen watched her sidelong. Was she ill? Had she recently undergone some great sorrow, or shock? She seemed composed enough — too composed, considering the wine she had drunk: muscatel, champagne, the various wines Navarth had ordered to accompany the dinner... Well, it made no difference to him, Gersen reflected. His business was with Viole Falushe. Though here at the Hotel Prince Franz Ludwig, in the company of Navarth and Zan Zu, Viole Falushe seemed unreal... With an effort Gersen brought himself back to the business at hand. How easy to be seduced by richness, elegance, exquisite food, the golden light of chandeliers! He asked, "If Viole Falushe is not to be found here, where do you propose to look?"

"I have no set scheme," Navarth explained. "We must move as the mood takes us. Do not forget that Viole Falushe long ago regarded me as an exemplar. Is it not reasonable to suppose that his program will merge with our own?"

"Reasonable indeed."

"We will test the theory."

They lingered over coffee, trifles of fragrant pastry, quarter-gills of krystallek; then Gersen paid the dinner check, well over SVU 200, and they departed the Hotel Prince Franz Ludwig.

"Now where?" asked Gersen.

Navarth ruminated. "We are somewhat early. Still, at Mikmak's Cabaret there is always amusement of one kind or another, if only in watching the good burghers at their decorous ease."

From Mikmak's Cabaret, they moved to Paru's, on to Der Fliegende Holländer, thence to the Blue Pearl: each new tavern and cabaret somewhat less genteel than the previous, or so it seemed. From the Blue Pearl Navarth led the way to the Sunset Café on the Boulevard Castel Vivence in Ambeules, thereafter to a succession of waterfront dives, beer-cellars and dance-halls. At Zadiel's All-World Rendezvous, Gersen interrupted one of Navarth's dissertations. "Is it here that we can expect Viole Falushe?"

"Where else but here?" demanded the mad poet, now somewhat drunk. "Where the heart of Earth beats the thickest blood! Thick, purple, smelling of must: like crocodile blood, the blood of dead lions. Never fear! You will see your man!...What was I discussing? My youth, my squandered youth! At one time I worked for Tellur Transit, investigating the contents of lost suitcases. Here, perhaps, I gained my deepest insight into the structure of the human soul..."

Gersen sat back in his chair. In the present circumstances passive wariness was the optimum course. To his surprise he found himself slightly drunk, though he had attempted moderation. The colored lights, the musics, Navarth's wild talk were probably no less responsible than the alcohol. Zan Zu was as remote as ever; looking sidelong at her, as he had tended to do all evening, Gersen wondered: what goes on in this umbral creature's mind? What does she hope from life? Does she daydream, does she yearn for a handsome lover, does she ache to travel, to visit the outworlds?

From the ancient cathedral on Flamande Heights came twelve reverberating strokes of the bass bell. "The hour is midnight," croaked Navarth. He rose swaying to his feet, looked from Gersen to Zan Zu from Eridu. "Now we proceed."

"Where now?" asked Gersen.

Navarth pointed across the street, to a long low pavilion with an eccentric roof and festoons of green lights. "I suggest the Celestial Harmony Café, the rendezvous of travelers, spacemen, offworld wanderers, wayward vagabonds such as ourselves."

To the Celestial Harmony Café they walked, Navarth declaiming upon the poor quality of life in present day Rolingshaven. "We are stagnant, slowly decaying! Where is our vitality? Drained to the outworlds! We have bled our life away! On Earth remain the sickly, the depraved, the cryptic thinkers, the sunset wanderers on the mud-flats, the pornoids and involutes, the great epicures, the timid dreamers, the mediaevalists."

"You have traveled the Oikumene?" Gersen inquired.

"Never has my foot lost contact with the soil of Earth!"

"In which of the categories, then, are you included?"

Navarth waved his arms on high. "Have I not inveighed against categories? Here is the Celestial Harmony Café! We arrive at the peak of the evening!"

They entered, threaded their way to a table, and Navarth instantly ordered a magnum of champagne. The café was crowded; voices, clatter, and shuffle competed with boisterous jigs played by an orchestra of fife, concertina, euphonium, banjo, while the clientele danced, cavorted, kicked and pranced after the modes familiar to them. A long bar on a level somewhat higher than the main floor ran the width of the building. Men standing at the railing were silhouetted against the orange and green lights of the bar. At the tables of the main floor sat men and women of every age, race, social condition and degree of sobriety. Most wore European garments, but a few displayed the costumes of other regions and other worlds. Hostesses formal and self-appointed roved here and there, soliciting drinks, dispensing ribald repartee, arranging assignations. The musicians presently took up other instruments: a baritone lute, viola, flute and tympanet, with which they accompanied a troupe of tumblers. Navarth drank champagne with indefatigable zest.

Zan Zu from Eridu looked this way and that, whether from interest, uneasiness, or a sense of suffocation Gersen could not be sure. Her knuckles were white where she held the goblet. She turned her head suddenly, met his gaze; her lips quivered in the faintest possible ghost of a smile. Or an embarrassed grimace... She raised the goblet, and sipped her champagne.

Navarth's gayety was at its height. He sang to the music, tapped the table with his fingers, reached to embrace the hostesses, who sidestepped with an air of boredom.

As if struck by a new thought he turned to consider Zan Zu, then inspected Gersen, as if puzzled why Gersen were not more enterprising. Gersen could not resist another glance at Zan Zu, and whether through wine, the colored lights, the ambiance of the evening, the guttersnipe tossing pebbles from a dock was gone. Gersen stared at her. The transformation was astonishing. She was magic, a creature of entrancing intensity.

Navarth was watching, gayety suddenly abandoned. Gersen turned, Navarth looked quickly away. What am I up to? Gersen wondered. What is Navarth up to?...Reluctantly Gersen rejected the concepts which had surged up into his mind. He settled back into his chair.

Zan Zu, the girl from Eridu, looked somberly down at her goblet. With relief? Sadness? Boredom? Gersen was at a loss to decide. The ways of the girl's mind seemed important indeed. What was he getting into, he asked himself with a pang of bitter anger. He glared at Navarth, who met his gaze blandly. Zan Zu sipped her champagne.

Navarth intoned: "The Vine of Life grows a single melon. The color of the heart is unknown until the rind is split."

Gersen looked out across the tables. Navarth filled his goblet; Gersen drank...Navarth was right. For a gain so wild, so delicious, so magic, there must be an initial abandon, a burning of bridges...What of Viole Falushe? What of his basic momentum? And as if in response to the thoughts Navarth seized his arm. "He is here."

Gersen roused himself from his brooding. "Where?"

"There. At the bar."

Gersen scanned the line of men who stood along the railing. Their silhouettes were nearly identical, some looked this way, some that; some held mugs or flasks; others leaned with elbows on the railing. "Which is Viole Falushe?"

"See the man who watches the girl? He can see no one else. He is fascinated."

Gersen searched along the line of men. None seemed to be paying any great attention. Navarth whispered in a husky voice: "She knows! She is even more aware than I!"

Gersen glanced at the girl, who seemed uneasy; her fingers fumbled with the stem of the goblet. As he watched, she glanced across the room at one of the dark shapes. How she had divined the attention was beyond Gersen's comprehension.

A waiter approached the girl, spoke into her ear: Gersen could not hear what was said. Zan Zu looked down at the champagne goblet, twisted the stem between her fingers...She came to some decision, and putting her hands on the table she rose to her feet. Gersen felt a surge of passion. Ignoble to sit quietly, to allow this to happen! He had been affronted. He was being pillaged of something which, while it had never belonged to him, nevertheless was his own. With a spasm of terror he wondered if it were too late. He lurched forward. He put his arm around the girl's waist, drew her down upon his lap. She turned him an astounded glance, like one suddenly waking from sleep. "Why did you do that?"

"I don't want you to go."

"Why not?"

Gersen could not bring himself to speak. Zan Zu sat passively, if somewhat primly. Gersen noticed that there were tears in her eyes, that her cheeks were wet. Gersen kissed her cheek; Navarth gave vent to a mad cachinnation. "Never, never does it end!"

Gersen put Zan Zu back on her chair, but held his hand over hers. "What never will end?" he asked in an even voice.

"I too have loved. But what of that? The time for love is past. Now there will be trouble, of course. Do you not understand the sensitivity of Viole Falushe? He is as strange and delicate as a fern-frond. He cannot bear deprivation; it sets his teeth on edge and makes him ill."

"This did not occur to me."

"You have acted altogether wrongly," scolded Navarth. "His thoughts were totally for the girl. You need only have followed her, and there would have been Viole Falushe."

"Yes," muttered Gersen. "True... True... I now understand that." He glowered at the wine goblet, then back at the line of silhouettes. Someone was watching; he could sense the attention. There was trouble on the way. He was not in optimum condition, he had not trained in weeks. Additionally he was half-drunk.

A man walking past seemed to slip. He reeled into the table, upset wine into Gersen's lap. He looked into Gersen's face with eyes the color of bone. "Did you trip me, you sneak? I've a mind to spank you like a child."

Gersen studied the man. He had a slab-sided face, close-cropped yellow hair, a short neck as wide as his head. His body was stocky and muscular, the body of a man who spent much of his life on one of the heavy planets. "I don't believe I tripped you," said Gersen. "But sit down. Join us for a glass of wine. Ask your friend to join us, as well."

The white-eyed man paused to consider a moment. He came to a decision. "I demand an apology!"

"Certainly," said Gersen. "It was on the tip of my tongue. If in any way I am responsible for causing you inconvenience, I am sorry."

"This is not enough! I despise foul baboons like yourself who insult one, then think to smirk themselves free of the consequences."

"This is your privilege," said Gersen. "Despise whom you like. But why not bring your friend over to join us? We could find much to talk about. You are from which world?" He raised his glass to drink.

The white-eyed man struck down the glass. "I insist that you leave the premises. You have offended me sufficiently."

Gersen looked across the white-eyed man's shoulder. "Your friend comes, in spite of your asinine braying."

The white-eyed man turned to look; Gersen kicked at his knee, hacked into the bulwark of a neck. Seizing one of the man's arms, Gersen heaved and sent him spinning across the dance-floor. The white-eyed man bounced erect without effort, and came back in a running crouch. Gersen pushed a chair into his face; the white-eyed man swept it aside, while Gersen struck him in the stomach. This was ribbed with muscle and hard as oak. The white-eyed man hunched his shoulders, jumped for Gersen, but four bouncers had appeared. Two propelled Gersen to the rear entrance and ejected him; two more escorted the white-eyed man to the front entrance.

Gersen stood disconsolately in the street. The entire evening: a botchery. What had got into him?

The white-eyed man might well be circling the building to find him. Gersen stepped back into the shadows. After a moment he started cautiously around to the front. At the corner waited the white-eyed man. "Dog's-meat. You kicked me, you struck me. It is my turn."

"Best that you go your way," said Gersen in a mild voice. "I am a dangerous man."

"What do you think of me?" The white-eyed man approached; Gersen backed away, in no mood for rough-housing. He carried weapons, but on Earth killing was not taken lightly... The white-eyed man sidled forward. Gersen's heel came in contact with a bucket. He picked it up, slung it into the white-eyed man's face, and was quickly around the corner. The white-eyed man came after him. Gersen held out his hand to display his projac. "See this? I can kill you."

The white-eyed man stood back, teeth glinting in contempt. Gersen went to the front entrance of the Celestial Harmony Café, the white-eyed man following at a distance of thirty feet.

The table was vacant. Navarth and Zan Zu were gone. The lounging figure at the railing? Lost among the others.

The white-eyed man waited beside the building. Gersen reflected a moment. Then slowly, as if in a reverie, he moved off down the boulevard and turned into a dark side street.

He waited. A minute passed. Gersen slid twenty feet farther along to a more favorable position, all the time watching the gap where street met boulevard. But no one passed in front, no one came to investigate. Gersen waited ten minutes, watching both ways, presently craning his neck to peer up, on the chance that his enemy was coming over the roofs… At last he returned to the boulevard. The botchery was complete. The white-eyed man, the most immediate link with Viole Falushe, had not bothered to pursue Gersen's acquaintance.

Seething with frustration, Gersen rode out Boulevard Castel Vivence to the Fitlingasse. The tug had departed; the houseboat, once more sound of hull, rode dark and silent on the water. Gersen alighted from the cab, went out to stand on the dock. Silence. Lights from Dourrai glinted on the estuary.

Gersen shook his head in mournful amusement. What more could be expected from an evening with a mad poet and a girl from Eridu?

He returned to the cab and was conveyed to the Rembrandt Hotel.

CHAPTER VII

The girl I met in Eridu
Was kind beyond belief;
The hours that I spent with her
Were hours far too brief.

Where willows shade the river-bank,
She urged that I recline.
She fed me figs and poured me full
Of pomegranate wine.

I told of force and time and space,
I told of hence and yonder;
I asked if she would come with me
To know my worlds of wonder.

She clasped her knees; her voice was soft:
"It dazes me to ponder
The blazing stars and tintamars,
The whirling ways you wander!

"You are you and I am I,
And best that you return.
And I will stay in Eridu
With all this yet to learn."

...Navarth

AT TEN O'CLOCK the following morning Gersen returned to the houseboat. All was changed. The sun was yellow and warm. The sky, shining blue with the blue of Earth, was flecked here and there with fair-weather clouds. Navarth sat hunched on his foredeck, sunning himself.

Gersen descended the ladder, walked along the landing. He stopped by the gangplank. "Ahoy. May I come aboard?"

Navarth slowly turned his head, inspected Gersen with the hooded yellow eyes of a sick chicken. He shifted his gaze to watch a string of barges sliding silently along on jets of ionized water. He spoke in an even voice: "I have no sympathy for persons of weak liver, who raise their sails only to drift downwind."

Gersen took the remark as implicit permission to board the boat. "My shortcomings aside, what eventuated?"

Navarth querulously brushed away the question. "We have strayed. The quest, the undertaking—"

"What quest? What undertaking?"

"—leads by a devious route. First there is sunlight. The road is broad and white, but soon it narrows. At the end is an awesome tragedy. A thousand mind-splitting colors, possibly the sunset... If I were young once more, how I would alter events! I have been blown by winds like a bit of trash. You will find it the same. You failed to seize the occasion! Each chance comes a single time—"

Gersen found the remarks uninspiring. "All this to the side, did you speak last night to Viole Falushe?"

Navarth raised a skinny hand in the air, the palm cupped forward. "Tumult! A reel of shapes! Angry faces, flashing eyes, a struggle of passions! I sat with a roaring in my ears."

"What then of the girl?"

"I agree in every respect. Magnificent."

"Where is she? Who is she?"

Navarth's attention became fixed upon an object in the water: a white and grey seagull. Evidently he planned no meaningful responses.

Gersen went on patiently: "What of Viole Falushe? How did you know he would be at the Celestial Harmony Café?"

"Nothing could be simpler. I told him that we would be there."

"When did you inform him?"

Navarth made a fretful movement. "Your questions are tiresome. Must I set my watch by yours? Must I wisely consult with you? Must I—"

"The question seemed simple enough."

"We live by different referents. Transpose, if you like; I cannot."

Navarth was plainly in a cantankerous mood. Gersen said soothingly, "Well then, for one reason or another, we missed Viole Falushe last night. How do you suggest that we find him now?"

"I make no more suggestions...What is your concern with Viole Falushe?"

"You forget that I have already explained this to you."

"To be sure...Well, as to arranging a meeting, this is no great problem. We will invite him to a small entertainment. A banquet perhaps."

Something in Navarth's tone, or perhaps the quick glittering glance which accompanied the words, put Gersen on his guard.

"You think he would attend?"

"Certainly, if it were a carefully planned affair."

"How can you be sure? How do you know definitely that he is on Earth?"

Navarth raised a monitory finger. "Have you ever watched a cat walk through the grass? At times it halts, with one paw raised, and calls out. Is there a reason to these sounds?"

Gersen could not trace the linkage of ideas. He said patiently, "What of this party, or banquet, whatever it is to be?"

"Yes, yes, the party!" Navarth had become interested now. "It must be exquisitely arranged, and it will cost a great deal. A million SVU."

"For one party? One banquet? Who is to be invited? The population of Sumatra?"

"No. A small affair of twenty guests. But arrangements must be made and quickly. I am a source, an inspiration for Viole Falushe. In sheer majesty he has excelled me. But I will prove that in a smaller compass I am superior. What is a million SVU? I have dreamed away more than this in an hour."

"Very well," said Gersen. "You shall have your million." A day's income, he reflected.

"I will need a week. A week is hardly enough. But we dare delay no longer."

"Why not?"

"Viole Falushe returns to the Palace of Love."

"How do you know?"

Navarth looked off across the water. "Do you realize that a crook of my finger disturbs the farthest star? That every human thought disturbs the psychic parasphere?"

"This is the source of your knowledge: psychic perturbations?"

"As good a method as any other. But now as to the party: there are conditions. Art implies discipline; the more excellent the art, the more rigorous the discipline. Hence you must concede to certain limitations."

"What are they?"

"First the money. Bring me a million SVU immediately!"

"Yes, of course. In a sack?"

Navarth gave an indifferent wave of the hand. "Secondly, I am in charge of arrangements. You may not interfere."

"Is this all?"

"Thirdly, you must conduct yourself with restraint. Otherwise you will not be invited!"

"I would not care to miss this party," said Gersen. "But I too will make conditions. First, Viole Falushe must be present."

"Never fear as to that! Impossible to keep him away."

"Secondly, you must identify him to me."

"No need. He will identify himself."

"Third, I want to know how you plan to invite him."

"How else? I call him by telephone, just as I call my other guests."

"What is his number code?"

"He can be reached by coding SORA-6152."

Gersen nodded. "Very well. I will bring you your money at once."

Gersen returned to the Rembrandt Hotel, where he ate a reflective lunch. How mad was Navarth? His spasms of lunacy alternated with periods of canny practicality, both somehow conducing to Navarth's convenience. The call-code SORA-6152, now; Navarth had yielded it with suspicious facility...Gersen could no longer restrain his curiosity. He went to a nearby booth, blanked the lens, touched the buttons. The presentation appeared: the outline of a startled human face. A voice spoke: "Who calls?"

Gersen frowned, bent his head forward. The voice spoke again: "Who calls?" It was Navarth's voice.

Gersen said, "I wish to speak to Viole Falushe."

"Who calls?"

"One who wishes to make his acquaintance."

"Please leave your name and call number; in due course you may receive a return call." And Gersen thought to hear a poorly-suppressed chuckle.

Thoughtfully he left the booth. Galling to be outwitted by a mad poet. He went to the Bank of Vega, called for and received a million SVU in cash. He packed the notes into a case, returned by cab out Boulevard Castel Vivence to the Fitlingasse. As he alighted he saw Zan Zu, the girl from Eridu, emerging from a fishmonger's shop with a paper cornucopia full of fried smelt. She wore her black skirt, her hair was a tousle, but some of the magic of two nights before still hung about her. She went to sit on an old baulk, and looking out across the estuary munched the fish. Gersen thought she appeared tired, listless, a trifle haggard. He proceeded to the houseboat.

Navarth took the money with a noncommittal grunt. "The party then, seven days hence."

"Have you issued invitations?"

"Not yet. Leave all to me. Viole Falushe will be among the guests."

"I presume you will call him at SORA-6152?"

"Of course." Navarth nodded three times, with great gravity. "Where else?"

"And Zan Zu — she is to come?"

"'Zan Zu'?"

"Zan Zu, the girl from Eridu."

"Oh — that one. It might not be wise."

The man's name was Hollister Hausredel; his position: registrar at the Philidor Bohus Lyceum. He was a man of early middle-age, with an almost total lack of distinguishing characteristics. He wore modest gray and black and lived in one of the Sluicht apartment towers with his wife and two small children.

Gersen, deciding that his business with Hausredel would go best at maximum distance from the school, approached him as he left the tube escalator a hundred yards from his apartment building.

"Mr. Hausredel?"

"Yes?" Hausredel was somewhat startled.

"I wonder if we might talk for a moment or two." Gersen indicated a nearby coffee bar. "Perhaps you would have a cup of coffee with me."

"What do you want to talk about?"

"A matter concerning a service you can do for me, to your profit."

The talk went without difficulty; Hausredel was more flexible than his superior, Dr. Willem Ledinger. On the following day Hausredel met Gersen at the coffee bar, with a large paper envelope. "Here we are. All went well. You have the money?"

Gersen passed across an envelope. Hausredel opened the flap, counted, tested one or two of the notes with his fake-meter. "Good. I hope I have helped you as much as you have helped me." And shaking Gersen's hand warmly, he departed the coffee bar.

Gersen opened the envelope. He extracted two photographs copied from those in the school archives. For the first time Gersen saw the face of Vogel Filschner. It was a sullen face. Black eyebrows canted down over burning black eyes, the mouth hung in a discontented droop. Vogel had not been a handsome boy. His nose was long and lumpy, his cheeks were puffy with baby fat, his black hair was overlong and even in the photograph seemed unclean. A more striking contradiction to the popular image of Viole Falushe was hard to imagine... But of course this was Vogel Filschner at the age of fifteen, and many changes had undoubtedly taken place.

The other picture was that of Jheral Tinzy: a delightfully pretty girl: her black hair glossy; her mouth pursed as if she were restraining a mischievous secret. Gersen studied the picture at length. It afforded him rather more perplexity than illumination, inasmuch as the face in the photograph was almost exactly that of Zan Zu, the girl from Eridu.

Thoughtfully Gersen examined the remaining material in the envelope: information regarding other members of Vogel Filschner's class with the present whereabouts, when it was known.

Gersen returned to the picture of Jheral Tinzy. The coquetry was absent in the face of Zan Zu: otherwise one was a replica of the other. The resemblance could not be accidental.

Gersen rode by tube to Station Hedrick in Ambeules, took the now familiar route up Boulevard Castel Vivence.

The time was early evening; sunset color still lingered along the estuary. The houseboat was dark; no one responded to Gersen's rapping. He tested the button: the door slid open.

Gersen entered, the lights came aglow. He went to Navarth's telescreen. The code, as he had expected, was SORA-6152. The crafty Navarth! To the side was an index. Gersen looked through the listings, finding nothing of interest. He scrutinized the wall, the underside of the shelf, the top molding of the telescreen, on the chance that Navarth might have noted down a number he did not care to entrust to his index, finding nothing. From the shelf Gersen took down an untidy portfolio, containing ballads, odes, dithyrambs: *A Growl for Gruel, The Juices I Have Tramped, I Am a Darting Minstrel, They Pass!, Drusilla's Dream, Castles in the Clouds and the Anxieties of Those Who Live Directly Below by Reason of Falling Objects and Wastes.*

Gersen put the poems aside. He inspected the bedrooms. On the ceiling of that occupied by Navarth was the photograph of a naked woman, twice life-size, arms high and outspread, legs extended and stretched apart, hair afloat, as if she were engaged in a vigorous leaping calisthenic. Navarth's wardrobe contained a fantastic assortment of costumes, of every style and color; on a shelf were hats, caps, and helmets. Gersen explored the drawers and cabinets, finding many unexpected objects, but none which seemed to bear upon the matter at hand.

There were two other small bedrooms, both furnished in a rather spartan manner. One of these was pervaded with faint sweet perfume: violet, or lilac; in the other was a desk, and here, by a window overlooking the estuary, Navarth evidently created his poetry. The desk was crammed with notes, names, apostrophes and allusions: a discouraging volume of material which Gersen did not even trouble to explore.

He returned to the main saloon and pouring himself a glass of Navarth's fine *moscato,* dimmed the lights, settled into the most comfortable chair.

An hour passed. The last traces of afterglow departed the sky; the lights of Dourrai glistened on the waves. A dark shape became visible, a hundred yards offshore: a small boat. It approached the houseboat; there was the rattle of oars being shipped and footsteps on the deck. The door slid back. Zan Zu entered the half-dark saloon. She gasped in fear and sprang back.

Gersen caught her arm. “Wait, don’t run away. I’ve been waiting to talk to you.”

Zan Zu relaxed, came into the saloon. Gersen turned up the lights. Zan Zu sat warily on the edge of a bench. Tonight she wore black trousers, a dark blue jacket; her hair was tied back with black ribbon, her face was white and wan.

Gersen looked at her a moment. “Are you hungry?”

She nodded.

“Come along then.”

In a nearby restaurant she ate with an appetite which nullified Gersen’s doubts as to the state of her health. “Navarth calls you Zan Zu; is that your name?”

“No.”

“What is your name?”

“I don’t know. I don’t think I have a name.”

“What? No name? Everyone has a name.”

“I don’t.”

“Where do you live? With Navarth?”

“Yes. For as long as I remember.”

“And he has never told you your name?”

“He has called me by many names,” said Zan Zu somewhat ruefully. “I rather like not having a name; I am anyone I wish to be.”

“Who would you like most to be?”

She flashed Gersen a sardonic glance, gave her shoulders a shrug. Hardly a talkative girl, thought Gersen.

She asked a sudden question: “Why are you interested in me?”

“For various reasons, some complicated, some simple. To begin with, you’re a pretty girl.”

Zan Zu considered the statement a moment. “Do you think so indeed?”

“Hasn’t anyone else told you as much?”

“No.”

Strange, thought Gersen.

"I talk to very few men. Or women. Navarth tells me there is danger."

"What kind of danger?"

"Slavers. I don't care to be a slave."

"Understandable. Aren't you afraid of me?"

"A little."

Gersen signaled a waiter. After consultation he ordered a large piece of cherry torte floating in whipped cream, which was set before Zan Zu from Eridu.

"Well then," said Gersen, "have you been to school?"

"Not a great deal." Gersen learned that Navarth had taken her here and there to odd corners of the world: remote villages and islands, gray cities of the north, resorts of Sinkiang, the Sahara Sea, the Levant. There had been an occasional tutor, seasons at somewhat unusual schools, much reading of Navarth's books. "Not a very orthodox education," Gersen remarked.

"It suits me well enough."

"And Navarth — what is his relationship to you?"

"I don't know. He has always been there. Sometimes he is —" she hesitated. "Sometimes he is kind, other times he seems to hate me... I don't understand, but then I am not particularly interested. Navarth is Navarth."

"He's never mentioned your parents?"

"Never."

"Haven't you asked him?"

"Oh yes. Several times. When he is sober he becomes flamboyant: 'Aphrodite rose from sea-foam. Lilith was the sister of an ancient god. Arrenice sprang to life when lightning struck a rose tree.' And I may select a source at my own discretion."

Gersen listened, surprised and amused.

"When Navarth is drunk, or when he is exalted with poetry, he tells me more, but perhaps it is less: he frightens me. He speaks of the 'journey'. I ask 'journey where?' and he won't say. But it must be something terrible... I don't want to go."

She fell silent. The conversation, so Gersen noticed, had not diminished the gusto with which she attacked the torte. "Has he ever mentioned a man named Viole Falushe?"

"Perhaps. I have not listened."

"Vogel Filschner?"

"No…Who are these men?"

"The same man. Using different names. Do you remember, at the Celestial Harmony Café, the man who stood by the railing?"

Zan Zu looked down into her coffee cup, gave a slow thoughtful nod.

"Who was he?"

"I don't know. Why do you ask?"

"Because you started to go to him."

"Yes. I know."

"Why? If you don't know him?"

The girl twisted the cup back and forth, watching the swirls of black liquid. "It's hard to explain. I knew he was watching me. He wanted me to come. Navarth had brought me there. And you were there. As if everyone wanted me to go to him. As if I were — something to be sacrificed. I was dizzy. The room was unsteady. Perhaps I had drunk too much wine. But I wanted to have it all over with. If this were my fate, I would know…But you wouldn't let me go. I remember this much. And I…" She stopped, and took her hands away from the coffee cup. "Anyway, I know you mean me no harm."

Gersen said nothing. Zan Zu asked tentatively, "Do you?"

"No. Are you finished?"

They returned to the houseboat, which was as they had left it. "Where is Navarth?" Gersen asked.

"He prepares for his party. He is tremendously excited. Since you have come all is different."

"And after I left the Celestial Harmony Café the other night, what happened?"

Zan Zu frowned. "There was talk. It seems there were lights in my eyes, orange and green blurs. The man came to the table, and stood looking down at me. He spoke to Navarth."

"Did you look at him?"

"No. I don't think so."

"What did he say to Navarth?"

Zan Zu shook her head. "There was a sound in my ears, like rushing water, or the roar of the wind. I didn't hear. The man touched my shoulder."

"And after that — what?"

Zan Zu grimaced. "I don't remember... I can't remember."

"She was drunk!" cried out a voice. Navarth rushed into the saloon. "Carefully drunk! What are you doing aboard my private houseboat?"

"I came to learn how you are spending my money."

"All is as before. Now depart at once."

"Come, come," said Gersen patiently. "This is a cavalier tone to take to the man who repaired your houseboat."

"After first stoving it in? Bah! Has there ever been an act to equal it?"

"I understand that in your youth you contrived a few outrages of your own."

"'In my youth'?" sputtered Navarth. "I have contrived outrages all my life!"

"What of the party?"

"It is to be a poetic episode, an exercise in experiential art. I think it best that you do not attend this particular party, as —"

"What? I'm paying for it! If I don't come, give me back my money."

Navarth flung himself petulantly into a chair. "I expected you to take this line."

"I'm afraid so. Where is the party to be held?"

"We meet at the village Kussines, twenty miles to the east. The rendezvous is precisely at the hour of two in the afternoon, in front of the inn. You must wear harlequinade and a domino."

"Viole Falushe is to come?"

"Indeed, indeed; have I not made all clear?"

"Not altogether. All are to wear dominoes?"

"Naturally."

"How will I recognize Viole Falushe?"

"What a question to ask. How can he hide? Black radiation hangs about him. He exudes a dread sensation."

"These qualities may be obvious," said Gersen. "Still — how else may he be identified?"

"You must determine this at the time. At the moment, I do not know myself."

CHAPTER VIII

AT TEN MINUTES BEFORE the appointed hour, Gersen parked his rented air-car in a meadow on the outskirts of Kussines and alighted. A cloak concealed the harlequinade; he carried the domino in his pocket.

The afternoon was soft and sunny, fragrant with the exhalations of autumn. Navarth could hardly have hoped for a finer day, thought Gersen. He checked his garments carefully. The harlequinade offered little scope for concealment, but Gersen had made the best of the situation. Inserted horizontally into his belt was a blade of thin keen glass, the buckle serving as a handle. Under his left arm hung a projac; in his right sleeve was poison. Thus encumbered, Gersen swept his cloak about him and marched into the village: a collection of ancient black iron and melt-stone structures on the shore of a small lake. The setting was bucolic and charming, almost mediaeval; the inn, perhaps the newest structure of the village, was at least four hundred years old. As Gersen approached, a young man in gray and black stepped forward. "For the afternoon party, sir?"

Gersen nodded and was led to a dock at the edge of the lake where a canopied boat awaited. "Domino, please," said the young man in uniform. Gersen donned the mask, stepped aboard the boat and was conveyed to the opposite shore.

It seemed that he was one of the last to arrive. At a semi-circular buffet stood perhaps twenty other guests, all self-conscious in their costumes. One who could only be Navarth came forward, divested Gersen of his cloak. "While we wait, taste this vintage; it is supple and light and will amuse you."

Gersen took the wine and stepped aside. Twenty men and women:

which was Viole Falushe? If he were present, he was not readily apparent. A slender young woman stood stiffly nearby, holding her goblet as if it contained vinegar. Navarth had allowed Zan Zu to the party after all, thought Gersen. Or dragooned her into coming, to judge by her attitude. He counted. Ten men, eleven women. If parity of sexes were to be observed, there still remained at least one man to arrive. Even as Gersen counted the white-canopied punt drifted into the dock; a man stepped ashore. He was tall, lean; his manner combined indolent ease with a taut wariness. Gersen inspected him carefully. If this were not Viole Falushe, he must be considered the most likely candidate... The man slowly approached the group. Navarth hurried forward with a crouch that was almost servility, took the cloak which the man tossed to him. With the cloak hung on its peg, a goblet of wine in the newcomer's hand, Navarth's ebullience returned. He waved his arms, walked back and forth with long springing strides. "Friends and guests, all are now arrived: a chosen group of nymphs and under-gods, poets and philosophers. Notice, as we stand here in the meadow, our patterns of orange and red, and black and red; we contrive an unconscious pavane! We are performers, participants and spectators at the same time! The frame within which spontaneity is confined — the theme, so to speak — is that which I have ordained; the variations, the intricacies, counterplay and development is our mutual concern. We must be subtle and free, carefully reckless, at all times consonant; our figures must never leave the chord!" Navarth held his goblet up to a shaft of sunlight, drank with a grand flourish, pointed dramatically through the trees. "Follow me!"

Fifty yards away was a charabanc with a tasseled yellow canopy, sides enameled in red, orange and green. Benches cushioned in bright orange plush ran along the sides, in the center kneeling marble satyrs supported a marble slab on which were dozens of bottles of every size, shape and color, all containing the same soft wine.

The guests climbed aboard, the charabanc slid off, silent and easy on its repulsion skids.

Through a beautiful park drifted the charabanc. Magnificent vistas opened to all sides. The guests gradually discarded restraint; there was conversation and laughter, but for the most part all were content to sip the wine and enjoy the autumn scenery.

Gersen scrutinized each man in turn. The last man to arrive still seemed the most likely candidate for the identity of Viole Falushe; Gersen thought of him as Possibility No. 1. But at least four others were tall, lean, dark, composed: Possibilities No. 2, No. 3, No. 4, No. 5.

The charabanc halted, the group stepped down into a meadow sprinkled with purple and white asters. Navarth, hopping and skipping like a young goat, led the group under a grove of tall trees. The time was now about three o'clock; afternoon sunlight slanted through the masses of golden leaves, to play upon a great rug of tan and golden silk with a border of gray-greens and blues. Beyond stood a silken pavilion supported by white spiral poles.

Spaced around the rug were twenty-two tall peacock-tail chairs. Beside each stood an antique tabouret of ebony inlaid with mother-of-pearl and cinnabar, with a vermilion bowl of crystallized spice on each. Working by some mysterious rationale Navarth arranged his guests in the splendid chairs. Gersen found himself at one end of the rug with Zan Zu several chairs distant, and the various Possibilities at the far side. From somewhere came music, or more accurately, near-music: a succession of wry quiet chords, sometimes so soft as to be unheard, sometimes so complex as to be equivocal and perplexing, never completing or fulfilling a progression, always of a haunting sweetness.

Navarth took his own place, and all sat quietly. From the pavilion came ten young girls naked but for golden slippers and yellow roses over their ears. They bore trays on which were goblets of heavy green glass, containing the same delicate wine as before.

Navarth remained in his chair; the other guests were content to do likewise. Sun-drenched yellow leaves floated down to the golden rug; an aromatic odor hung in the air. Gersen sipped his wine cautiously; he could not afford to be lulled, soothed. Close at hand was Viole Falushe, a situation for which he had paid a million SVU. The sly Navarth had not kept the letter of his promise. Where was the "aura of black radiation" Navarth had mentioned? It seemed to hang heaviest around Possibilities No. 1, No. 2 and No. 3, but in this regard Gersen was disinclined to trust his parapsychic powers.

A tension, an expectancy, began to be felt. Navarth sat crouched in the chair, as if already bemused. The naked girls, dappled by sunlight and leaf-shadow, poured wine, moving slowly, as if walking under water... Navarth lifted his head, as if hearing a voice or a far sound. He spoke, in an exultant voice, and the vagrant chords seemed to match themselves to the rhythm of his speech, creating music. "Some here have known emotion in many phases. No one can know every emotion, for these are both infinite and fugitive. Some here are unaware, untouched, unexplored — and know it not. See me! I am Navarth, called the mad poet! But is not every poet mad? It is inevitable. His nerves are conductive and transport uncontainable gushes of energy. He fears: how he fears! He feels the movement of time; between his fingers it is a warm pulsing, as if he grasped an exposed artery. At a sound — a distant laugh, a ripple of water, a gust of wind — he becomes sick and faints — because never in all the extent of time can this sound, this ripple, this gust recur. Here is the deafening tragedy of the 'journey' which we all undertake! Would the mad poet want it any differently? Never exulting? Never desperate? Never clasping life against his bare nerves?" Navarth leapt to his feet and danced a jig. "All here are mad poets. If you would eat, the delicacies of the world await. If you would reflect, sit in your chairs and watch the fall of the leaves. Notice how slow is their motion; here time has slowed on our behalf. If you would exalt yourself, this magnificent vintage never cloys nor stupefies. If you would explore erotic proximities, or middle distances, or indistinct horizons: bowers and dells surround us." His voice descended an octave; the chords became measured and slow. "There can be no light without shade, no sound without silence. Exultation skips along the verge of pain. I am the mad poet, I am Life! Hence, by the inevitable consequence, Death is here as well. But where Life cries out its meanings, Death sits quiet. Look then among the masks!"

And Navarth pointed from one silent harlequin to another, around the circle. "Death is here, Death watches Life. It is not witless, aimless Death. It is Death with a snuff cap, intent on a single candle. So — do not fear, unless you have cause to fear..." Navarth turned his head. "Listen!"

From far away came a merry sound: music. It grew louder and louder still, and into the glade marched four musicians: one with castanets, one with guitar and two fiddlers, and they played the most impelling and merry of jigs, enough to set the pulses racing. Suddenly they stopped short in their music. The castanet player brought forth a flute and now the music was of a heart-breaking melancholy. And playing in this fashion they moved off through the trees and presently were lost to hearing. The soft indecisive chords went on as before, without beginning or end, as easy and natural as breathing.

Gersen had become uneasy. Circumstances were moving beyond his control. In this harlequinade, he felt inept. Was this another of Navarth's crafty ploys? Were Viole Falushe to stand before him now and announce himself, Gersen could never act. The autumn air was heavy with haze; the wine had made him maudlin. He could never spill blood on the magnificent rug of tawny tan and gold. Nor even on the carpet of golden leaves beyond.

Gersen leaned back in his chair, amused and disgusted with himself. Very well then; for the moment he would sit and reflect. Some of the other guests were stirring. Perhaps Navarth's talk of death had chilled them, for they moved tentatively and carefully. Gersen wondered to whom Navarth had referred, in his talk of death...The girls moved sedately along the line of chairs, pouring wine. As one bent near Gersen, he caught the scent of her yellow rose; straightening, she smiled at him, and passed on to the next guest.

Gersen drank the wine. He leaned back in the chair. Even if he had become detached and passionless, he could yet speculate. Certain of the guests had risen to their feet and leaving their high-backed chairs, mingled and talked in soft husky voices. Possibility No. 1 stood brooding. Possibility No. 2 stared fixedly at Zan Zu. Possibility No. 3, like Gersen, sprawled in his chair. Possibilities No. 4 and No. 5 were among those talking.

Gersen looked toward Navarth. What next? Navarth's intention must extend beyond the instant. What more had he planned? Gersen called to him. Navarth turned aside reluctantly.

Gersen asked, "Is Viole Falushe here?"

"Tish!" exclaimed Navarth. "You are a monomaniac!"

"I have been told as much before. Well, is he here?"

"I invited twenty-one guests. Counting myself, twenty-two are present. Viole Falushe is here."

"Which is he?"

"I don't know."

"What? You don't know?" Gersen sat upright, aroused from his lethargy by Navarth's double-dealing. "We must have no misunderstanding, Navarth. You accepted a million SVU from me, agreeing to fulfill certain conditions."

"And I have done so," snapped Navarth. "The simple truth is that I do not know in what semblance Viole Falushe currently walks. I knew the boy Vogel Filschner well. Viole Falushe has altered his face and his manner. He might be one of three or four. Unless I were to unmask this group, send away those I recognized until one remained, I could not give you Viole Falushe."

"Very well, this we shall do."

Navarth would not submit. "My life might well be slid from my body by one route or another. I object to this. I am a mad poet, not a lummox."

"Immaterial. This is how we will act. Be so kind as to summon your candidates into the pavilion."

"No, no!" croaked Navarth. "It is impossible. There is an easier way. Watch the girl. He will go to her. And then you will know."

"A half-dozen might go to her."

"Then claim her. Only one man would challenge you."

"And if no one challenges?"

Navarth held out his arms. "What can you lose?"

Both turned to look toward the girl. Gersen said, "What can I lose indeed?...What is her relationship to you?"

"She is the daughter of an old friend," declared Navarth suavely. "She is, in effect, my ward; I have been at pains to nurture her and bring her nicely to maturity."

"And this now accomplished, you offer her here and there to passing strangers?"

"The conversation becomes tiresome," said Navarth. "Look. A man approaches the girl!"

Gersen swung around. Possibility No. 2 had approached Zan Zu and was talking in a manner unmistakably ardent. Zan Zu listened politely. As in the Celestial Harmony Café, Gersen felt a surge of emotion: lust?

jealousy? protective instinct? Whatever the nature of the urge, it compelled him to step forward and join the two.

"You are enjoying the party?" Gersen asked with factitious good-fellowship. "A wonderful day for such an outing. Navarth is a magnificent host; still he has introduced no one to no one. What is your name?"

Possibility No. 2 answered courteously: "Navarth doubtless has good reason for the neglect; best that we do not divulge our identities."

"Sensible," said Gersen. He turned to Zan Zu. "Still, what is your opinion?"

"I have no identity to divulge."

Possibility No. 2 suggested: "Why not approach Navarth and inquire his thoughts on the subject?"

"I think not. Navarth would become confused. He has propounded a fallacy. He seems to advocate intimate relationships between walking costumes. Is this feasible? I doubt it. Certainly not at the level of intensity Navarth would insist upon."

"Quite so, quite so," said Possibility No. 2. "Be a good fellow and leave us to ourselves. The young lady and I were enjoying a private discussion."

"My apologies for interrupting you. But the young lady and I already had planned to gather flowers from the meadow."

"You are mistaken," said Possibility No. 2. "When all wear harlequinade, error is easy."

"If there has been error, it is for the best, as I prefer this delightful young flower-picker to the last. Be so good as to excuse us."

Possibility No. 2 was amiability itself. "Really, my good fellow, your facetiousness has run its course. Surely you must see that you are intruding?"

"I think not. In a party of this sort, where experience is to be clasped to the naked nerves, where Death walks, there is wisdom in flexibility. Notice the woman yonder. She appears loquacious and prepared to discuss every subject in your repertory. Why not join her and chat away to your heart's content?"

"But it is you she admires," said Possibility No. 2 brusquely. "Be off with you."

Gersen turned to Zan Zu. "Apparently you must make the choice. Conversation or wildflowers?"

Zan Zu hesitated, looking from one to the other. Possibility No. 2 fixed her with a gaze of burning intensity. "Choose, if there indeed is a choice — between this lout and myself. Choose — but choose carefully."

Zan Zu demurely turned to Gersen. "Let us pick flowers."

Possibility No. 2 stared, looked away toward Navarth as if to call upon him to intercede, then thought better of it and walked away.

Zan Zu asked, "Are you really anxious to pick wild flowers?"

"You know who I am?"

"Of course."

"I don't care to pick wild flowers, unless you do."

"Oh... What then do you want of me?"

Gersen found the question hard to answer. "I do not know myself."

Zan Zu took his arm. "Let us go to look for flowers, and perhaps we will find out."

Gersen looked around the group. Possibility No. 2 watched from a distance. Possibilities No. 1 and No. 3 appeared to pay them no heed. He started off through the trees, Zan Zu leaning on his arm. Gersen put his arm around her waist; she sighed.

Possibility No. 2 gave a quick jerk of the shoulders, and by this motion seemed to cast off restraint. He came after Gersen with soft portentous strides; in his hand he carried a small weapon. Behind, so Gersen saw in a near-instantaneous glimpse, stood Navarth, looking after, his posture a curious superimposition of shame on glee.

Gersen pushed Zan Zu to the ground, ducked behind a tree. Possibility No. 2 halted. He turned toward Zan Zu, and to Gersen's shocked amazement, pointed his weapon. Gersen leapt from behind the tree, struck the man's arm; the weapon threw a sear of energy into the ground. The two confronted each other, eyes blazing mutual hate... A shrill blast of whistle. From the forest came the thud of heavy feet; gendarmes swarmed forth, a dozen or more, urged by a lieutenant in a golden helmet and a furious old man in brocaded gray.

Navarth stepped forward haughtily. "What is the meaning of this intrusion?"

The old man, who was short and overweight, bounded forward to shake his fist. "What the devil are you up to, trespassing upon my private property? You are a jackanapes! And these naked girls — an absolute scandal!"

In a stern voice Navarth demanded of the lieutenant: "Who is this old rogue? What right does he have to intrude upon a private party?"

Now the old man, stepping forward, discerned the rug, and went pale. "Behold!" he whispered huskily. "My priceless silk Sikkim rug! Spread out for these rascals to cavort upon. And my chairs, oh my precious Bahadurs! What else have they stolen?"

"This is balderdash!" stormed Navarth. "I have rented these premises and hired the furniture. The owner is Baron Caspar Heaulmes, who is at a sanatorium for his health."

"I am Baron Caspar Heaulmes!" cried the old man. "I do not know your name, sir, behind that ridiculous mask, but I perceive you to be a blackguard! Lieutenant, do your duty. Take them all away. I insist on the fullest investigation!"

Navarth threw his hands into the air, and argued the case from a dozen viewpoints, but the lieutenant was inexorable. "I fear I must take all into custody. Baron Heaulmes is making a formal complaint."

Gersen, standing to the side, had been watching with great interest, simultaneously noting the movements of Possibilities No. 1, No. 2, No. 3. Whichever was Viole Falushe — and it would seem to be Possibility No. 2 — he would be sweating heavily at this moment: once he were arrested and taken into court, his identity must become known.

Possibility No. 1 stood dour and dismal; Possibility No. 2 was carefully assessing the situation, looking this way and that; Possibility No. 3 seemed unconcerned, even amused.

The lieutenant by this time had seized Navarth, charging him with trespass, theft, offenses against public morality and simple assault: the latter arising from his attempt to kick Baron Heaulmes. The remaining gendarmes now commenced to herd the guests toward a pair of carcel-wagons which had descended to the meadow. Possibility No. 2 loitered at the edge of the group and taking advantage of Navarth's obstreperous behavior slipped behind a tree. Gersen raised up a shout; a pair of gendarmes looked around, bawled peremptory orders and marched forward to conduct Possibility No. 2 to the carcel-wagons. Possibility No. 2 jumped back among the trees; when the gendarmes ran in pursuit, there came a dire flash of radiation: once, twice, and two men lay dead. Possibility No. 2 sprinted away through the forest and was lost to view. Gersen gave chase, but halted after a hundred yards, fearing ambush.

Shedding mask, he ran to the semi-circular buffet beside the pond, where he found and donned his cloak. The punt ferried him across the lake to the outskirts of Kussines.

Five minutes later he reached his air-car and took it aloft. He hovered several minutes, searching the air-space. If Possibility No. 2 had arrived by air-car, he must likewise be taking himself aloft. And also, thought Gersen, patrol craft would be converging on the scene of the murders. One man in harlequinade looked much like another; the sooner he was gone the better. And Gersen flew full speed back toward Rolingshaven.

Chapter IX

From the Rolingshaven *Mundus*:

> Kussines, September 30: Two agents of the County Gendarmerie this afternoon were murdered by a guest at a mysterious orgy on the estate of Baron Caspar Heaulmes at Kussines. In the confusion attendant upon the violence the murderer made good a temporary escape and is believed to be hiding in the woods. His name has not yet been made public.
>
> Host and ringleader at the bacchanalian fête was the notorious poet and free-thinker Navarth, whose escapades have long edified the citizens of Rolingshaven…

The article goes on to describe the circumstances of the murder. The names of the persons taken into custody are listed.

—~~—

From the Rolingshaven *Mundus*:

> Rolingshaven, October 2: Victim of an inexplicable attack was Ian Kelly, 32, of London, who last night was waylaid in the Bissgasse and viciously beaten to death. There is no clue as to the identity of his assailant, and no apparent motive. Kelly figured in the news two days ago as a guest at the poet Navarth's fantastic party on the estate of Baron Caspar Heaulmes. Police are working on the theory that the two circumstances are connected.

Article for *Cosmopolis*:

VIOLE FALUSHE

by Navarth

PART I: THE BOY

Notorious as much for his fascinating Palace of Love as for the ghastly score of his crimes is Viole Falushe, the Demon Prince. Who is he, what is he? I, perhaps better than anyone alive, am able to calculate his motives and analyze his acts. I have little knowledge of the man as he is today. If he were to pass me on the street I would not recognize him. But I can say this much: judging by Viole Falushe as a youth, I find the popular concept of Viole Falushe — which is to say, a man handsome, elegant, gay, romantic — impossible to credit. The notion is, in fact, startling and ludicrous.

I first met Viole Falushe when he was fourteen. His name was then Vogel Filschner. If the man resembles the boy, his celebrated amours can only have been achieved through duress or drugs. As all know, I am jealous of my reputation for dispassionate candour, and to this end interviewed all the women who, as girls, knew Vogel Filschner well. I withhold their names, for obvious reasons. Representative comments:

"— a boy preoccupied with every sort of nastiness."

"Vogel was utterly repellent, though there were boys far uglier than he in our class. Four years I knew him, and instead of learning to take pains with himself he became worse."

"I could never bear to sit next to Vogel. He smelled badly, as if he never changed his socks or his underwear. I'm sure he never washed his hands and possibly never bathed."

"Vogel Filschner! I suppose it was not all his fault. His

mother must have been a sloven. He had disgusting personal habits, such as picking his nose and examining the yield, making queer gulping noises, and above all *smelling*."

These are representative remarks; indeed, some of the milder comments. I am a man, above all, fair and judicious; hence I quote none of the more extravagant anecdotes.

Let me describe Vogel Filschner as I knew him. He was tall and arachnid, with spindly legs and an unhealthy round belly. To complete the somewhat spider-like illusion were his round cheeks and pink proboscis of a nose. To his credit he admired my poetry, though I fear that Vogel distorted my doctrines beyond recognition. I preach augmented existence; Vogel wanted me to approve his solipsistic ruthlessness.

The first occasion I was approached by Vogel Filschner was at the time of my celebrated contretemps with Dame Amelie Pallemont-Dalhouse, in connection with my sponsorship of her daughter Earline, which of course is a fascinating tale in itself. In any event, Vogel appeared one morning with some wretched doggerel he had written. It seems that Vogel's juices were flowing, that he was in love with a pretty girl who needless to say was far from flattered by the compliment...

The article continued for several pages.

—~—

ON OCTOBER 3 NAVARTH, having paid exemplary damages of SVU 50,000 to Baron Caspar Heaulmes, was discharged from the court, which likewise dismissed charges against Navarth's guests.

Gersen met Navarth on the mall in front of the Justice Courts. Navarth at first made as if he would pass without deigning to recognize Gersen, but Gersen finally was able to divert him to the table of a nearby café.

"Justice, bah!" Navarth made a grimace toward the courts. "Think of it! Money I must pay that vindictive and sanctimonious unmentionable! He should have indemnified me! Did he not disrupt the party? What did he hope to gain, running forth from the forest like that?" Navarth paused to moisten his throat with the beer Gersen had ordered. "It is enough to turn a man sour." He set the mug down with a thump and turned a yellow glance toward Gersen. "What do you want of me now? Another exercise in bathos? I warn you, I will not be so malleable a second time."

Gersen displayed the newspaper articles dealing with the event. Navarth refused to look at them. "A wretched lot of nonsense, sheer scurrility. You journalists are all alike."

"I notice that yesterday a certain Ian Kelly was murdered."

"Yes, poor Kelly. Did you come to the arraignment?"

"No."

"Then you missed your chance, because among the crowd was Viole Falushe. He is the most sensitive of men and cannot forget an injury. Ian Kelly was unlucky enough to resemble you in size and manner." Navarth shook his head ruefully. "Ah, that Vogel! He detests frustration as a bee-sting."

"Do the police know the murderer is Viole Falushe?"

"I told them he was a man I met in a bar. What else could I say?"

Gersen had no reply to make. He indicated the article once more. "Twenty names are listed, which refers to Zan Zu?"

Navarth made a contemptuous gesture toward the article. "Select as you like. One is as accurate as the next."

"One of these names must refer to her," said Gersen. "Which?"

"How should I know what name she chooses to supply the police? I believe I will drink more beer. The argument has parched my throat."

"I see here a 'Drusilla Wayles, age 18'. Is this she?"

"Quite possibly, possibly indeed."

"And this is her name?"

"Merciful Kalzibah! Must she own a name? A name is a weight! A chain to a set of uncontrolled circumstances. To own no name is to own freedom! Are you so stolid then that you cannot imagine a person without a name? She is what one chooses to call her."

"Strange," said Gersen. "She exactly resembles the Jheral Tinzy of thirty years ago."

Navarth jerked back in his chair. "How do you know this?"

"I have not been idle. For example, I have produced this." Gersen produced a dummy *Cosmopolis*. From the cover looked the face of young Vogel Filschner superimposed upon the outline of a tall ominous gray figure. Below was the caption: THE YOUNG VIOLE FALUSHE: *Vogel Filschner as I knew him, by Navarth.*

Navarth seized the dummy, read the article aghast. He raised his hands to his head. "He'll kill us all! He'll drown us in dog-vomit! He'll grow trees in our ears!"

"The article seems balanced and judicious," said Gersen. "Certainly he can take no offense at facts!"

Navarth read further, and went into a new paroxysm of dismay. "You have signed my name! I never wrote all that!"

"It's all true."

"The more so! When is this to be published?"

"In a week or two."

"Impossible. I forbid it."

"In that case, return me the money I lent you, that you might finance your party."

"'Lent'?" Navarth was shocked anew. "That was no loan! You paid me, you hired me to produce a party, at which Viole Falushe would be present."

"You did neither. Baron Heaulmes, it is true, truncated your party, but this is no affair of mine. And where was Viole Falushe? You can point to the murderer, but this means nothing to me. Please return the money."

"I cannot! I have spent money like water! And Baron Heaulmes demanded his pound of flesh."

"Well, return me the nine hundred thousand SVU you have left."

"What? I have no such sum on hand!"

"Perhaps we can set aside a portion as your payment for this article, but—"

"No, no! The article must not be published!"

"Best that we have a complete understanding," said Gersen. "You have not told me all."

"For which I am grateful. You have published the rest." Navarth kneaded his forehead. "These have been terrible days. Have you no pity for poor old Navarth?"

Gersen laughed. "You plotted to get me killed. You knew that Viole Falushe would attempt to possess Drusilla Wayles, or Zan Zu, whatever her name. You knew that I would not allow it. Ian Kelly paid his life in my place."

"No, no, nothing like that! I hoped you would kill Viole Falushe!"

"You're a devious villain. What of Drusilla, how was she to fare? Did you consider her?"

"I consider nothing," said Navarth huskily. "I cannot allow myself to ponder. If I lifted the partition between my two brains for so much as an instant…"

"Tell me what you know."

With extreme reluctance Navarth obeyed. "I must go back to Vogel Filschner once more. When he kidnapped the choral society, Jheral Tinzy escaped. That you know. But she was the cause of the crime and the parents of the other girls blamed her… It became very hard, very rough. There were threats, names called in public…"

Navarth had come under similar attack. One day he proposed to Jheral Tinzy that they run away together. Jheral, bitter and disillusioned, was in a mood for anything. They went to Corfu where they spent three years, and every day Navarth loved Jheral Tinzy more ardently than the day previously.

One terrible day Vogel Filschner appeared at the door of their little villa. He was no longer the old Vogel, though his appearance was much the same. He stood more erect, but the most striking change was his new personality. He had become hard, sure, firm; his eyes were bright, his voice assured. Evil-doing clearly was good for him.

Vogel made a great show of amity to Navarth. "Past is past. Jheral Tinzy? I want nothing from her. She has given herself to you; she is sullied. I am fastidious in this respect; I take no woman fresh from another man's use. Be assured, she never will know an iota of my love… She should have waited. Yes. She should have waited. Because she might have known I would return… But now my love for Jheral Tinzy is gone."

Navarth was somewhat reassured. He brought out a bottle; they sat in the garden, ate oranges, drank ouzo. Navarth became very drunk, and fell asleep. When he awoke Vogel Filschner was gone. Jheral Tinzy was gone as well.

A day later Vogel Filschner reappeared. Navarth was in a frenzy. "Where is she? What have you done with her?"

"She is well and safe."

"What of your promise? You told me you had no more love for her!"

"This is true. The promise shall be kept. Jheral will never know my love, nor the love of any other man. Do you underestimate my emotion, poet? Love can turn to hate in a flicker of time. Jheral will serve, and serve well. She would not gratify my love, but she will appease my hate."

Navarth threw himself at Vogel Filschner, but Vogel vaulted over the wall, and Navarth was left alone.

Nine years later Viole Falushe made contact with Navarth by telescreen, but now his face was blanked. Navarth heard only his voice. Navarth asked for the return of Jheral Tinzy, and Viole Falushe agreed. Two days later a child three years old was brought to Navarth. Viole Falushe called again. "I have done as I promised. You have Jheral Tinzy again."

"Is it her daughter?"

"It is Jheral Tinzy, this is all you need know. I put her into your charge. Keep her, nurture her, guard her, see that she remains undefiled — for one day I will return for her." The screen went dead. Navarth turned to inspect the girl. Even now he could see her resemblance to Jheral... What to do? Navarth considered the child with mingled emotion. He could regard her neither as a daughter nor as a manifestation of his former love. He felt antagonism: there would always be a bittersweet ambiguity in their relationship, for Navarth was unable to love impersonally; the object of his love must relate to himself.

Navarth exemplified his contradicting impulses in his rearing of the girl. He fed her, provided shelter, both of the most casual and desultory sort. Otherwise the girl was independent. She became moody and uncommunicative; she made no friends and presently gave up asking questions.

As she matured her resemblance to Jheral Tinzy became ever more striking: she was Jheral Tinzy indeed, and her presence tormented Navarth with memories of the past.

A dozen years passed, but Viole Falushe had made no appearance. Still Navarth never dared hope that Viole Falushe had forgotten; indeed he became ever more obsessed with the certainty that Viole Falushe would presently arrive and take the girl away. He tried from time to time to acquaint the girl with the danger represented by Viole Falushe, but his approach varied with his mood, and he was never sure that she understood him. He attempted to seclude her, a task rendered difficult by the girl's unpredictable habits, and he took her off to remote corners of the Earth.

When the girl was sixteen, they lived in Edmonton, Canada, the goal of hordes of pilgrims who came to gaze upon the Sacred Shin. Navarth reasoned that here, among the interminable festivals, processions and sacerdotal rites, they might well live unnoticed.

But Navarth was wrong. Viole Falushe by some means knew his whereabouts. One night the telescreen lit up to show a tall figure standing against a flashing blue background which obscured his features. Navarth nevertheless recognized Viole Falushe and despondently called out "Show" to the telescreen.

"Well, Navarth," said Viole Falushe, "what do you do in the Holy City? Have you become a devout Kalzibahan that you live almost in the shadow of the Shin?"

"I study," muttered Navarth. "I derive a sense of purpose from the pervasive zeal."

"And what of the girl? I refer to 'Jheral'. She is well, I trust?"

"She was in fair condition last evening. I haven't seen her since."

Viole Falushe stared fixedly at Navarth, with only the glitter of his eyes giving dimension to his silhouette. "Is she pure?"

"How would I know?" demanded Navarth crossly. "I can't watch her day and night. In any event, what affair is it of yours?"

If anything, the intensity of Viole Falushe's glance increased. "It is my affair in all respects, to such a degree that you would never imagine!"

"Your language is extravagant," sniffed Navarth. "I can hardly believe you to be serious."

Viole Falushe laughed softly. "Someday you will visit the Palace of Love, old Navarth; someday you will be my guest."

"Not I!" declared Navarth. "I am a new Antaeus; never may I detach my toe from Earth; if necessary I will fall flat on my face and cling with both hands!"

"Well then, summon the girl, call 'Jheral' before the screen so that I may see her." An odd note had entered Viole Falushe's voice: sweetness and tenderness burdened with an almost insupportable rage.

"How can I call her when I don't know her whereabouts? She may be prowling the streets, or canoeing on the lake, or lying in someone's bed —"

A hoarse sound interrupted Navarth. But Viole Falushe's voice was mild. "Never say that, old Navarth. She was given into your care; I intended that you give her proper instruction. Have you done so? I suspect not."

"The best instruction is living itself," declared Navarth bluffly. "I am no pedant, as you well know."

There was a moment's silence. Then Viole Falushe said: "Do you know why I put the girl in your care?"

"My own motivations confuse me," said Navarth. "How should I know yours?"

"I will tell you. Because you know me well, you know what I require without explicit instructions."

Navarth blinked. "I had not considered the matter in this light."

"Then, old Navarth, you are remiss."

"I have heard this accusation a hundred times."

"But now you know what I expect. I hope you will repair your neglect."

The screen went dead. Navarth in a fury of frustration and resentment went striding out along the Great Nave, that avenue extending from the Plaza of Beatitudes to the Temple of the Shin. But the press of pilgrims irked him, and he took refuge in a tea-house, where he drank four cups of strong tea before he was sufficiently composed to think.

Specifically, Navarth wondered, what did Viole Falushe expect? He had a romantic interest in the girl, he wanted her inculcated, preconditioned, receptive. Navarth could not restrain a wild cackle of mirth, which aroused surprised glances from the other patrons of the tea-house, most of them black-clad pilgrims.

Viole Falushe wanted him to make the girl conscious of the great honor which awaited her; he wanted her preconditioned, predisposed, already fervent...The pilgrims, fresh from ceremonies at the temple, were regarding him with suspicion. Navarth jumped to his feet, departed the tea-room. There was no further reason to remain in Edmonton. As soon as possible he took the girl back to Rolingshaven.

Once or twice he mentioned Viole Falushe to the girl, in a tone of dejection, for now he had come to think of the girl as doomed; to such effect that on one occasion the girl ran away. Fortuitously the event occurred immediately before one of Viole Falushe's visits to Earth. When he telephoned Navarth demanding to see the girl, Navarth was forced to blurt forth the truth. Viole Falushe spoke in a mild voice: "Best that she be found, Navarth."

But Navarth made no attempt to find the girl until he was sure Viole Falushe had departed from Earth — here Gersen interposed a question: "How could you be sure?"

Navarth attempted to evade the question, but finally admitted that Viole Falushe, during his visits to Earth, could be telephoned at a particular code number. "Then you could call him now?"

"Yes, yes, of course," snapped Navarth. "If I wanted to do so, which I do not." He continued his story, but now he became cautious, using many flamboyant gestures, shifting his yellow glance all around with only an occasional brief flicker for Gersen.

It seemed that when Gersen appeared on the scene, Navarth sensed that here might be a weapon to be used against Viole Falushe (an aspect to the account Navarth left unspoken). With the utmost caution, committing no overt acts, always leaving himself lines of retreat, Navarth tried to arrange for the discomfiture or destruction of Viole Falushe. Events however superseded his plans. "And now," quavered Navarth, pointing a long finger at the *Cosmopolis* dummy, "this!"

"You believe Viole Falushe would react unfavorably to the article?"

"Indeed, indeed! He is the least forgiving of men; it is the key to his soul!"

"Perhaps then we had best discuss the article with Viole Falushe himself."

"What benefit can derive from that? He will merely have more time to generate a suitable response."

Gersen pondered. "Well then, it seems that we had best publish the article in its present form."

"No, no!" cried Navarth. "Have I not made all clear? He would punish us in equivalence to his annoyance, and he uses a subjective judgment! This article would offend him to an unprecedented fury; he hates his childhood, he only comes to Ambeules to gloat and work mischief on his old enemies. Do you know what happened to Rudolph Radgo, who jeered at Vogel Filschner's pimples? Rudolph Radgo's face is a garden of carbuncles, through Sarkovy poison. There was Maria, who moved her seat because Vogel's rheums and snivelings upset her. Maria now lacks all trace of a nose. Twice she has had grafts, twice she has suffered the loss of her new member; she is not to have a nose for all her life. So you see, it is not wise to offend Viole Falushe..." Navarth craned his neck. "What are you writing?"

"This is interesting new material; I am incorporating it into the article."

Navarth threw his hands up so wildly that his chair almost overturned. "Have you no prudence?"

"Perhaps if we discussed the article with Viole Falushe he might authorize its publication."

"It's you who are mad, not I!"

"We can only try."

"Very well," croaked Navarth. "I have no choice. But I warn you, I disavow all connection with the article!"

"As you wish. Shall we make our call here, or at the houseboat?"

"At the houseboat."

They left the plaza, rode the tube to Ambeules, and were conveyed to the Fitlingasse by surface wagon.

The houseboat floated serene and quiet on the estuary. "Where is the girl?" asked Gersen. "Zan Zu, Drusilla, whatever her name?"

Navarth refused to answer. Gersen's question, so he implied, was like asking the color of the wind. He hopped on down the ladder, jumped aboard the boat, and with a desperate tragic gesture, flung wide the door. He stalked to the telescreen, pushed buttons, spoke a muffled activant word. The presentation sprang to life: a single frail lavender flower. Navarth turned to look at Gersen. "He is available; when off Earth the pattern is blue."

They waited. From the telescreen came a wisp of tender melody, then after a moment or two a voice: "Ah Navarth, my ancient companion. With a friend?"

"Yes, an urgent matter. This is Mr. Henry Lucas, representing *Cosmopolis* magazine."

"A journal with an honored tradition! But have we not met? There is about you a disturbing familiarity."

"I was on Sarkovy recently," said Gersen. "As I recall, your name was in the air."

"A miasmic planet, Sarkovy. Nevertheless, one with a certain macabre beauty."

Navarth spoke. "I have had a misunderstanding with Mr. Lucas, and I wish specifically to disavow responsibility for his actions."

"My dear Navarth, you alarm me! Mr. Lucas is surely a man of courtesy."

"You shall see."

"As Navarth has mentioned I work for *Cosmopolis*," said Gersen. "In fact I am a senior official. One of our writers prepared a rather sensational article. I suspect the writer of over-enthusiasm and therefore checked with Navarth, who reinforced my doubts. It seems that the writer came upon Navarth in an exalted mood, and on the basis of a casual word went to enormous lengths of research and produced the article."

"Ah yes, the article. You have it with you?"

Gersen displayed the dummy. "It is included here. I insisted on checking the facts, apparently to good avail. Navarth insists that our writer took the most extreme liberties. He feels that in all fairness you should be allowed to authenticate the article before publication."

"Sound notion, Navarth! Well then, allow me to examine this alarming effusion; I'm sure it can't be all that grim."

Gersen slipped the magazine into the transcription rack. Viole Falushe read. From time to time he made sudden apparently involuntary noises: hisses between the teeth, small throaty sounds. "Turn the page, please." His voice was light and mild. Presently he said: "Yes. I have finished." There was a moment's silence, then he spoke again, and now the voice, superficially jocular, rang with a tinny overtone. "Navarth, you have been singularly reckless, even for an exhilarated poet."

"Bah," muttered Navarth. "Did I not disassociate myself from this entire farrago?"

"Not completely. I notice matters which are magnified and distorted in a manner possible only to a mad poet. You have been indiscreet."

Navarth said bravely, "Candour is never indiscreet. Truth, which is to say, the reflection of life, is beautiful."

"Beauty is in the eye of the beholder," said Viole Falushe. "I for one find little beauty in this abusive article. Mr. Lucas is quite correct in seeking my reaction. The article may not be published."

For some fantastic reason Navarth saw fit to grumble. "What good is notoriety if your friends are unable to profit from it?"

"Exploitation of notoriety and humiliation of your friends are not identical," spoke the mild voice. "Can you imagine my distress if this article appeared and exposed me to ridicule? I would be forced to demand amends for all concerned, which is only simple justice. Since by an act of yours, my feelings are injured, then by other acts you must atone until my feelings are whole again. It is not enough to assert that I am over-sensitive. If you hurt me, then you must assuage the hurt, no matter how disproportionate the effort."

"Truth reflects the cosmos," argued the mad poet. "To expunge truth, one must destroy the cosmos. This is the disproportionate act!"

"Aha!" declared Viole Falushe. "But the article is not necessarily truth! It is a point of view, an image or two snatched out of context. I, the person most intimately concerned, denounce the point of view as a flagrant distortion."

"I would like to make a suggestion," said Gersen. "Why not allow *Cosmopolis* to present the real facts; or that is to say, the facts from your own point of view? No doubt you have a statement to make to the folk of the Oikumene, who are fascinated by your exploits, whether or not they approve of them."

"No, I think not," said Viole Falushe. "Such an article would seem self-inflation or worse, a rather spurious apologia. Basically I am a modest man."

"But are you not an artist as well?"

"Certainly. On the truest and noblest scale. Artists before me have conveyed their assertions by abstract symbology; the spectators or audience has always been passive. I use a more poignant symbology, essentially abstract but palpable, visible and audible — in short a symbology of events and environments. There are no spectators, no audience, no passivity. There are only participants. They encounter experience at its keenest. No man has dared conceive on so vast a scope before!" Here Viole Falushe gave a slow strange chuckle. "With the exception perhaps of my megalomaniac contemporary Lens Larque, though his concepts are less fluid than my own. But I dare to say it: I am perhaps the supreme artist of history. My subject is Life; my medium is Experience; tools are Pleasure, Passion, Pungence, Pain. I arrange the total environment, in order to suffuse the total entity. This of course is the rationale of my estate, popularly known as the 'Palace of Love'."

Gersen nodded sagely. "Precisely what the folk of the Oikumene are anxious to learn! Rather than publish a vulgar exposé of this sort —" Gersen tapped the dummy with the back of his hand "— *Cosmopolis* would like you to explain your thesis. We want photographs, charts, odor swatches, sound impressions, portraits; above all we want your expert analysis."

"Possible, possible."

"Good. To this end let us meet together. Name a time and place and I will be there."

"The place? Where else? The Palace of Love. Each year I welcome a group of guests. You shall be in the current contingent, and mad old Navarth as well."

"Not I!" protested Navarth. "My feet have never yet lost contact with Earth; I do not care to risk the clarity of my vision."

Gersen also demurred. "The invitation, though tempting, is not particularly convenient. I would prefer to meet you tonight, here on Earth."

"Impossible. On Earth I have enemies, on Earth I am a shadow; no man can point and say, "There stands Viole Falushe." Not even my dear friend Navarth, from whom I have learned much of value. A lovely party, that, Navarth! Magnificent, worthy of a mad poet. However, I am disappointed in the girl I gave you to nurture, and I am disappointed in you. You have exercised neither the tact, the imagination, nor the creative direction for which I had hoped. Consider the girl in the light of what she is and what she might be! I had expected a new Jheral Tinzy: gay and grave, sweet as honey, tart as lime, with a brain full of stars, ardent yet innocent. What do I find? A wanton, a hoyden, a sour-faced ragamuffin, completely irresponsible and undiscerning. Imagine! In preference to me, she chose a certain Ian Kelly, an insolent, unworthy person, far better dead. I find the situation incomprehensible. The girl clearly had not been well-trained. Surely she knows of me and my interest in her?"

"Yes," said Navarth mulishly. "I have pronounced your name."

"Well, I am not quite satisfied, and I am sending her elsewhere for corrective training by less gifted but more disciplined tutors. I think it likely that she will join us at the Palace of Love — Ah, Navarth? You spoke?"

"Yes," said Navarth in a dull voice. "I have decided to advantage myself of your invitation. I will visit your Palace of Love."

"All very well for you artists," said Gersen hurriedly. "But I am a busy man. Perhaps a brief conference or two here on Earth —"

"But I have already left Earth," said Viole Falushe in a voice of gentle reproach. "I hang here in orbit only until I hear that my plans for the young minx have been implemented... So you must come to the Palace of Love."

The violet flower flashed green, faded and shifted to a delicate pale blue. The connection had been broken.

Navarth sat sprawled in his chair a long two minutes, head askew, chin on his chest. Gersen stood looking out the window, sensible of a sudden new hollowness... Navarth lurched to his feet, went out on the front deck. Gersen followed. The sun was setting into the estuary; the tiled roofs of Dourrai glowed bronze; the rotting black wharves and docks stood forth in queer shapes and angles; all was invested with an unreal melancholy.

Gersen presently asked, "Do you know how to reach the Palace of Love?"

"No. He will inform us. He has a mind like a filing cabinet; no detail evades him." Navarth swung his arms indecisively, then went inside, to return with a tall slender black-green bottle and two goblets. He broke off the seal, poured. "Drink, Henry Lucas, whatever your name, whatever your trade. Within this bottle is the wisdom of the ages, tincture of Earth-gold. Nowhere is tipple to equal this; it is unique to old Earth. Mad old Earth, like mad old Navarth, yields its best in its serene maturity. Drink of this precious elixir, Henry Lucas, and count yourself fortunate; normally it is reserved for mad poets, tragic pierrots, black angels, heroes about to die..."

"Cannot I be counted among these?" muttered Gersen, more to himself than Navarth.

As was his habit Navarth raised the goblet into the sunlight, of which only a few smoky orange rays remained. He tossed half a cupful into his mouth, stared out across the water. "I leave Earth. The withered leaf is lifted by the wind. Look, look, look!" In sudden excitement he pointed to the somber sun-trail along the estuary. "The road ahead, the way we must go!"

Gersen sipped the liquor, which seemed to explode into a spray of multi-colored lights. "There is no doubt but what he has taken the girl?"

Navarth's mouth twisted awry. "I have no doubt as to this. He will punish her, hissing like a serpent. She is Jheral Tinzy, and once again she has rebuffed him... so once again she will return to her infancy."

"You are sure she is Jheral Tinzy? Not someone who resembles her closely?"

"She is Jheral Tinzy. There are differences, significant differences. Jheral was frivolous and a trifle cruel; this one is somber, pensive, and never thinks of cruelty... But she is Jheral Tinzy."

They sat, each occupied with his own thoughts. Dusk fell across the water; lights commenced to shine from the far slopes. A uniformed messenger alighted from his air-car, descended the ladder. He called from the landing: "A delivery for 'the poet Navarth'."

Navarth lurched to the gangplank. "I am he."

"Thumbprint here, please."

Navarth returned with the delivery: a long blue envelope. Slowly he opened it, withdrew the enclosure. At the top was the lavender flower of the screen presentation. The message read:

Go Beyond to Sirneste Cluster, in Aquarius Sector. Deep within the cluster hangs the yellow sun Miel. The fifth planet is Sogdian upon which, at the south of the hour-glass continent, you will discern the city Atar. In one month's time go to Rubdan Ulshaziz at his agency and say: "I am guest to the Margrave."

CHAPTER X

Excerpt from the televised debate at Avente, Alphanor, on July 10, 1521, between Gowman Hachieri, Counsel for the Planned Progress League, and Slizor Jesno, Fellow of the Institute, 98th Degree:

HACHIERI: Is it not true then that the Institute originated as a cabal of assassins?

JESNO: To the same degree that the Planned Progress League originated as a cabal of irresponsible seditionists, traitors, suicidal hypochondriacs.

HACHIERI: This is not a pertinent response.

JESNO: The elasticities, the areas of vagueness surrounding the terms of your question do indeed encompass the exact truth of the situation.

HACHIERI: What, then, in inelastic terms, is the truth?

JESNO: Approximately fifteen hundred years ago, it became evident that existing laws and systems of public safety could not protect the human race from four bland and insidious dangers: First, universal and compulsory dosage of drugs, tonics, toners, conditioners, stimulants and prophylactics administered through the public water supply. Second, the development of genetic sciences, which allowed and encouraged various agencies to alter the basic character of Man, according to contemporary biological and political theory. Third, psychological control through media of public information. Fourth, the proliferation of machinery and systems which in the name of progress and social welfare tended to make enterprise, imagination, creative toil and the subsequent satisfactions obsolete if not extinct.

I will not speak of mental myopia, irresponsibility, masochism, or the efforts of persons nervously groping for a secure womb to re-enter: this is all irrelevant. The effect however was a situation analogous to the growth of four cancers in a human organism; the Institute came into being by much the same progress that the body generates a prophylactic serum.

WITH TREPIDATION DAMPENED BY FATALISM, Navarth boarded Gersen's Distis Pharaon. Standing in the saloon, looking right and left, he spoke in a tragic voice: "So at last it has happened! Poor old Navarth, pried away from his source of strength! See him now — a huddle, a sack of tired bones. Navarth! You failed to discriminate in your company! You befriended waifs and criminals and journalists; for your tolerance you are to be wafted away into space."

"Compose yourself," said Gersen. "It's not all that bad."

As the Pharaon lifted from Earth Navarth gave a hollow groan, as if a spike were being driven into his foot.

"Look out the port," suggested Gersen. "See old Earth as you have never seen it before."

Navarth inspected the great blue and white globe and reluctantly agreed that the vista was of majestic dimensions.

"Now Earth recedes," said Gersen. "We point ourselves toward Aquarius, we engage the intersplit. Suddenly we are insulated from the universe."

Navarth pulled at his long chin. "Strange," he admitted. "Strange that this shell can convey us so far so fast. Somewhere there is mystery. It impels one to theosophy: to the worship of a space-god, or a god of light."

"Theory dissolves the mystery, though it lays bare a cryptic new stratum. Quite likely there is an endless set of these layers, mystery below mystery. Space is foam, matter particles are nodes and condensations. The foam fluxes, at varying rates; the average activity of these minuscule fluxes is Time."

Navarth cautiously moved across the ship. "It is all very interesting. Had I followed an early bent, I might have been a great scientist."

The voyage proceeded. Navarth was a rather trying companion, ebullient one moment, morose the next. At one time he simultaneously became afflicted with claustrophobia and agoraphobia, and lay on a settee with his feet bare and a cloth pulled over his head. On other occasions he sat by the port watching the stars pass, crowing with amazement and glee. Another time he became interested in the workings of the intersplit and Gersen explained it as well as he could: "Space-foam is whorled into a spindle; the pointed ends crack and split the foam, which has no inertia; the ship, inside the whorl, is insulated from the effects of the universe; the slightest force propels it at an unthinkable rate. Light curls through the whorl, we have the illusion of seeing the passing universe."

"Hmm," mused Navarth. "How small can the units be made?"

Gersen could give no definite answer. "Quite compact, I suppose."

"Think! If you carried one on your back you could become invisible!"

"To drift a million miles with each breath."

"Unless a person anchored himself. Why isn't this done?"

"The intersplit would break the connection; no anchor would hold."

Navarth argued the point at length, and lamented his previous ignorance. "Had I known previously of this marvellous device, I might have contrived a useful new machine!"

"The intersplit has been known for a long time."

"But not to me!" And Navarth went off to brood.

Through the hither stars of Aquarius flew the Pharaon; the Pale, that invisible barrier theoretically separating order from chaos, fell behind. Ahead glowed Sirneste Cluster: two hundred stars like a swarm of bright bees, controlling planets of every size and description. Gersen located Miel with some difficulty, and presently the fifth planet Sogdian hung below, of Earth-size and atmospheric type, like most of the settled planets. The climate appeared temperate; the polar ice was of small extent; the equatorial zone showed expanses of desert and jungle. The hour-glass continent was evident at once, and the macroscope located the city Atar.

Gersen sent down a request for landing clearance; it received no acknowledgment, which Gersen took as a sign that landing formalities were unknown.

He settled toward the planet and Atar spread below: a small pink and white city surrounding an inlet of the ocean. The spaceport was operated in the manner standard at all the outer worlds: as soon as Gersen had landed, two port officials approached, exacted a fee and departed. There were no de-weaselers, a sign that the world was not a haven for pirates, raiders and slavers.

No public conveyance was available; Gersen and Navarth walked a half mile to the town. The people of Atar, dark-skinned folk with hair dyed orange, wearing white pantaloons and wide complicated white turbans, regarded them with great curiosity. They spoke an incomprehensible language, but Gersen by dint of repeating, "Rubdan Ulshaziz? Rubdan Ulshaziz?" presently learned the whereabouts of the man he sought.

Rubdan Ulshaziz operated an import and export agency near the ocean. He was a bland dark-skinned man dressed like the others in loose pantaloons and turban. "Gentlemen, I welcome you. Will you drink punch?" He poured out tiny cuplets of thick cold fruit syrup.

"Thank you," said Gersen. "We are guests of the Margrave, and were instructed to come to you."

"Of course, of course!" Rubdan Ulshaziz bowed. "You will now be conveyed to the planet where the Margrave has his little estate." Rubdan Ulshaziz favored them with a lewd wink. "Excuse me a little moment; I will instruct the person who is to conduct you." He disappeared behind a portière, presently to return with a dour-seeming man with close-set eyes, who puffed nervous clouds of smoke from an acrid cheroot. Rubdan Ulshaziz said, "This is Zog, who will escort you to Rosja."

Zog blinked, coughed, spat a shred of tobacco to the floor.

"He speaks only the language of Atar," continued Rubdan Ulshaziz. "He will not be able to offer a description of your destination. Are you ready?"

"I need equipment from my spaceboat," said Gersen. "And the spaceboat itself: is it safe?"

"As safe as if it were a tree; I will go bond on this. If you do not find all correct upon your return, seek out Rubdan Ulshaziz and demand an accounting. But what do you wish from your ship? The Margrave furnishes everything, even to new garments."

"I need my recorder," said Gersen. "I plan to take photographs."

Rubdan Ulshaziz made a suave gesture. "The Margrave supplies all equipment of this sort, the most modern combinations. He wants his guests to arrive unburdened by possessions; though he is indifferent to their psychic baggage."

"In other words," said Gersen, "we are not to carry any personal belongings with us?"

"None whatever. The Margrave supplies everything. His hospitality is all-inclusive. You have locked, sealed and coded your spaceship? Good; then from this moment forward you are a guest of the Margrave. If you will accompany Fendi Zog…" He signaled Zog with a peremptory twist of the hand. Zog inclined his head and Gersen and Navarth followed him to an open area behind the warehouse. Here was an air-car of a design unfamiliar to Gersen, and, so it seemed, to Zog as well. Sitting at the controls, Zog tested first one, then another, squinting at the rather haphazard arrangement of knobs, grips and voice sensors. Finally, as if tiring of the uncertainty, he pushed at a cluster of finger-flicks. The air-car jerked aloft, darted across the tree-tops, with Zog crouching over the controls and Navarth calling out in wrath.

Zog finally took command of the air-car; they flew twenty miles south across the cultivated plots and stock-pens surrounding Atar, to a field on which rested a late-model Baumur Andromeda. Once again Zog betrayed signs of uncertainty. The air-car swooped, bucked, wallowed, finally sank to rest; Navarth and Gersen alighted with alacrity. Zog signaled them toward the Andromeda; they climbed aboard and the port closed behind them. Through a transparent panel in the partition separating the saloon from the forward compartment, they saw Zog settling himself at the controls. Navarth called out an instant protest; Zog squinted back through the panel, bared yellow teeth in what might have been meant as a smile of reassurance, and drew a curtain.

The magnetic lock clicked shut on the intervening door. Navarth sank back in dismay. "Life is never so sweet until it becomes at hazard. What a sour trick for Vogel to play on his old preceptor!"

Gersen indicated the pleated burlap screen which covered the ports. "He also wants to preserve his mystery."

Navarth shook his head in bewilderment. "What use is knowledge to minds benumbed by fright?...Why do we wait? Does Zog consult the Operator's Manual?"

The Andromeda lurched and rose at an alarming rate, almost hurling Gersen and Navarth to the floor; Gersen grinned to hear Navarth's roar of protest. The sun Miel, as it could be glimpsed through the burlap, swung right and left, then rolled down and out of sight below the hull. Off through the cluster flew the Andromeda, and it seemed as if Zog changed course several times, whether from inaccuracy, poor spacemanship, or a desire to confuse his passengers.

Two hours passed: a yellow-white sun bulked large behind the screened ports; below hung a planet the configuration of which could not be discerned by reason of the curtain. With an impatient ejaculation, Navarth went to pull the curtain aside. A crackle of blue sparks struck out at his fingertips; Navarth fell back with a startled cry. "This is an imposition!" he exclaimed. "Ill usage indeed!"

From an unseen diaphragm a recorded voice spoke: "As cherished guests, you will wish to please your host by adhering to certain standards of courtesy and restraint. It is not necessary to define these standards; they will be clear to all persons of delicacy. The stimulus provides a jocular reminder to the insensitive or thoughtless."

Navarth made a surly sound in his throat. "There's a smug dog for you. What harm in peering forth from the port?"

"Evidently the Margrave hopes to conceal the location of his headquarters," said Gersen.

"Balderdash. What is to prevent a man searching the cluster until he finds the Palace of Love?"

"There are hundreds of planets," Gersen pointed out. "Very likely other discouragements as well."

"He need fear no intrusion from me," sniffed Navarth.

The Andromeda settled upon a field surrounded by blue-green gum trees, of distinctly terrestrial derivation. Zog immediately unsealed the port, a process which Gersen watched first with amazement, then quizzical amusement. Wary of unseen microphones, he communicated none of his ideas to Navarth.

They alighted into the morning glare of a yellow-white sun, much like Miel in color and radiance. The air was pungent with the odor of the gum trees and native vegetation: shrubs with lustrous black stalks, black and scarlet leaf-disks; blue spikes with fluttering dark blue vanes; puffs of cottony membrane enclosing tomato-red nodes. There were also clumps of terrestrial bamboo and grass and a thicket of blackberry bushes.

"Bizarre, bizarre," muttered Navarth, looking about. "There is fascination to be found on these far worlds!"

"This is almost like Earth," said Gersen. "But other areas may be dominated by local plants; then you will see the truly bizarre."

"No scope even for a sane poet," grumbled Navarth. "But I must put aside my individuality, my pitiful small cell of sentience. I have been snatched from Earth, and no doubt my bones will rot in this strange soil." He picked up a clod, crushed it between his fingers, let the fragments fall to the ground. "It looks like soil, it feels like soil — but it is star-stuff. We are far from Earth...What? And we are to be marooned as well, with neither a crust nor a bottle of wine?" For Zog had returned within the Andromeda and was sealing the port. Gersen took Navarth's arm, hustled him across the meadow. "Zog has a reckless temperament; he may take off on intersplit and carry away ship, meadow, shrubs, grass and two passengers, if we stand too near. Then you could well sing of bizarre circumstances."

But Zog raised the ship on its ionic pencils; Gersen and Navarth watched it dwindle into the bright blue sky. "So here we are, somewhere in Sirneste Cluster," said Navarth. "Either the Palace of Love is nearby or Viole Falushe has performed another of his grotesque jokes."

Gersen went to the edge of the meadow, looked through the screen of trees. "Grotesque joke or not, here is a road, and it must lead somewhere."

They set out along the road, between hedges of tall black rods, with scarlet leaf-disks clattering and chattering in the wind. The road wound around a knob of black schist, swung up a steep rise: gaining the crest they looked out upon a valley and a small city only a mile or two distant.

"Is this the Palace of Love?" wondered Navarth. "Hardly what I expected: far too neat, too precise... And what are those circular towers?" The towers to which Navarth referred rose at regular intervals across the city. Gersen could only suggest that they contained offices or apartments, or perhaps served to house civic functionaries.

As they started down the hill, a vehicle approached at a great rate: a bumping thudding platform supported by rolling air-cushions. Standing at the controls was a gaunt stern person in a brown and black uniform, who on closer inspection proved to be a woman. She halted the car, inspected the two with a skeptical gaze. "You are the Margrave's guests? Step aboard then."

Navarth took exception to the woman's tone. "Were you supposed to meet the ship? This is inefficiency; we were forced to walk!"

The woman gave him a scornful half-smile. "Get aboard, unless you care to walk more."

Gersen and Navarth climbed aboard, Navarth fuming with indignation. Gersen asked the woman, "What city is that?"

"It is City Ten."

"And what is your name for this planet?"

"I call it Fool's World. Other folk may call it what they like." Her mouth snapped shut like a trap. She swung the vehicle around, started back down the road, the bladders pounding, Gersen and Navarth clinging tight to avoid being hurled into the ditch. Navarth bawled orders and instructions, but the woman drove even more furiously and did not slow until they entered the city by a curving tree-shaded avenue; whereupon her pace became extremely sedate, and Gersen and Navarth were exposed to the curious stares of the city's inhabitants. These were a people without distinctive peculiarity other than the fact that the heads of the men were shaved clean as an egg: eyebrows, scalp, and beard; while the women affected an elaborate coiffure of long varnished spikes, occasionally tipped with flowers or other ornaments. Both men and women wore garments of extravagant cut and color, and carried themselves with a peculiar mixture of swagger and furtiveness;

speaking emphatically in low voices, laughing in loud brash bays, only to stop short, look in all directions, then continue with their mirth.

The vehicle passed one of the towers Navarth had noted: a structure of twenty stories, each apparently consisting of six wedge-shaped apartments.

Navarth spoke to the woman: "What is the purpose of the towers which rise so prominently?"

"It is where the taxes are collected," was the reply.

"Aha then, Henry Lucas, you are correct: the towers house civic functionaries."

The woman turned Navarth a caustic gray glance. "They do, indeed. Indeed and indeed."

Navarth paid her no further heed. He pointed to one of the numerous cafés along the boulevard, patronized principally by men. "These rascals have much idle time," Navarth noted. "See how they loll and take their tipple! Viole Falushe is less than harsh with his subjects, if such they be!"

The vehicle swung into a turn-around, halted before a long two-floored building. On the verandah sat a number of men and women in various costumes, obviously outworlders. "Off then, shag-heads!" said the woman driver tersely. "Here is the inn; I have done my stint."

"Incompetently, and in a surly manner," declared Navarth, rising and preparing to alight. "Your own head, incidentally, would never be the worse for a few changes. Perhaps a full beard, as a start."

The woman touched a button; the bed of the vehicle tilted; Navarth and Gersen were forced to jump to the ground. The vehicle departed, with Navarth making an insulting gesture at the woman's back.

A footman came forward to meet them. "You are guests of the Margrave?"

"This is correct," said Navarth. "We have been invited to the Palace."

"During the wait, you will be housed at the inn."

"Wait? Of what duration?" demanded Navarth. "I assumed that we would be taken directly to the Palace."

The footman bowed. "The Margrave's guests assemble here; all go forth together. I presume there are five or six others yet to come, this being the usual number. May I show you to your rooms?"

Gersen and Navarth were conducted to cubicles eight feet on a side, each containing a low narrow bunk, a wardrobe, a lavatory, ventilated only by the lattice in the door. Navarth was housed next to Gersen, and his complaints were clearly audible. Gersen smiled to himself. For reasons known best to himself, such was the style in which Viole Falushe wished his guests to wait.

Within the wardrobe were Earth-style garments of a light crisp fabric. Gersen washed, removed his beard with a depilatory, changed into fresh garments and went out upon the verandah. Navarth had preceded him, and already was holding forth to the eight people, four men and four women, who sat there. Gersen took a seat to the side and considered the group. Beside him sat a portly gentleman wearing the black neck-band and beige skin-tone currently fashionable on the Mechanics Coast of Lyonesse, one of the Concourse planets. He was, so Gersen discovered, a manufacturer of bathroom fixtures named Hygen Grote. His companion, Doranie, almost certainly not his wife, was a cool wide-eyed blonde woman with only an ultra-fashionable hint of bronze skin-luster.

A pair of serious young women sat quietly to the side: sociology students at Sea Province University near Avente. Their names were Tralla Callob and Mornice Whill; they seemed awed, half-alarmed, and sat close to each other, feet flat on the floor, knees pressed tight together. Tralla Callob was not unattractive, though she seemed unaware of this and took no pains to make the most of herself. Mornice Whill was victimized by over-large features and a truculent conviction that every man in the group intended assault upon her chastity.

More relaxed was Margray Liever, a middle-aged woman from Earth who had won first prize in a television contest: her 'heart's desire'. She had chosen a visit to Viole Falushe's 'Palace of Love'. Viole Falushe had been amused and obliging.

Torrace daNossa was a musician, a man of sophistication and elegance, perhaps a trifle soft, more than a trifle vain, and with an effortless ease of manner which made meaningful conversation difficult. He was visiting the Palace of Love preparatory to composing an opera entitled *The Palace of Love.*

Lerand Wible was a marine architect of Earth, who recently had constructed a sailboat of ultimate design. The fin was osmium, the sails were tall air-foils of metal-plated foam, self-supporting and unstayed. Sails and fin extended at opposite diameters of a metal slip-ring; the hull floated always upright, in its most efficient hydrodynamic posture. Both hull and fin were coated with a water repellent, reducing skin friction to a minimum, while ducts expelled air to minimize turbulence. Wible had met Viole Falushe in connection with his fanciful scheme for a sea-going palace, ring-shaped to enclose a central lagoon.

Skebou Diffiani was a taciturn man with a head of coarse black hair, a black tightly-curled beard, an expression conveying disdain and suspicion of all the others. He was a native of Quantique, which went far to explain his aloof manner. His occupation was day-laborer; his inclusion in the group could be explained only as a caprice of Viole Falushe.

Margray Liever had been the first to arrive, five of the long local days before. Then Tralla and Mornice had come, then Skebou Diffiani. Lerand Wible and Torrace daNossa were next, followed by Hygen Grote and Doranie.

Navarth plied all with questions, pacing the verandah, darting side-glances right and left. But no one knew more than he did; none knew where lay the Palace of Love, or the time of departure. The uncertainty troubled no one; in spite of the constricted chambers, the hotel was reasonably comfortable, and there was the city to be explored: a puzzling, mysterious city, with latencies and undercurrents some of the guests found fascinating, others disturbing. A gong summoned the group to lunch, which was served on a back court under black, green and scarlet trees. The cuisine was uncomplicated: pastry wafers, poached fish, fruit, a cool pale-green beverage, cakes of spiced currants. During the meal six new guests arrived and were brought immediately to the court for lunch. They were Druids of Vale, or Virgo 912 VII, and apparently consisted of two families, though such relationships were shrouded in secrecy. There were two Druids, two Druidesses, two adolescents. All wore similar garments: black gowns, black cowls, long-toed black slippers. Druids Dakaw and Pruitt were tall and saturnine; Druidess Wust was thin, sinewy, with a hollow-cheeked face, Druidess Laidig was portly and imposing. The lad Hule was sixteen or seventeen, extremely handsome, with sallow clear skin and clear dark eyes. He spoke little and smiled never, surveying all with a troubled gaze. The girl Billika, about the same age, was likewise pale, with something of the same troubled gaze, as if she constantly strove to balance sets of irreconcilable relationships.

The Druids sat together, ate hurriedly with cowls drawn forward and only occasional mutters of conversation. After lunch when the guests returned to the verandah, the Druids came purposefully forward, introduced themselves with brave cordiality, and took seats among the others.

Navarth came to question them, but their evasiveness was a match for his curiosity, and he learned nothing. The talk became general, reverting, as it always did, to the city, the name of which was either City Ten or Kouhila. The subject of the towers arose: what was their function? Did they contain business offices, as Doranie suggested, or were they residences? Navarth reported the explanation of the woman in the uniform: that the towers were tax-gathering agencies, but the rest of the group found the idea far-fetched. Diffiani made the somewhat brutal assertion that the towers were brothels: "Notice: early in the morning girls and young women arrive; later the men come."

Torrace daNossa said, "The hypothesis is one which leaps to mind, but the women leave when they will; and they seem to include every stratum of society, which is hardly typical."

Hygen Grote gave a sly wink to Navarth. "There is a simple way to resolve the question. I suggest that we deputize one of our number to make direct inquiry."

Druidesses Laidig and Wust snorted and drew their cowls close around their faces; the girl Billika licked her lips nervously. Druids Dakaw and Pruitt looked off in different directions. Gersen wondered why the Druids, notoriously prim, had ventured on the journey to the Palace of Love, when their sensibilities could not but fail to be outraged. Mysteries everywhere...

A few minutes later Gersen and Navarth went for a stroll through the city, examining stalls, stores, workshops and residences with the untroubled curiosity of tourists. The people watched them with indifference and perhaps a tinge of envy. They seemed prosperous, gentle, easy of disposition; still Gersen sensed a pervading quality he could not define: nothing so coarse as fear, or discord, or anxiety... A wide tree-shaded café tempted Navarth; Gersen pointed out that they lacked money.

Navarth brushed the matter aside, and insisted that Gersen join him for a glass of wine. Gersen shrugged, followed Navarth to a table. Navarth signaled the proprietor. "We are guests of the Margrave Viole Falushe; we have no coin of the city. We intend to patronize your café and you may send the account to the hotel for collection."

The proprietor bowed punctiliously. "It shall be as you wish."

"Then we will drink a flask of whatever wine you consider suitable for this time of day."

"At once, sir."

The wine was served, a pleasant beverage which Navarth found somewhat too delicate. They sat watching folk walk past. Directly opposite rose one of the cryptic towers, which, now, in the middle afternoon showed no great activity.

Navarth summoned the proprietor to order another flask of wine, and, indicating the tower, asked, "What goes on in yonder tower?"

The proprietor seemed puzzled by the question. "It is like all the rest: where we pay our taxes."

"But why so many towers then? Would not a single tower suffice?"

Now the proprietor was amazed. "What, sir? For so many people as live here? Hardly possible!"

With this Navarth was forced to be satisfied.

Returning to the hotel they found that two more guests had arrived, both men of Earth: Harry Tanzel of London, Gian Mario of no fixed address. Both were well-favored men, tall, keen-faced, dark-haired, of ages not immediately apparent. Tanzel was perhaps the handsomer of the two; Mario was more energetic and vital.

The local day was a long twenty-nine hours; when night finally arrived the guests retired without protest to their cubicles, only to be awakened at midnight by a gong and summoned to a midnight meal, in accordance with local custom.

The following morning saw the arrival of Zuly, a tall languorous dancer from the world Valhalla, Tau Gemini VI. She comported herself with the most exquisite mannerisms, to the suspicion and perturbation of the Druids, especially young Hule who could not keep his eyes away from the woman.

Immediately after the morning meal Gersen, Navarth and Lerand Wible went walking beside the canal which ran behind the hotel. Today appeared to be a holiday: the people of the city wore garlands; some were drunk; others sang songs in praise of Arodin, evidently a folk-hero or ruler.

"Even on a holiday," said Navarth, "they go to pay their taxes."

"Nonsense," said Wible. "When do men go to pay taxes with so jaunty a step?" The three paused to watch men going and coming from the tall tower. "Definitely, it is a brothel. It can be nothing else."

"But so public? So industrious? We may be misled by appearances."

"Conceivably. Do you wish to enter the place?"

"No indeed; if brothel it is, I am unfamiliar with their methods and might perform some unorthodox act, to the discredit of us all."

"You are unusually cautious," remarked Gersen.

"I am on a strange planet," sighed Navarth. "I lack the strength I derive from the soil of old Earth. But I am curious; we shall resolve the question once and for all. Come." He led the way to the pavilion where they had been served the day before, and scanned the tables. A portly middle-aged gentleman in a wide-brimmed green hat sat looking off along the boulevard, a small jug of wine at his elbow.

Navarth approached him. "Your pardon, sir. As you can see, we are strangers here. One or two of your customs puzzles us, and we wish to learn how matters stand."

The middle-aged man heaved himself erect, and after a moment's hesitation pointed to the other chairs. "I will explain as best I can, though there is small mystery here. We do as best we can and live according to our lights."

Navarth, Gersen and Wible seated themselves. "First of all," Navarth inquired, "what is the function of that tower yonder, where so many people go in and out?"

"Ah, there. Yes. That is our local agency of tax collection."

"Tax collection?" asked Navarth, with a triumphant glance at Wible. "And the folk who go in and out pay taxes?"

"Exactly. The city is under the wise sponsorship of Arodin. We are prosperous because taxes suck away none of our wealth."

At this Lerand Wible made a skeptical sound. "How is this possible?"

"Is it not the same elsewhere? The money collected is the money which otherwise would be spent on frivolity. The system is beneficent to all. Every girl of the region must serve five years, performing a stipulated number of services per day. Naturally the more attractive girls fulfill their quota sooner than those who are plain, and there is consequently a considerable incentive to maintaining pulchritude."

"Aha!" said Wible. "In effect — a civic brothel."

His informant shrugged. "Call it what you wish. There is no diminution of resource; the yield is devoted to civic expense; there is no outcry at the collection of tax and the tax collectors find their work not irksome; or if they do, they can make in lieu payments — which usually happens should the girl wed before her service is complete. Then, of course, we have our obligation to Arodin, which each of us discharges by the payment of a two-year-old child. Thereupon we pay no more taxes, except for an occasional special assessment."

"No one complains when their child is taken?"

"Usually not. The child is taken to a crèche immediately after birth, so that no bonds of affection are formed. Folk breed children early to discharge their obligation as rapidly as possible."

Wible exchanged glances with Navarth and Gersen. "And what happens to the children?"

"They go to the account of Arodin. The unsuitable are sold to the Mahrab; the satisfactory serve at the great Palace. I gave a child ten years ago; I now owe tax to no one."

Navarth could contain himself no longer. Leaning forward in his chair he pointed a knobby finger. "So this is why you sit here blinking so smugly in the sun? Where is your guilt?"

"'Guilt'?" The man raised his hands to adjust his wide-brimmed hat in puzzlement. "There is no guilt. I have performed my duty. I gave my child; I patronize the civic brothel twice a week. I am a free man."

"While the child you gave is now a ten-year-old slave. Somewhere he, or she, toils that you may sit here with your belly on your lap!"

The man rose to his feet, face pink with fury. "This is incitement, a serious offense! What then do you do here, you plucked, foolish old fowl? Why do you come to this city if you don't fancy our ways?"

"I did not select your city as a destination," said Navarth with dignity. "I am a guest of Viole Falushe, and remain here only pending his notification."

The man laughed: a harsh throbbing chortle. "This is the outworld name for Arodin. You come to enjoy the Palace, and you have not even paid!" He pounded the table once with his fist and marched out of the café. Other patrons who had been listening pointedly turned their backs. Presently the three returned to the hotel.

Even as they arrived, the thud of the bladder-buggy sounded at the end of the boulevard. It rumbled up to the hotel, halted. A man alighted, turned to help a young woman who, ignoring the hand, jumped to the ground. Navarth gave a raucous cry of surprise. The young woman, attired in fashionable Alphanor-style garments, was Navarth's erstwhile ward, known as Zan Zu, Drusilla and otherwise.

Navarth took her aside, pelted her with questions: What had happened to her; where had she been pent?

Drusilla could tell him little. She had been shoved into an air-car by the white-eyed man, conveyed to a space-vessel, placed in the custody of three grim women. Each of them wore a heavy gold ring; after the poison sprayed from the rings was demonstrated upon a dog, no further threats or warnings were necessary.

Drusilla was taken to Avente on Alphanor, lodged at the splendid Hotel Tarquin. The women were watchful as hawks, speaking seldom, never more than two or three feet away, the gold rings a sinister glitter. They took her to concerts, restaurants, fashion shows, cinematic displays, museums and galleries. They urged her to buy clothes, to tone her skin, to make herself chic: all of which Drusilla resisted, from sullen perversity; whereupon the women bought the clothes, toned her skin, arranged her hair. Drusilla retaliated by sagging, drooping, contriving to look as uncouth as possible. Finally the women took her to the spaceport; they boarded a spaceship which conveyed them to Sirneste Cluster and the planet Sogdian. They arrived at the agency of Rubdan Ulshaziz at Atar simultaneously with another guest for the Palace of

Love, Milo Ethuen, who stayed in Drusilla's company the remainder of the journey. The three women came as far as the Kouhila space field, then returned to Atar with Zog. Navarth and Gersen looked around to inspect Ethuen, who now sat on the verandah with the others: a man not unlike Tanzel and Mario, with a brooding face, dark hair, long arms and sensitive hands.

The manager of the hotel came forth upon the verandah. "Ladies and gentlemen, I am pleased to announce that your wait is at an end. The guests of the Margrave are assembled; you must now set forth on your journey to the Palace of Love. Please follow me; I will conduct you to your conveyance."

Chapter XI

Excerpt from the televised debate at Avente, Alphanor, July 10, 1521, between Gowman Hachieri, Counsel for the Planned Progress League and Slizor Jesno, Fellow of the Institute, 98th Degree:

HACHIERI: You admit that the Institute arranges assassination for persons striving to improve the human condition?

JESNO: You beg the question.

HACHIERI: Do you murder anyone whatever?

JESNO: I don't care to discuss tactical theory. There are very few such events.

HACHIERI: But they occur.

JESNO: Only in the case of absolutely flagrant offenses against the human organism.

HACHIERI: Is not your definition of 'offense' arbitrary? Are you not simply opposed to change? Are you not conservative to the point of stagnation?

JESNO: To all three questions: no. We want natural organic evolution. The human race, needless to say, is not without flaws. When elements of the race attempt to cure these ills: to create an 'ideal man' or an 'ideal society', there is the certainty of overcompensation in one or another direction. The flaws, with the reaction to the flaws, create a distortion factor, a filter, and the final product is more diseased than the original. Natural evolution, the slow abrasion of man against his environment, has slowly but definitely improved the race. The optimum man, the optimum society may never eventuate. But there will never be the nightmare of the artificial man or the artificial 'planned progress' which the League advocates: not so long as the human race generates that highly active set of antibodies known as the Institute.

HACHIERI: This is a resonant speech. It is superficially persuasive. It is ridden with maudlin fallacy. You want man to evolve through 'abrasion against his environment'. Other human beings are part of the environment. The League is part of the environment. We are natural; we are neither artificial nor sick. The ills of the Oikumene are by no means obscure or mysterious; they are susceptible to remedy. We of the League propose to take action. We do not intend to be dissuaded or intimidated. If we are threatened, we shall take measures to protect ourselves. We are not helpless. The Institute has tyrannized society long enough. It is time that new ideas permeated the human community.

BEHIND THE HOTEL waited a long omnibus with six bladder wheels and a canopy of rosy-pink silk. Amid banter, laughing and repartee, the guests — eleven men, ten women — climbed aboard, settled themselves upon cushions of purple satin. The bus trundled across the canal and away to the south; Kouhila with its tall towers was left behind.

For an hour the guests rode past carefully-tended farms and orchards, toward a line of wooded hills, and speculation was rife as to the exact location of the Palace of Love. Hygen Grote went so far as to push into the forward compartment and make inquiry of the driver. This was the gaunt woman in the brown and black uniform. Hygen Grote was rebuffed, and returned to his seat grinning ruefully and shaking his head. Up into the hills rolled the bus, under tall umbrella-shaped trees with glossy black trunks and green-yellow leaf-disks. From somewhere in the distance came the melodious hooting of tree-dwelling creatures; enormous white moths fluttered through the shade, which became ever more dank, ever more pungent with the reek of lichens and large-leafed shrubs. At the ridge the road broke out into a dramatic blaze of sunlight; ahead spread a vast blue ocean. The bus plunged down a steep straight road and halted at a dock. Here waited a glass-hulled yacht with blue decks and a white metal superstructure. Four stewards in dark blue and white uniforms assisted the guests from the bus, conducted them to a building of white coral blocks, where they were asked to change into new garments: white yachting costumes, with rope sandals, loose white linen caps. The Druids protested vigorously on doctrinal grounds. They flatly refused to part with their cowls; and so they boarded the yacht, the men attired in white trousers and jackets, the women in white skirts and jackets, with heads encowled in black as before.

The time was sunset; the yacht would not get under way until the morrow. The passengers assembled in the saloon, where they were served Earth-type cocktails, and presently dinner. The two younger Druids, Hule and Billika, wore their cowls rather more loosely than their parents, thereby incurring reprimands.

After dinner the three young men, Mario, Tanzel and Ethuen, played deck tennis with Tralla and Mornice. Drusilla huddled disconsolately near Navarth, who conducted the strangest of conversations with Druidess Laidig. Gersen sat to the side watching, propounding speculations, wondering where his responsibilities lay and to whom. From time to time Drusilla wistfully looked across the saloon toward him. Clearly she dreaded the future. With good reason, thought Gersen. He could think of no way to reassure her. Zuly the dancer, supple as a white eel, walked around the deck with daNossa. Skebou Diffiani the Quantique stood by the rail, thinking the mysterious thoughts of his race, with an occasional contemptuous glance toward daNossa and Zuly.

Billika shyly came up to talk to Drusilla, followed by Hule, who seemed to find Drusilla attractive. Billika, somewhat flushed, had been tasting wine. She wore her cowl artfully disarranged to show her curly brown hair: a situation which did not evade the notice of Druidess Laidig, who, however, was unable to detach herself from Navarth.

Margray Liever chatted with Hygen Grote and his companion Doranie, until Doranie became bored and went to saunter along the deck, where, to Hygen Grote's annoyance, she was joined by Lerand Wible.

The Druids were the first to bed, followed by Hygen Grote and Doranie.

Gersen went out on the deck, looked up at the sky where the stars of Sirneste Cluster blazed. To the south and east heaved the waters of an ocean whose name he did not know. Not far distant Skebou Diffiani leaned on the rail, looking across the same ocean...Gersen returned within. Drusilla had gone to her stateroom. On the sideboard the stewards had arranged a collation of meats, cheese, fowl, aspic, a selection of wines and liquors.

Zuly conversed in low tones with daNossa. Margray Liever now sat alone, a vague smile on her face; was she not achieving her heart's desire? Navarth had become somewhat drunk and was swaggering about, spoiling for an opportunity to produce a dramatic scene. But everyone else was relaxed and gave him no scope. Navarth finally threw up his hands and went off to bed. Gersen, after a last look around, followed.

Gersen awoke to the pitch and roll of the yacht. The time was shortly after dawn: sunlight slanted into the cabin through the section of hull above the waterline; below dark blue water surged past, not yet illuminated by the sun.

Gersen dressed, went to the saloon, to find himself the earliest riser. Land lay four or five miles off the starboard beam: a narrow beach, a wooded foreshore backed by low hills, with the hint of purple mountains in the distance.

Gersen went to the buffet, helped himself to breakfast. As he ate other guests appeared, and presently the entire complement sat in the saloon, devouring grills and pastries, drinking hot beverages, marveling at the scenery and the easy motion of the yacht.

After breakfast Gersen went out upon the deck, where he was joined by Navarth, foppish in his white yachting costume. The day was perfect; sunlight glinted on the blue swells; clouds soared above the horizon. Navarth spat over the side, contemplated the sun, the sky, the sea. "The journey begins. It must start like this, innocent and pure."

Gersen understood Navarth's meaning well enough. He made no comment.

Navarth spoke again, in a voice even more gloomy. "No matter what else you say of Vogel, he knows how to do a thing well."

Gersen inspected the gold buttons on his jacket. They seemed no more than buttons. In response to Navarth's puzzled stare he said mildly, "Such articles have been known to conceal spy-cells."

Navarth laughed hoarsely. "Not likely. Vogel may well be aboard, but he won't be eavesdropping. He'd be afraid of hearing something unpleasant. It would spoil the trip for him."

"You think he's aboard then?"

"He's aboard, no fear. Would he miss an experience like this? Never! But who?"

Gersen considered. "He's not you nor I, nor the Druids. He's not Diffiani."

"He would not be Wible, a different type altogether, too fresh and fair and round. He would not be daNossa, though it's barely possible. Barely possible he's one of the Druids. But I think not."

"That leaves only three. The tall dark men."

"Tanzel, Mario, Ethuen. He could be any of these."

They turned to consider the three men. Tanzel stood on the bow, looking ahead across the ocean. Ethuen sat sprawled in a deck-chair, talking to Billika, who squirmed in mingled embarrassment and pleasure. Mario, the last to arise, had just finished breakfast, and was stepping out on deck. Gersen tried to match each of them to what he knew of Viole Falushe. Each was tense, yet elegant, each might have been Possibility No. 2, the murderer in harlequinade who had fled on long legs from Navarth's party.

"Any could be Viole Falushe," said Navarth.

"And what of Zan Zu — Drusilla — whatever her name?"

"She is doomed." Navarth threw his hands up in the air and stalked away.

Gersen looked toward Drusilla, as he had decided to think of her. She stood talking to Hule, the young Druid, who in the fervor of the moment had let fall his cowl. A handsome lad, thought Gersen: earnest, with a look of internal tension which women must eventually find provocative. Indeed Drusilla was examining him with some small interest. Druidess Wust barked a sharp order. Hule guiltily snapped up his cowl and slunk away.

Gersen went over to Drusilla. She gave him a look of wary welcome.

"Were you surprised to see us at the hotel?" Gersen asked.

She nodded. "I had never expected to see you again." After a moment's hesitation she asked, "What's going to happen to me? Why am I so important?"

Gersen, still in doubt regarding spy-cells, spoke cautiously: "I don't know what will happen. I will protect you if I can. You're important because you resemble a girl Viole Falushe once loved and who scorned him. He may be aboard the yacht; he may be one of the passengers. So you must be very careful."

Drusilla turned a fearful look around the deck. "Which one?"

"You remember the man at Navarth's party?"

"Yes."

"He will be a man like that."

Drusilla winced. "I don't know how to be careful. I wish I were someone else." She looked over her shoulder. "Can't you take me away?"

"Not now."

Drusilla bit her lip. "Why did it have to be *me*?"

"I might answer if I knew who you were to begin with. Zan Zu? Drusilla Wayles? Jheral Tinzy?"

"I'm none of them," she said in a dolorous voice.

"Who are you?"

"I don't know."

"You don't have a name?"

"The man at the dock saloon called me Spooky...That's not much of a name. I'll be Drusilla Wayles." She looked at him carefully. "You're not really a journalist, are you?"

"I am Henry Lucas, a monomaniac. And I mustn't talk to you too much. You know why."

Drusilla's face lost its momentary animation. "If you say so."

"Try to identify Viole Falushe," said Gersen. "He will want you to love him. If you don't, he'll hide his anger, but you may know by a glance, a threat, a look on his face. Or while he flirts with someone else he will watch to see if you notice."

Drusilla pursed her lips doubtfully. "I'm not very discerning."

"Do your best. But be careful. Don't bring trouble on yourself. Here comes Tanzel."

"Good morning, good morning," said Tanzel breezily. He spoke to Drusilla. "You look as if you've lost your last friend. That's not the case, you know, not with Harry Tanzel aboard! Cheer up! We're off to the Palace of Love!"

Drusilla nodded. "I know."

"Just the place for a pretty girl. I'll personally show you all the sights, if I can fight off my competitors."

Gersen laughed. "No competition here. I can't take time from my job, much as I'd like to."

"Job? At the Palace of Love? Are you an ascetic?"

"Simply a journalist. What I see and hear will show up in *Cosmopolis*."

"Keep my name out of it!" warned Tanzel facetiously. "Someday I'll be a married man; I'd never live down that kind of fame."

"I'll be discreet."

"Good. Come along now." Tanzel took Drusilla's arm. "I'll help you with your morning constitutional. Fifty times around the deck!"

They walked off, Drusilla with a last forlorn glance over her shoulder at Gersen.

Navarth sidled up. "There's one of them. Is he the man?"

"I don't know. He's starting strong."

Three days the yacht plied the sunny seas: for Gersen three pleasant days though the hospitality came from a man he intended to kill. There was an effortless quality to the hours, a dream-like isolation, and each person's characteristic style was intensified, becoming a thing larger than life. Attitudes and rigidities relaxed: Hule allowed his cowl to hang loose and finally discarded it altogether; Billika, more tentatively, did the same, whereupon Zuly in a spirit of cool mischief offered to arrange her hair. Billika hesitated, then, with a sigh of hedonistic abandon, assented. So Zuly shaped and clipped, to accentuate Billika's pale, wide-eyed delicacy, to the amazement of all the men aboard. Druidess Laidig cried out in anger; Druidess Wust clicked her tongue; the two Druids were startled; but all the others begged them not to browbeat the girl. Such was the atmosphere of ease and gayety that Druidess Laidig at last fell to laughing at Navarth, and Billika managed to slip away quietly. Not long after, Druidess Laidig allowed her own cowl to hang loose, as presently did Druid Dakaw. Druid Pruitt and Druidess Wust held to the full rigor of their habit, but tolerated the delinquency of the others with no more than an occasional disparaging glance or muttered sarcasm.

Tralla, Mornice and Doranie, noting the attention paid to the younger girls, became extremely enthusiastic and gay: clearly none planned to rebuff any attempted gallantry.

Each afternoon the yacht halted to drift on the ocean. All who chose plunged into the clear water, while others went below to watch through the glass hull. These latter included the older Druids, Diffiani (who participated in no activity except eating and drinking), Margray Liever, who professed a fear of deep water, and Hygen Grote, who could not swim. The others, even Navarth, donned the swimsuits provided by the yacht and splashed in the warm ocean.

At dusk of the second evening, Gersen took Drusilla to the bow, refraining from any intimacy of contact which might infuriate Viole Falushe, should he be watching. Drusilla seemed to feel no such constraint, and Gersen became aware, with a bitter-sweet pang, that the girl was in some degree infatuated with him. Gersen, as susceptible as anyone else, fought back his inclinations. Even if he succeeded in destroying Viole Falushe, what then? There was no place for Drusilla in the harsh future he had laid out for himself. Still, the temptation remained. Drusilla, with her somber moods, her sudden flashes of joy, was fascinating... But circumstances were as they were, and Gersen kept his conversation to the business at hand. Drusilla had noticed nothing. Mario, Ethuen, Tanzel — all plied her with attention. As Gersen had instructed, she showed favoritism to none... Even as they stood in the bow watching the sunset, Mario came to join them. After a moment or two Gersen excused himself, and returned to the promenade. If Mario were Viole Falushe, it would not do to antagonize him. If he were not, then Viole Falushe, watching balefully from elsewhere, would be reassured that Drusilla preferred no single person.

The morning of the fourth day found the yacht cruising among small islands lush with vegetation. At noon the yacht approached the mainland, drifted up to a dock. The voyage was over. The passengers disembarked regretfully, with many a backward glance; Margray Liever frankly wept.

In a structure beside the dock the guests were issued new garments. For the men there were loose velvet blouses in the softest and richest of colors: moss-green, cobalt-blue, dark maroon, with loose black velvet trousers fastened below the knees with scarlet ribbons. The women received the same style blouses in paler shades, with striped matching skirts. All were issued soft velvet berets, square, loose, with an intriguing tassel.

When all had reassembled, they were served lunch, then ushered to a great wooden wagon with six green and gold wheels, a dark green canopy supported by spiral posts of a beautiful dark wood.

The wagon set off along a coastal road. Late in the afternoon the track veered inland, over rolling grassy hills spangled with flowers, and the ocean was lost to sight.

Soon there were trees, tall and solitary, much like Earth trees, but conceivably indigenous; then clumps and groves. At dusk the wagon halted beside one such grove. The guests were conducted to a hostel built high in the tree-tops; led along swaying walkways to small wicker tree houses.

Supper was served on the ground, to the light of a great cackling fire. The wine seemed stronger than usual, or perhaps all were in a mood to drink. Everyone seemed larger than life; the twenty-one were the only people alive in the universe. Toasts were drunk, including several to 'our unseen host'. The name 'Viole Falushe' was never mentioned.

A troupe of musicians appeared with fiddles, guitars, pipes; they played wild wailing tunes, which set the heart pounding and the head swaying. Zuly leapt to her feet, improvised a dance as wild and abandoned as the music.

Gersen forced himself to sobriety: at times like this it was most important to watch. He saw Lerand Wible whisper to Billika; a moment later she sidled away and off into the shadows, and too was gone. The Druids and Druidesses were rapt with the dancing, sitting with heads back, eyes half-closed. Only Hule noticed. He looked thoughtfully after the two, then crept quietly up to Drusilla and whispered in her ear.

Drusilla smiled. She turned a flicker of a glance toward Gersen, and said something in a soft voice. Hule nodded without enthusiasm, seated himself close beside her, and presently put his arm around her waist.

A half hour passed. With only Gersen seeming to notice, Wible and Billika were once more among the group, Billika with eyes bright and mouth soft. It seemed that only a moment later Druidess Laidig bethought herself of Billika and sought around to locate her. There sat Billika. Something was amiss, something was new and different: Druidess Laidig could sense this much, but there was nothing else — to see... Her suspicion lulled, she returned to her enjoyment of the music.

Gersen watched Mario, Ethuen, Tanzel. They sat with Tralla and Mornice, but it seemed as if their eyes wandered toward Drusilla. Gersen chewed his lip. Viole Falushe — if indeed he were among the guests — did not seem disposed to yield his identity...

Wine, music, firelight! Gersen leaned back, aware of giddiness. Who among the group was watchful, who attentive? That person would be Viole Falushe! Gersen saw no one who seemed other than relaxed. Druid Dakaw was asleep. Druidess Laidig was nowhere to be seen. Skebou Diffiani also had disappeared. Gersen chuckled and leaned toward Navarth to share the joke, then thought better of it. The fire became embers; the musicians wandered away like figures in a dream. The guests roused themselves and went by swaying walkways to their wicker cabins. If other assignations had been made, if other trysts were kept, Gersen had no knowledge of them.

In the morning the guests assembled for breakfast to find that the wagon was gone, and there was speculation as to what mode of transport next would be offered them. After breakfast a steward pointed out a path. "There we will go; I have been requested to guide. If all are ready, I suggest that we set off, for there is far to go before evening."

Hygen Grote spoke in an astonished voice, "You mean to say, we *walk*?"

"Exactly this, Lord Grote. There is no other way to our destination."

"I never expected all this backing and filling," complained Grote. "I thought that when we were invited to the Palace of Love, an air-car simply took us there."

"I am only a servant, Lord Grote; I can offer no explanation."

Grote turned away, not completely pleased. But he had no choice. Presently his spirits rose and he was the first to start singing an old walking song of his fraternity at Lublinken College.

Over low hills, through glades and groves, went the path. They walked over a wide meadow, startling a number of white birds into flight; they descended a valley to a lake, where lunch awaited them.

The steward would not allow an overlong rest. "There is still far to go, and we cannot walk fast for fear of tiring the ladies."

"I'm already tired," snapped the Druidess Wust. "I don't intend to move another step."

"Anyone who wishes may return," said the steward. "The path is plain, and there is staff to assist you along the way. But now it is time for the rest of us to go on. It is afternoon, and a wind is rising."

Indeed a breeze with a hint of coolness blew small wavelets across the lake, and the western sky was paved with herringbone clouds.

Druidess Wust elected to continue with the group, and all set off along the shore of the lake. Presently the path turned aside, mounted a slope and struck off across a parkland of tall trees and long grass. On and on trudged the party, with the wind at their backs. With the sun declining behind a range of mountains, they halted for pastries and tea. Then off once more with the wind sighing through the branches.

As the sun sank behind the mountains the party entered dank heavy woods, which seemed all the darker for the going of the sun.

The pace was slow; the older women were tired, though only Druidess Wust complained. Druidess Laidig wore a grim expression while Margray Liever strolled along with her customary small smile. Hygen Grote had lapsed into sulky silence, except for an occasional terse word to Doranie.

The woods seemed endless; the wind, now distinctly cool, roared through the upper branches. Dusk fell over the mountains; at last the party stumbled into a clearing to find a rambling old forest lodge of timber and stone. The windows glowed with yellow lights, smoke drifted from a chimney; within must be found warmth and food and good cheer.

And so it was. The tired travelers, climbing stone steps to the porch, entered a vast beamed parlor, with bright rugs on the floor and a roaring blaze in the fireplace. Some of the group sank gratefully into deep chairs, others chose to go to their rooms to refresh themselves. Once again new clothing was issued: for the men black trousers and short jackets with a dark brown cummerbund; for the ladies long trailing black gowns with white and brown flowers for the hair.

Those who had bathed and dressed returned to the parlor, to the envy of those who still sat tired and dirty; presently all had bathed and changed into the new dark garments.

Mulled wine was served, and presently a hearty forest dinner: goulash, bread and cheese, red wine, and all the toil of the day was forgotten.

After dinner the guests gathered around the fireplace to sip liquors, and now the talk was loud and brave, everyone speculating as to where lay the Palace of Love. Navarth struck a dramatic pose in front of the fire. "It is plain!" he cried in a great brassy voice. "Or is it not? Does not everyone understand, or is it left to old Navarth the poet to illuminate?"

"Speak, Navarth!" called Ethuen. "Reveal to all your insight. Why cherish them for your private pleasures?"

"I have never had that intention: all will know what I know; all will feel what I feel. We are midway along the journey! Here is where the carelessness, the amplitude, the calm ease depart. The winds arose at our back and hurried us through the woods. Our refuge is medievalism!"

"Come now, old man," chaffed Tanzel. "Speak so we can understand you."

"Those who understand me will do so; those who cannot will never do so. But all is clear. He knows, he knows!"

Druidess Laidig, impatient with hyperbole, spoke crossly, "He knows *what? Who* knows what?"

"What are we all but perambulatory nerves? The artist knows the linkage of nerve with nerve!"

"Speak for yourself," muttered Diffiani.

Navarth performed one of his extravagant gesticulations. "He is a poet like myself! Did I not teach him? Every pang of the soul, every wry ache of the mind, every whisper of blood —"

"Navarth! Navarth!" groaned Wible. "Enough! Or at any rate, something different… Here we are, in this strange old lodge; a perfect refuge for ghosts and wipwarks."

Druid Pruitt spoke sententiously, "This is our lore: each man and each woman is a living seed. When his planting time comes, he is delved and covered, and finally comes forth as a tree; and each soul is distinct. There are birches and oaks and lavengars and black paneys…"

The talk proceeded. The younger and more energetic folk explored the ancient structure and played hide-and-seek in the long hall, among the billowing amber curtains.

Druidess Laidig became uneasy, and craned her neck to find Billika. At last she hoisted herself to her feet and went off, looking here and there, presently to return with a downcast Billika. Druidess Laidig muttered something to the Druidess Wust, who jumped up and went off down the hall. There were loud echoing voices in the hall, then silence, and a moment later Wust returned with Hule, who seemed sullen.

Three minutes later Drusilla came back to the saloon. Her face was flushed, her eyes alive with something between mirth and mischief. The dark gown suited her beautifully; she had never looked more beautiful. She crossed the room and slipped into the seat beside Gersen.

"What happened?" he asked.

"We played a game in the hall. I hid with Hule, and watched, as you told me, to see who would be most angered."

"And who was?"

"I don't know. Mario says he loves me. Tanzel was laughing, but he was annoyed. Ethuen said nothing and would not look at me."

"What were you doing, that they should be angry? Don't forget, it's dangerous to thwart people."

Drusilla's mouth drooped. "Yes. I forgot… I should feel frightened… I *do* feel frightened when I think about it. But you will take care of me, won't you?"

"I will if I can."

"You can. I know you can."

"I hope I can ... Well, what was going on to annoy Mario, Tanzel and Ethuen?"

"Nothing very much. Hule and I sat in an old couch that was turned backwards. Hule wanted to kiss me, and I let him. The Druidess found us and embarrassed Hule dreadfully. She called me names: 'harlot!' 'lilith!' 'nymph!' " Drusilla imitated Wust's peculiar grating voice to an exactitude.

"And all heard?"

"Yes. All heard."

"Who seemed the most upset?"

Drusilla shrugged. "Sometimes I think one, then the other. Mario seems the softest. Ethuen has the least humor. Tanzel is sometimes sarcastic."

Obviously, thought Gersen, there had been much which he had missed. "Best that you do not hide with anyone, not even Hule. Be pleasant to each of the three, but prefer none."

Drusilla's face became bleak and drawn. "I am frightened, really. When I was with the three women I thought I might run away. But I feared the poison in their rings. Do you think they would have killed me?"

"I don't know. But for now, go to bed and sleep. And open your door to no one."

Drusilla rose to her feet. With a final cryptic glance at Gersen, she went to the stairs, ascended to the balcony and entered her chamber.

One by one the group dwindled, and at last Gersen sat alone gazing into the dying fire, waiting for he knew not what ... The balcony lights were dim; a balustrade obscured his vision. A shape drifted up to the door of one of the chambers, which quickly opened and closed.

Gersen waited another hour, while the fire became embers and the wind blew spatters of rain against the dark windows. There was no further activity. Gersen went to his own bed.

The chamber which had received the visitor, so Gersen noted the next morning, was that of Tralla Callob, the sociology student. He watched to see upon whom her eyes rested, but could be sure of nothing.

This morning all wore similar costumes: grey suede trousers, a black blouse, a brown jacket, an intricate black hat which was almost a helmet, with ear flaps flaring rakishly outward.

Breakfast, like the meal of the night before, was simple and substantial; as they ate, the pilgrims cast appraising glances at the sky. Ragged patches of mist blew over the mountain; directly overhead was a thin overcast, breaking at the east into tattered clots of nimbus: an outlook not too cheerful.

After breakfast the steward marshaled the pilgrims, evading questions put to him.

"How far must we walk today?"— this from Hygen Grote.

"I really don't know, sir. I have never heard the distance mentioned. But the sooner we start, the sooner we arrive."

Hygen Grote gave a despondent snort. "This certainly wasn't what I expected... Well, I'm as ready as I'll ever be."

The path led south from the clearing; all turned to take a final look at the somber old lodge before it passed from sight.

For several hours the trail wound through the woods. The sky remained overcast; the gray-mauve light which penetrated the trees invested the moss, the ferns, the occasional pale flowers, with a peculiarly rich color. Rocky outcrops began to be seen, with black and red lichen; everywhere were fragile little growths not dissimilar to the fungus of Earth, but taller and many-tiered, exhaling a bitter old-age smell when crushed.

The path began to rise, the woods fell below. The pilgrims found themselves on a rock-strewn slope, with mountains looming to the west. At a stream they paused to drink and catch their breath, and the steward distributed sweet biscuits.

To the east spread the forest, gloomy and dark; above loomed the mountain. Hygen Grote again deprecated the difficulty of the way, to which the guide made the blandest of replies: "There is much in what you say, Lord Grote. But as you know, I am only a servant, with orders to make the journey as convenient and interesting as possible."

"How can trudging these weary miles be interesting or convenient?" grumbled Grote, to be answered by Margray Liever: "Come now, Hygen. The scenery is delightful. Look at the view. And did you not enjoy the romantic old lodge? I did."

"I am sure that this is the hope of the Margrave," said the steward. "And now, Lords and Ladies, best that we continue."

The trail slanted up the mountain slope; soon Druidess Laidig and Doranie were falling behind, and the steward courteously slowed the pace. The path entered a stony gulch and the ascent became less steep.

Lunch was brief and austere, consisting of soup, biscuits and sausage; then once again the pilgrims set off along the trail. Wind began to strike down the mountainside, a few cold gusts at a time; overhead dark gray clouds raced to the east. Up the bleak mountainside plodded the pilgrims, and the city Kouhila, the glass-hulled yacht, the green and gold wagon were only remote memories. Margray Liever remained cheerful, and Navarth swung along grinning, as if at some malicious joke. Hygen Grote gave up complaining, saving his breath for the exertion of moving uphill.

Halfway through the afternoon a rain squall drove the party to shelter under a jut of rock. The sky was dark; an unreal gray light washed the landscape. The pilgrims in their costumes of black and umber were as if derived from the same stone and soil as the mountain itself.

The trail entered a stony gorge. The pilgrims plodded forward in silence, the badinage and gentilities of the first few days put aside. There was another brief shower which the steward ignored, for the light was waning. The gorge widened, but the way ahead was blocked by a massive stone wall, topped by a row of iron spikes. The steward went to a black-iron postern, raised a knocker, let it fall. After a long minute, the portal creaked back to reveal a crooked old man in black garments.

The steward addressed the pilgrims. "Here is where I leave you. The path lies beyond; you need only follow. Make the best haste possible, because darkness is not far away."

One by one the group passed through the gap; the portal clanged shut behind them. For a moment they milled uncertainly, looking this way and that. The steward and the old man had gone; there was none to direct them.

Diffiani pointed: "There, the path. It leads up toward the height."

Painfully the pilgrims proceeded. The path traversed a stony barren, crossed a river, once more slanted up through the blowing wind.

Finally, just as the light failed, the path came out on the ridge. Diffiani, in the lead, pointed ahead. "Lights. A hospice of some sort."

The group straggled forward, bending to the wind-gusts, turning faces away from driven drips of rain. A long low stone structure bulked against the sky; one or two of the windows showed a wan yellow illumination. Diffiani found a door, pounded on it with his fist. It creaked open, a woman peered forth. "Who are you? Why do you come so late?"

"We are travelers, guests for the Palace of Love," bawled Hygen Grote. "Is this the way?"

"Yes, this is the way. Enter then. Were you expected?"

"Of course we were expected! Is there lodging for us here?"

"Yes, yes," quavered the old woman. "I can give you beds, but this is the old castle. You should have gone by the other path. Enter then. I must look about. You have supped, I trust?"

"No," said Grote despondently, "we have not."

"Perhaps I can find gruel. What a shame the castle is so cold!"

The pilgrims passed into a bleak courtyard, lit by a pair of feeble lamps. The old woman conducted them one at a time to tall-ceilinged chambers in various quarters of the castle. These were austere, gloomy, decorated to the precepts of some long-forgotten tradition. Gersen's chamber contained a cot, a single lamp of red and blue glass. Three walls were black iron, relieved by patterns of rust. In one of the walls was a door. The fourth wall was paneled in dark waxed wood and carved with enormous grotesque masks. There was neither fire nor heating; the room was chill.

The old lady, breathless and anxious, told Gersen, "When food is ready you'll be summoned." She pointed to the door. "Yonder is the bath, with precious little warm water. One must make do." And she hurried away. Gersen went into the bathroom, tested the shower; the water ran hot. He stripped off his clothes, bathed, then rather than dressing in sodden clothes, he stretched out on the cot and covered himself with a quilt. Time passed; Gersen heard a distant gong strike nine times. There might be supper, again there might not…The warmth of the shower made him drowsy; he fell asleep. Vaguely he heard the gong strike ten times, then eleven. Evidently there was to be no supper… Gersen turned over and went back to sleep.

Twelve strokes of the gong. Into the room came a slender maiden with silky blonde hair. She wore a skin-tight garment of blue velvet, blue leather slippers with rolled toes.

Gersen sat up in bed. The maiden spoke, "We have now prepared a meal; all are aroused, all are summoned to eat." She rolled a wardrobe cart into the room. "Here are garments; do you require assistance?" Without waiting for response she brought under-linen to Gersen. Presently he was clothed in beautiful fabric after a style quaint, ornate and complicated. The maiden dressed his hair, applied gallantry-disks to his cheeks, sprayed him with scent. "My Lord is magnificent," she murmured. "And now: a mask, which tonight is of necessity."

The mask consisted of a black velvet casque fitting down to the ears, with a black visor, a nose-cup, a chin-guard; only Gersen's cheeks, mouth and eyes were bare. "My Lord is now mysterious as well," said the maiden in the softest of voices. "I will lead you, for the way is by the old corridors."

She took him down a draughty staircase, along a dank echoing corridor, with only the feeblest of lamps to light the way. The walls, once splendid in patterns of magenta, silver and gold, were faded and blotched; the tiles of the floor were loose...The maiden halted by a heavy red portière. She looked sidelong at Gersen and put her finger to her lips; with the dim light glowing on her blue velvet garment, glinting in her hair, she seemed dream-stuff, a creature too exquisite to be real. "Lord," she said, "within is our banquet. I must urge you to mystery, for this is the game all must play and you may not speak your name." She pulled aside the portière; Gersen stepped through, into a vast hall. From a ceiling so high as to be unseen hung a single chandelier, casting an island of light around a great table laid with linen, silver and crystal.

Here sat a dozen people in the most elaborate of costumes, wearing masks. Gersen examined them; but recognized none. Were they his fellows along the journey? He could not be sure...Others entered the room. Now they came by twos and threes, all masked, all moving with an air of wonder.

Gersen recognized Navarth, whose swaggering gait was unmistakable. The girl, was she Drusilla? He could not be certain.

Forty people had entered the room, converging slowly upon the table. Footmen in silver and blue livery assisted all to seats; poured wine in the goblets, served from silver trays.

Gersen ate and drank, aware of a peculiar confusion, almost bewilderment. Where and what was reality? The rigors of the journey seemed as remote as childhood. Gersen drank somewhat more wine than he might have under different circumstances ... The chandelier exploded in a dazzling burst of green light, then went out. Gersen's eyes projected orange after-images into the dark; from around the table came whispers and hisses of surprise.

The chandelier slowly returned to normal. A tall man stood on a chair. He wore black garments and a black mask; he held a goblet of wine in his hand. "Guests," he said, "I make you welcome. I am Viole Falushe. You have attained the Palace of Love."

Chapter XII

Avis rara, black mascara
Will you stay to dine with me?
Amanita botulina
Underneath my upas tree.

This dainty tray of cloisonné
Contains my finest patchouli.
Aha, my dear! What have we here?
A dead mouse in the potpourri.

With mayonnaise the canapés,
Ravished from a sturgeon's womb;
With silver prong we guide along
The squeaking oyster to his doom.

A samovar of hangdog tea:
A cup, or are you able?
Antimony, macaroni
On my hemlock table.

... Navarth

—∾—

"There are many varieties of love," said Viole Falushe in a pleasant husky voice. "The range is wide, and all have contributed to the creation of the Palace. Not all of my guests discover this, and not every phase is yielded to them. For some the Palace will seem little more than a holiday resort. Others will be haunted by what has been described as unnatural beauty! This is everywhere: in every detail, every view. Others will revel in ardor, and here I must offer information."

Gersen studied Viole Falushe with a rapt intensity. The tall masked figure stood spare, straight, arms at sides: Gersen turned his head this way and that, trying to identify the figure, but the chandelier hanging directly above the man distorted his contours.

"The people at the Palace of Love are amiable, gay and beautiful, and fall into two categories," said Viole Falushe. "The first are servants. They are pleased to obey every wish of my guests, every whim or caprice. The second class, the happy people who inhabit the Palace, are as independent in their friendships as I myself. They are to be identified by their garments, which are white. Hence, your choice is wide."

Gersen sought around the table, trying to find Tanzel, or Mario or Ethuen and thus eliminate them from suspicion. In this effort he was unsuccessful. Among the forty were a dozen persons who might be any of the three. He turned back to listen to Viole Falushe.

"Are there restrictions? A person who went mad and began to kill would naturally be restrained. Then again, all of us here cherish our privacy, one of our most delightful prerogatives. Only the most thoughtless person would intrude where he was not wanted. My personal apartments are sufficiently secluded; you need not apprehend an accidental intrusion; this is almost impossible." Viole Falushe turned his head slowly, looked around the room. No one spoke; the room was heavy with expectancy.

Viole Falushe spoke on. "So now: the Palace of Love! At times in the past I have arranged small dramas of which the participants were never aware. I have contrived moods in artful sequence. I have employed tragic contrasts to heighten the delectation. On this occasion there will be no such program. You will be free to do as you like, to create your own drama. I advise restraint. The rare jewels are the most precious. The degree of austerity I myself practice would astound you. My great pleasure is creation: of this I never tire. Some of my guests have complained of a gentle melancholy which hangs in the air; I agree that the mood exists. The explanation, I believe, arises from the fugacity of beauty, the tragic pavane to which all of us step. Ignore this mood;

why brood, when there is so much love and beauty here? Take what is offered; have no regrets: a thousand years from now it will be all the same. Satiety is a problem, but it is your own. I cannot protect you. The servants are to serve; command them. The residents who wear white are to woo, to beguile. I pray that you do not become infatuated either with the Palace or its people; such a situation presents difficulties. You will not see me, though spiritually I am always in your midst. There are no spy devices, no sound transmitters, no vision cells. Upbraid me if you choose, revile me, praise me — I cannot hear. My only reward is the act of creation and the effect it produces. Do you wish to look forth on the Palace of Love? Turn then in your seats!"

The far wall slid away; daylight poured into the hall; before the guests spread a landscape of mind-wrenching beauty: wide lawns, feathery green bower-trees, tall black cypress, twinkling birch; ponds, pools, marble urns, pavilions, terraces, rotundas: constructed to an airy delicate architecture that seemed almost to float.

Gersen, like the others, had been startled by the sudden opening of the wall. Recovering he jumped to his feet, but the man in black had disappeared.

Gersen sought out Navarth. "Who was it? Mario? Tanzel? Ethuen?"

Navarth shook his head. "I did not notice. I have been looking for the girl. Where is she?"

With a sudden sinking feeling Gersen swung around. None of the people in the room was Drusilla. "When did you see her last?"

"When we arrived, when we came into the courtyard."

Already the journey seemed remote. Gersen muttered: "I hoped to protect her. I told her so. She trusted me."

Navarth made an impatient motion. "You could have done nothing."

Gersen went to the window, looked across the panorama. To the left was the sea, a group of distant islands. To the right mountains reared ever higher and harsher, with cliffs falling to the valley floor. Below was the Palace: a loose grouping of terraces, halls and pleasaunces. A door slid aside to reveal a descending staircase. One by one the guests descended to the valley.

—ꟾꟾꟾ—

The precincts of the Palace occupied a roughly hexagonal area perhaps a mile on a side. The base was the north cliff, with the Palace at its midpoint. The second side, clockwise, was demarcated by a line of rocky crags, the gaps between which were choked by rank thorny thickets. The third side was white beach and warm blue sea. The fourth and fifth sides were less distinct, and merged into the natural landscape. The sixth side, angling back to the cliff, was demarcated by a line of carefully cultivated flower beds and fruit trees arranged against a rude stone wall. Within the area were three villages, innumerable glades, gardens, waterways. The guests wandered where they chose, spent the long days in whatever fashion seemed most pleasurable. Bright mornings, golden afternoons, evenings and nights: one by one they drifted away.

The servants, as Viole Falushe had implied, were acquiescent and possessed of great physical charm. The folk in white, even more beautiful than the under-servants, were innocent and willful as children. Some were cordial, some were perverse and impudent; all were unpredictable. It seemed as if their sole ambition was to evoke love, to tantalize, to fill the mind with longing, and they became depressed only when guests found the under-servants preferable to themselves. They showed no awareness of the worlds of the universe, and only small curiosity, though their minds were active and their moods mercurial. They thought only of love, and the various aspects of fulfillment. As Viole Falushe had hinted, infatuation too intense might lead to tragedy; of this danger the people in white were gravely aware, but made small effort to avoid the danger.

The mystery of the Druids' presence resolved itself. On the first day after arrival Dakaw, Pruitt, Laidig and Wust, with Hule and Billika in careful convoy, explored the precincts, and fixed upon a delightful little glade for their center of operations. To the back rose a line of black cypress, to right and left were lower trees and flowering shrubs, at the center was a great spraddle-rooted oak. In front of the glade a pair of shelters was erected: low domes of pale brown fiber. Here the group took up residence, and thereafter, each morning and afternoon held evangelical meetings, expounding the nature of their religion to all who came past. With great fervor they urged rigor, harshness, restraint and ritual upon the folk of the garden, who listened politely enough, but after the meetings enticed the Druids to relaxation and pleasure. Gersen decided that the whole affair was one of Viole Falushe's wry jokes: a game he had chosen to play with the Druids. The other guests arrived at the same conclusion, and attended the meetings to judge whose doctrines would triumph.

The Druids worked with great intensity, and built a fane of stones and twigs. Standing at the front one or the other would cry out: "Must you all then die to become dead? The mode to the Eternal is through minglement with a Vitality more enduring than your own. The source of all is the Triad Mag-Rag-Dag: Air, Earth and Water. This is the Holy Immanence, which combines to produce the Tree of Life! The Tree is the wise, the vital, the enduring! Look at lesser things: insects, flowers, fish, man. See how they grow, bloom, lapse, while the Tree in its placid wisdom lives on! Yea, you titillate your flesh, you gorge your stomach, you flood your brain with vapor: what then? How soon you die, while the noble Tree, with roots in Earth, holds innumerable leaves to the glory of the sky! Forever! And when your flesh sags and withers, when your nerves no longer leap, when your belly is sour, when your nose drips from the liquor you have misused — then is no time to worship the Tree! No, no, no! For the Tree will have none of your corruption. All must be fresh and good. So worship! Give over the sterile cavortings, the animal gratifications! Worship the Tree!"

The Palace folk listened with respect and awe. It was impossible to judge how deeply the Druid doctrine touched them. Meanwhile Dakaw and Pruitt began to dig a great hole under the oak, burrowing down between the sprawled roots. Hule and Billika were not allowed to dig and showed no disposition to do so; indeed they watched the process with horrified fascination.

The Palace folk, in their turn, insisted that the Druids participate in their festivities, arguing: "You wish us to learn your ways, but in all fairness you must know the way we live too, so that you may judge our lives and see if after all we are corrupt!" Grudgingly the Druids acquiesced, sitting in a huddled group and maintaining the closest possible strictures upon Hule and Billika.

The other guests watched with varied reactions. Skebou Diffiani attended the meetings with regularity and presently, to the astonishment of all, announced his intent to become a Druid. Thereafter he donned black robe and cowl and joined the others at their rituals. Torrace daNossa spoke of the Druids with pitying contempt; Lerand Wible, who along the way had displayed an interest in Billika, threw up his arms in disgust and stayed away; Mario, Ethuen and Tanzel went their own ways and were seen but seldom. Navarth had become obsessed. He roved the garden, morose, dissatisfied, looking this way and that. He took no joy in the beauty of the garden and went so far as to sneer at Viole Falushe's arrangements. "There is no novelty here: the pleasures are banal. There are no exhilarations, no staggering insights, no sublime sweep of mind. All is either gross or maudlin: the gratification of gut and gland."

"This may be true," Gersen admitted. "The pleasures of the place are simple and undramatic. But what is wrong with this?"

"Nothing. But it is not poetry."

"It is all very beautiful. To do Viole Falushe credit, he has avoided the macabre, the sadistic spectacles, which occur elsewhere, and he allows his servants a certain degree of integrity."

Navarth made a sour grumbling sound. "You are an innocent. The more exotic pleasures he reserves for himself. Who knows what goes on beyond the walls? He is a man to halt at nothing. And 'integrity' in these people? Bathos! They are dolls, toys, confections! No doubt many are the little children extorted from Kouhila: those he did not sell to the Mahrab. And when they lose their youth: what then? Where do they go?"

Gersen only shook his head. "I don't know."

"And where is Jheral Tinzy?" Navarth went on. "Where is the girl? What does he do with her? He has had her at his mercy."

Gersen gave a grim nod. "I know."

"You know," jeered Navarth, "but only after I reminded you. You are not only innocent; you are futile and foolish, no less than myself. She trusted you to protect her: and what have you done? Swilled and trolloped with the others, and this is the extent of your effort."

Gersen thought the outburst exaggerated but made a mild reply. "If I could contrive some feasible course of action, I would do so."

"And in the meantime?"

"In the meantime, I am learning."

"Learning what?"

"I find that none of the people here know Viole Falushe by sight. His offices seem to be somewhere back in the mountains; I can find them nowhere in the valley. I dare not try to cross the stone wall to the west, nor the thorn barrier to the east; I would certainly be apprehended, and, journalist or not, dealt with harshly. Since I have no weapons I can demand nothing. I must be patient. If I do not speak to him here at the Palace of Love, I will no doubt find opportunity elsewhere."

"All for your magazine, eh?"

"Why else?" asked Gersen.

They had come to the glade of the Druids. Dakaw and Pruitt were delving as usual below the great oak, where they had excavated a chamber tall enough for a man to stand erect.

Navarth approached, peered down into the sweating dust-streaked faces. "What do you do down there, you burrowing Druids? Are you not pleased with the vista above ground that you seek a new viewpoint below?"

"You are facetious," said Pruitt coldly. "Be on your way; this is holy soil."

"How can you be so sure? It looks like ordinary dirt."

Neither Pruitt nor Dakaw made response.

Navarth barked down, "What sort of mischief are you up to? This is no ordinary pastime. Speak now!"

"Go away, old poet," said Pruitt. "Your breath is a pollution and saddens the Tree."

Navarth moved back and watched the digging from a little distance. "I do not like holes in the ground," he told Gersen. "They are unpleasant. Look at Wible yonder. He stands as if he were overseer to the project!" Navarth pointed toward the entrance to the glade, where Wible stood, legs apart, hands clasped behind his back, whistling between his teeth. Navarth joined him. "The work of the Druids enthralls you?"

"Not at all," said Lerand Wible. "They dig a grave."

"As I suspected. For whom?"

"That I can't be sure. Perhaps you. Perhaps me."

"I doubt if they will inter me," said Navarth. "You may be more pliable."

"I doubt if they will inter anyone," said Wible, whistling once more through his teeth.

"Indeed? How can you be so sure?"

"Come to the 'consecration' and see for yourself."

"When does this rite occur?"

"Tomorrow night, so I have been informed."

Little music was to be heard on the grounds of the Palace; the quiet of the garden was as crystalline and clear as a dew-drop. But on the following morning the folk in white brought forth stringed instruments and for an hour played a wistful music rich with plangent overtones. A sudden shower sent all hurrying to the shelter of a nearby rotunda, where they stood chattering like birds, peering up at the sky. Gersen, contemplating their faces, thought how frail and tenuous was the connection between them and the guests. Did they know anything except frivolity and love? And there was the question raised by Navarth: what happened when they aged? Few in the garden were past the first bloom of their maturity.

The sun came forth; the garden glinted with freshness. Gersen, drawn by curiosity went to the Druids' glade. Within one of the shelters he glimpsed Billika's pale face. Then Wust came to stare at him from the doorway.

The long afternoon passed. Today a portent hung in the air, and uneasiness seemed to infect everyone. Evening arrived; the sun sank in a great tumult of clouds; gold, orange and red flamed overhead and far into the east. With the coming of dusk, folk of the garden went to the Druids' glade. To each side of the oak tree were fires, tended by Druidess Laidig and Druidess Wust.

Druid Pruitt emerged from his shelter. He went to the fane and began his address. His voice was heavy and resonant; he paused frequently, as if to hear the echoes of his words.

Lerand Wible approached Gersen. "I am speaking to everyone in our group. Whatever happens — do not interfere. Do you agree to this?"

"Naturally not."

"I didn't think you would. Well then —" Wible whispered a few words; Gersen grunted. Wible moved off to speak to Navarth, who tonight was carrying a staff. After Wible spoke, Navarth threw down his staff.

"— on each world a hallowed Tree: how does it become so? By the afflatus, by the concentration of Life. Oh worshipful Druids, who share the life of the First Germ, bring forth your awe, your most poignant dedication! What say we? Two are here, two have lived for this consecration. Come forth, Druids, go to the Tree!" From one shelter staggered Hule, from the other Billika. Baffled, dull-eyed as if bewildered or drugged, they stared this way and that, then saw the fires. Fascinated they approached, step by slow step. Silence was heavy in the glade. The two approached the tree, looked at the fires, then descended into the hole below the tree.

"Behold!" called Pruitt. "They enter the life of the Tree — oh blessed pair! — which now becomes the Soul of the World. Exalted children, lucky two! Forever and ever stand in sun, in rain, by day, by night; help us to truth!" Druids Dakaw, Pruitt and Diffiani began to spade earth into the hole. They worked with gusto. In half an hour the hole was full, the soil banked around the roots. The Druids marched around the tree, holding brands from the fire. Each called forth an invocation, and the ceremony ended with a chant.

The Druids customarily breakfasted at the refectory of the near village. The morning after the consecration they marched across the meadows, entered the refectory. Behind them came Hule and Billika. The Druids took their usual places, as did Hule and Billika.

Wust was the first to notice. She pointed a trembling finger. Laidig screamed. Pruitt leapt away, then turned and ran from the refectory. Dakaw fell back like a half-filled sack; Skebou Diffiani, sitting bolt upright, stared in puzzlement. Hule and Billika ignored the consternation they had caused.

Laidig, sobbing and gasping, reeled from the room, followed by Wust. Diffiani was the least disturbed. He spoke to Hule. "How did you get out?"

"By a tunnel," said Hule. "Wible caused a tunnel to be dug."

Wible came forward. "The servants are here to be used. I used them. We dug a tunnel."

Diffiani nodded slowly. He reached up, took off his cowl, inspected it, tossed it into a corner.

Dakaw, roaring, rose to his feet. He struck once at Hule, knocking him to the floor; then aimed a tremendous blow at Wible, who stepped back, grinning. "Go back to your tree, Dakaw. Dig another hole and bury yourself."

Dakaw marched from the inn.

Wust and Laidig were finally discovered, crouching in a bower. Pruitt had run south, beyond the precincts of the garden and was seen no more.

In some fashion the episode with the Druids had broken a web. The guests, looking at each other, knew that the end of their visit was approaching; that soon they would be departing the Palace of Love.

Gersen stood looking up at the mountains. Patience was well and good, but he might never be so close to Viole Falushe again.

He pondered the small clues he had gleaned. It seemed reasonable to suppose that the banquet hall communicated with Viole Falushe's apartments. Gersen went to examine the portal at the foot of the stairs. It showed a blank featureless face. The mountainside above was unclimbable.

To the east, where crags reared over the sea, Viole Falushe had set a thorn palisade. To the west the way was barred by a stone wall. Gersen turned to look south. If he made a long journey, circling the periphery of the garden, he would then be able to climb into the mountains to approach the area from above... This was the sort of purposeless activity Gersen detested. He would be moving without knowledge, without plan. There must be some better method... He could think of none. Very well, then: activity. He looked at the sun. Six hours of daylight remained. He must go far afield and trust to luck. If he were apprehended, he was Henry Lucas, journalist, in search of information: a statement of sufficient force unless Viole Falushe undertook to use a truth-extracting device... Gersen's flesh crawled. The sensation annoyed him. He had become soft, diffident, over-wary. Reproaching himself first for cowardice, then for wilful recklessness, he set forth, walking south, away from the mountains.

Chapter XIII

From *Worlds I Have Known,* by L.G. Dusenyi:

The municipal Temple at Astropolis is a splendid edifice of red porphyry, with a noteworthy altar of solid silver. The Astropolitans are divided into thirteen cults, each dedicated to a distinct Supreme Deity. To determine which image sits on high the Astropolitans each seven years conduct a Tournament of the Gods, with trials to measure Paramount Power, Inaccessible Loftiness and Ineffable Mystery.

At the first trial wooden god-images are mounted upon onagers, each hitched to a heavy log. The onagers then are urged around a track and the winning god is credited with Paramount Power.

At the second trial the images are thrust into a glass cauldron which is then sealed and inverted. The god which floats on high is credited with Inaccessible Loftiness.

The images are then concealed behind booths. Candidates for sacrifice are brought forward, and each attempts to guess the god behind each booth. The candidate with the lowest score receives unction and the blade, while the god who most efficiently conceals his identity is judged Ineffably Mysterious.

Over the past twenty-eight years the god Kalzibah has proved himself so consistently and the god Syarasis has so often failed that the Syaratics are gradually deserting the cult to become ardent Kalzibahans.

—∿∿—

THE GARDEN ENDED at a grove of indigenous trees, of a type Gersen had not seen before: tall, gaunt organisms with pulpy black leaves, from which dripped a musty unpleasant sap. Fearing poison, Gersen breathed as shallowly as possible, and was relieved to reach open ground with no other sensation than dizziness. To the east, toward the ocean, were orchards and cultivated soil; to the west a dozen long sheds were visible. Barns? Warehouses? Dormitories? Keeping to the shadow of the trees Gersen walked west, and presently came upon a road leading from the sheds toward the mountains.

No living creature was in sight. The sheds seemed deserted. Gersen decided not to explore them; they certainly were not the headquarters of Viole Falushe.

Across the road was a wild area overgrown with thorny scrub. Gersen looked dubiously down the road. Best to travel by the barrens; there would be less chance of discovery. He ducked across the road, struck off toward the mountains. The afternoon sun shone bright; the scrub was host to swarms of small red mites which set up an impatient whirring sound when disturbed. Stepping around a hummock — a hive or nest of some sort — Gersen came upon a bloated serpent-like creature with a face uncannily human. The creature saw Gersen with an expression of comical alarm, then, rearing back, displayed a proboscis from which it evidently intended to eject a fluid. Gersen beat a quick retreat, and thereafter walked more warily.

The road veered west, away from the garden. Gersen crossed once more and took shelter under a cluster of yellow bladder-plants. He considered the mountain, tracing a route which would bring him to the ridge. Unfortunately, while climbing, he would be exposed to the gaze of anyone who happened by... No help for it. He took a last look around, and seeing nothing to dissuade him, set forth.

The mountainside was steep, at times precipitous; Gersen made discouragingly slow progress. The sun swung across the sky. Below spread the Palace of Love and the garden. Gersen's chest pounded, and his throat felt numb, as if it had been anaesthetized... The influence of the noxious black-leaved forest? Ever higher, the panorama ever wider.

For a space the way became easier and Gersen angled toward the east, where presumably Viole Falushe maintained his headquarters.

Motion. Gersen stopped short. From the corner of his eyes he had seen — what? He could not be sure. The flicker had come from below and to his right. He scrutinized the face of the mountain, and presently saw what otherwise might have evaded his attention: a deep cleft or fissure with a bridge between two arched apertures, the whole camouflaged by a stone wall.

Clutching and straining, Gersen angled down toward the cleft, finally reaching a point thirty feet above the walkway. There was no means to descend. He could go neither forward nor up nor down. His fingers were tiring, his legs were cramped. Thirty feet: too far to jump. He would break his legs. Out upon the bridge came a pale stoop-shouldered man with a large moist head, a clipped shock of black-gray hair. He wore a white jacket, black trousers. It was the white jacket, Gersen now realized, which had originally drawn his attention. If the man should look up, if a dislodged pebble should strike the bridge, Gersen was lost... The man moved into the opposite aperture and out of sight. Gersen gave a fantastic gravity-defying leap, to throw himself into the angle of the cleft. He thrust out his legs, doubled his knees, pressing between the walls. Inch by inch he let himself down, gratefully jumping the final six feet. He stretched, massaged sore muscles, then limped over to the western doorway, into which the man had disappeared. A white-tiled hall led back fifty yards, broken by areas of glass and occasional doorways. Beside one of these glass areas stood the stoop-shouldered man, peering at something which had attracted his attention. He raised his hand, signaled. From somewhere beyond Gersen's range of vision came a heavy-shouldered man with a thick neck, narrow head, a coarse yellow brush of hair, white eyes. The two looked through the glass, and the white-eyed man seemed to be amused.

Gersen drew back. Crossing the walkway, he looked up the passage to the east, to see a single doorway at the far end. The walls and floor were white tile; ornate lamps scattered rays and planes of various colors.

With long stealthy strides Gersen went to the far door. He touched the open-button. No response. He sought for code points, or a lockhole, without success: the opening-mechanism was controlled from the other side. In one sense this was encouraging. The stoop-shouldered man had come this way, and it could only be to confer with whomever sat or stood or worked beyond the door.

It would not do to attract attention. Yet Gersen must do something and quickly. At any moment one of the two men might approach, and he had nowhere to hide. He scrutinized the door with great care. The latch was magnetic; retraction was accomplished by an electro-muscle. The escutcheon plate was fixed to the panel with adhesive. Gersen searched his pockets but found nothing of utility. Loping back down the hall, he reached up to the first lighting fixture, twisted loose a decorative metal cusp with a sharp point. Returning to the door he pried at the escutcheon plate, presently snapped it free, to reveal the mechanism of the open-button. Gersen traced the circuit, and with the point of his metal cusp shorted across the relay contacts. He touched the button. The door slid aside, silent as a whisper.

Gersen passed through the opening into an unoccupied foyer. He replaced the escutcheon plate and let the door slide shut.

There was much to see. The far end of the room was ripple glass. To the left an archway opened upon a flight of stairs. To the right were five cinematic panels, each displaying Jheral Tinzy in various guises at different stages of existence. Or were they five different girls? One, wearing a short black skirt, was Drusilla Wayles: Gersen recognized the expression on her face, the droop to her mouth, the restless habit of tossing her head to the side. Another, this a delightful imp in clown's regalia, cavorted on a stage. A Jheral Tinzy of thirteen or fourteen in the translucent white gown of a sleepwalker moved slowly across an eerie setting of stone, black shadow, sand. A fourth Jheral Tinzy, a year or two younger than Drusilla, wore only a barbaric skirt of leather and bronze. She stood on a stone-flagged terrace and seemed to be performing a religious ritual. A fifth Jheral Tinzy, a year or two older than Drusilla, walked briskly along a city street... Gersen glimpsed all this in the space of two seconds. The effect was fascinating, but he could not spare time to look. For beyond the ripple-glass wall was the distorted image of a tall spare man.

Gersen crossed the foyer on four silken strides. His hand went to the open-button of the door; he tensed, touched the button. The door failed to open. Gersen exhaled: a long slow sigh of frustration. The man turned his head sharply; all Gersen could see was distortion and blur. "Retz? Back once more?" he jerked his head suddenly forward; the glass was evidently permeable to his vision. "It's Lucas: Henry Lucas the journalist!" His voice took on a harsh edge. "There is a need for much explanation. What are you doing here?"

"The answer is obvious," said Gersen. "I came here to interview you. There seemed no other way."

"How did you find my office?"

"I climbed the mountain, jumped down where the walkway crosses the notch. Then I came along the passageway."

"Indeed, indeed. Are you a human fly to traverse the cliff?"

"It was not so difficult," said Gersen. "There would be no other opportunity."

"This is a serious annoyance," said Viole Falushe. "Do you recall my comments on the subject of privacy? I am rigid on this score."

"Your comments were addressed to your guests," said Gersen. "I am here as a man with a job to do."

"Your occupation gives you no license to break laws," Viole Falushe stated in a gentle voice. "You are aware of my wishes, which here, as elsewhere in the cluster, are law. I find your trespass not only insolent but inexcusable. In fact, it goes far beyond the brashness ordinarily tolerated in a journalist. It almost seems —"

Gersen interrupted. "Please do not let your imagination dominate your sense of proportion. I am interested in the photographs in the foyer. They seem to be the likeness of the young lady who accompanied us on our journey: Navarth's ward."

"This is the case," said Viole Falushe. "I have a strong interest in the young woman. I entrusted her upbringing to Navarth with unhappy results; she is a wanton."

"Where is she now? I have not seen her since we arrived at the Palace."

"She is enjoying her visit in circumstances somewhat different from yours," said Viole Falushe. "But why your interest? She is nothing to you."

"Except that I befriended her and tried to clarify certain issues which she found confusing."

"And these issues were?"

"You will allow me to use candor?"

"Why not? You can hardly provoke me more than you already have."

"The girl was fearful of what might happen to her. She wanted to live a normal life, but did not care to risk retaliation for actions she could not avoid."

Viole Falushe's voice trembled. "Is this how she spoke of me? Only in terms of fear and 'retaliation'?"

"She had no reason to speak otherwise."

"You are a bold man, Mr. Lucas. Surely you know my reputation. I subscribe to a doctrine of general equity: that he who commits a grievance must repair the effects of his act."

"What of Jheral Tinzy?" Gersen inquired, hoping to divert Viole Falushe.

"'Jheral Tinzy'." Viole Falushe breathed the name. "Dear Jheral: as wilful and promiscuous as the unfortunate girl whom you befriended. Jheral could never quite repay the damage she wrought upon me. Oh, those wasted years!" Viole Falushe's voice quavered; grief lay near the surface. "Never could she requite her wrongs, though she did her best."

"She is alive?"

"No." Viole Falushe's mood changed once more. "Why do you ask?"

"I am a journalist. You know why I am here. I want a photograph of Jheral Tinzy for our article."

"This is a matter I do not care to publicize."

"I am puzzled by the resemblance between Jheral Tinzy and the girl Drusilla. Can you explain this?"

"I could," said Viole Falushe. "But I do not choose to do so. And there still remains your intrusion, which has shocked me, to such an extent that I demand retribution." And Viole Falushe leaned negligently back against an article of furniture.

Gersen reflected a moment. Flight was futile. Attack was impossible. Viole Falushe certainly carried a weapon; Gersen had none. Galling though the situation might be he must persuade Viole Falushe to change his mind. He tried a reasonable approach. "Conceivably I violated the letter of your regulations, but what avail is an article on the Palace of Love without the comments of its creator? There is no communicating with you, since you choose to keep yourself aloof from your guests."

Viole Falushe seemed surprised. "Navarth knows my call-code well. A servant would have brought you a telephone unit; you might have called me at any time."

"This did not occur to me," said Gersen thoughtfully. "No, I had not considered the telephone. You say Navarth knows the code?"

"Certainly. It is the same as that which I use on Earth."

"The fact remains," said Gersen, "I am here. You have seen Part I of the projected article; Part II and III are even more highly colored. If we want to present your point of view, it is important that we speak together. So open the door and we will discuss the matter."

"No," said Viole Falushe. "It is my whim to remain anonymous, since I enjoy mingling with my guests... Well, then," he grumbled, "I suppose I must swallow my outrage. It is not just that you should evade your debt to me. Perhaps you will not in any event. For the moment, you may regard yourself as reprieved." He spoke a soft word that Gersen did not hear; a door opened in the foyer. "Go within; this is my library. I will speak with you there."

Gersen passed into a long room carpeted in dark green. A heavy table at the center supported a pair of antique lamps, a selection of current periodicals. One wall was lined with ancient books, the shelves sliding up or down through floor and ceiling to magazines above and below. There was a standard micro-reference system, a number of soft chairs.

Gersen looked around with a trace of envy; the atmosphere was quiet, civilized, rational, remote from the hedonistic life of the Palace. A screen glowed to reveal Viole Falushe sprawling in a chair. A light threw his form into silhouette; he was no more identifiable now than before.

"Very well then," said Viole Falushe, "so here we are. You have been making your photographic records, I believe?"

"I have several hundred pictures. More than necessary to cover the superficial aspects of the Palace: that which you display to your guests."

Viole Falushe seemed amused. "And you are curious as to what else occurs?"

"From a journalistic standpoint."

"Hm. What do you think of the Palace then?"

"It is remarkably pleasant."

"You have a reservation?"

"Something is lacking. Perhaps the flaw lies in your servants. They lack depth; they do not seem real."

"I recognize this," said Viole Falushe. "They have no traditions. The only remedy is time."

"They are also without responsibility. After all, they are slaves."

"Not quite, for they do not realize it. They consider themselves the Fortunate Folk, and such they are. It is precisely this unreality, this sense of faerie, that I have been at pains to develop."

"And when they age, what then? What becomes of the Fortunate Folk?"

"Some work the farms surrounding the gardens. Some are sent elsewhere."

"To the real world? They are sold as slaves?"

"All of us are slaves, in some wise."

"How are you a slave?"

"I am victim to a terrible obsession. I was a sensitive boy, cruelly thwarted; I daresay Navarth has provided the details. Rather than submit, I was forced, by my sense of justice, to seek compensation — which I am still seeking. I am a man much maligned. The public considers me a voluptuous sybarite, an erotic glutton. The reverse is true. I am — why mince matters? — absolutely ascetic. I must remain so until my obsession is relieved. I am a man cursed. But you are not interested in my personal problems, since naturally they are not for publication."

"Nevertheless I am interested. Jheral Tinzy is the source of your obsession?"

"Precisely." Viole Falushe spoke in a measured voice. "She has blighted my life. She must expunge this blight. Is this not justice? To date she has proved unwilling, incapable."

"How could she remove the obsession?"

Viole Falushe stirred fretfully in his chair. "Are you so unimaginative? We have explored the matter far enough."

"So Jheral Tinzy is yet alive?"

"Yes indeed."

"But I understood you to say that she was dead."

"Life, death: these are imprecise terms."

"Who then is Drusilla, the girl you left with Navarth? Is she Jheral Tinzy?"

"She is who she is. She made a dreadful mistake. She failed and Navarth failed, for Navarth should have schooled her. She is frivolous and wanton; she trafficked with other men, and she must serve as Jheral Tinzy served, and thus it shall be, ever and ever, until finally there is expiation, until I can feel soothed and whole. By this time there is a terrible score to pay. Thirty years! Think of it!" Viole Falushe's voice vibrated and cracked. "Thirty years surrounded by beauty, and incapable of enjoying it! Thirty long years!"

"I would not presume to give you advice," said Gersen, somewhat drily.

"I need no advice, and naturally what I tell you is in confidence. You would be ungracious to publish it. I would be grieved and forced to demand satisfaction."

"What then may I publish?"

"Whatever you like, so long as I am not injured."

"What of the other events here? What goes on at the other end of the hall?"

Viole Falushe considered him a moment. Gersen could sense but not see the smoulder in his eyes. But he spoke in a light voice: "This is the Palace of Love. I am interested in the subject, even fascinated, through the mechanism of sublimation. I have an elaborate program of research under way. I explore the emotion in artificial and arbitrary circumstances. I do not choose to discuss the matter any further at this time. Perhaps five years from now, or ten, I will publish a resumé of my findings. They will provide fascinating insights."

"In regard to the photographs in the foyer—"

Viole Falushe jumped to his feet. "No more! We have talked too much. I find myself uneasy. You have provoked this, hence I have arranged a similar uneasiness for you, which will go far to soothe me. Thereafter: caution, discretion! Make the most of your time, because shortly you must return to Reality."

"What of you? You remain here?"

"No. I shall also leave the Palace. My work here is accomplished, and I have an important mission on Alphanor, which well may change all... Be so good as to step into the hall. My friend Helaunce awaits you."

Helaunce, thought Gersen. This would be the white-eyed man. Slowly, with Viole Falushe watching him from the screen, Gersen turned, went to the door. The white-eyed man waited in the hall. He carried an object something like a flail: a rod terminating in a set of cords. He appeared to carry no other weapon.

"Remove your clothes," said Helaunce. "You are to be chastised."

"Best that you confine your chastisement to words," said Gersen. "Revile me all you like; in the meantime let us return to the garden."

Helaunce smiled. "I have my orders. Be as difficult as you like; the orders must and will be carried out."

"Not by you," said Gersen. "You are too thick and too slow."

Helaunce flourished the flail; the cords made a sinister crackling sound. "Quick, or you will make us impatient, and the punishment will be commensurate."

Helaunce was hard and tough, Gersen noted, obviously a trained fighter, perhaps as well-trained as himself. Helaunce was also thirty pounds heavier. If he had a weakness, it was not apparent. Gersen suddenly sat down in the hall, put his hands to his face, began to sob.

Helaunce stared in puzzlement. "Off with your clothes! Do not sit there!" He came forward, nudged Gersen with his foot. "Up."

Gersen jumped up with Helaunce's foot clamped to his chest. Helaunce hopped backward; Gersen gave the foot a cruel twist, applying torque to joints where muscles could interpose no protection. Helaunce cried out in agony, fell flat. Gersen wrested loose the flail, struck him across the shoulder. The cords hissed, crackled; Helaunce muttered.

"If you can walk," said Gersen, "be good enough to show me the way."

There was a step behind him: Gersen turned to glimpse a tall shape in black garments. Something splashed purple-white light into his brain; Gersen toppled, dazed.

There was half an hour of nightmare. Gersen slowly regained control of his faculties. He lay naked in the Garden, beside the white Palace wall. His clothes were stacked neatly beside him.

So much for that, thought Gersen. The project had failed. Not in disaster, for he still had his life. Gersen dressed himself, smiling grimly. There had been an attempt to humiliate him. It had not succeeded. He had paid, but pain, like pleasure, had no duration. Pride was an entity more persistent.

Gersen leaned against the wall until his brain cleared. His nerves still throbbed to the terrible flail. There were no bruises, no lacerations: no more than a few red welts. Gersen was hungry. And here was humiliation indeed: he must eat Viole Falushe's food; walk through the pleasant garden that Viole Falushe's brain had conceived...Gersen smiled again, even more wolfishly than before. He had known that his life might not be altogether graceful and easy.

The time was about dusk. The garden had never seemed more beautiful. Fireflies moved in the jasmine bushes; marble urns glowed against dark foliage as if exuding wan light of their own. A troupe of girls from one of the villages came capering past. Tonight they wore loose white pantaloons and carried yellow lanterns. Seeing Gersen, they circled around him singing a gay song, the words of which Gersen could not comprehend. One approached, held her lantern to Gersen's face. "Why so strange, guest-man? Why so gray? Come frolic, come join us!"

"Thank you," said Gersen. "I fear tonight I would frolic very poorly indeed."

"Kiss me," coaxed the girl. "Am I not beautiful? Why are you so sad? Because you must leave, forever and ever, the Palace of Love? And we will remain, and always be young and carry our lanterns through the night. Is this why you grieve?"

Gersen smiled. "Yes, I must return to a far world. And I am forlorn at the thought. But do not let me interfere with your joy."

The girl kissed his cheek. "Tonight is your last night, your last night at the Palace of Love! Tonight you must do all you have neglected so far; never will there be another time!" The girls continued on their way, with Gersen looking after them. "Do all I have neglected? I wish I could..." He went to a sunken terrace where guests sat dining. Navarth crouched over a bowl of goulash; Gersen joined him. An attendant wheeled forth a cart; Gersen, who had not eaten since morning, served himself. Navarth finally spoke: "What's happened? You appear well-used."

"I spent an afternoon with our host."

"Indeed. You spoke to him face to face?"

"Almost so."

"And you know then his identity? Mario? Ethuen? Tanzel?"

"I can't be sure."

Navarth grunted, and bent once more to the goulash.

"Tonight is the last night," Gersen said presently.

"So they tell me. I will be glad to go. There is no poetry here. It is as I have always set forth: joy comes of its own free will; it cannot be belabored. Look: a great palace, a magnificent garden with live nymphs and heroes. But where is the dreaming, the myth? Only simple-minded folk find joy here."

"Your friend Viole Falushe would be sorry to hear you say this."

"I cannot say less." Navarth turned Gersen a sudden sharp look. "Did you ask for the girl?"

"I did. I learned nothing."

Navarth closed his eyes. "I have become an old man, I am ineffectual. Henry Lucas, whatever your name, cannot you act?"

"Today I tried," said Gersen. "I was not made welcome."

The two sat in silence. Then Gersen asked, "When do we leave?"

"I know no more than you."

"We will do what we can."

Chapter XIV

From *The Avatar's Apprentice* in Scroll from the Ninth Dimension:

Struggling to the hill's crest Marmaduke searched for the blasted cypress which marked the hut of the symbologist. There stood the tree, haggard and desolate, and a hut nearby.

The symbologist gave him welcome. "A hundred leagues I have come," said Marmaduke, "to put a single question: 'Do the colors have souls?' "

"Did anyone aver otherwise?" asked the perplexed symbologist. He caused to shine an orange light, then, lifting the swing of his gown, cavorted with great zest. Marmaduke watched with pleasure, amused to see an old man so spry!

The symbologist brought forth green light. Crouching under the bench he thrust his head between his ankles and turned his gown outside to in, while Marmaduke clapped his hands for wonder.

The symbologist evoked red light, and leaping upon Marmaduke, playfully wrestled him to the floor and threw the gown over his head. "My dear fellow," gasped Marmaduke winning free, "but you are brisk in your demonstration!"

"What is worth doing is worth doing well," the symbologist replied. "Now to expatiate. The colors admit of dual import. The orange is icterine humor as well as the mirth of a dying heron.

"Green is the essence of second-thoughts, likewise the mode of the north wind. Red, as we have seen, accompanies rustic exuberance."

"And a second import of the red?"

The symbologist made a cryptic sign. "That remains to be seen, as the cat said who voided into the sugar bowl."

Amused and edified, Marmaduke took his leave, and he was quite halfway down the mountain before he discovered the loss of his wallet.

—~~—

THE LAST NIGHT at the Palace of Love was celebrated by a fête. There was music, intoxicating fumes, a whirl of dancers from the villages. Those who had formed attachments made woeful conversation or indulged in a final frenzy of passion. Others sat quietly, each in his private mood, and so passed the night. One by one the colored lights blinked and dimmed; the folk in white slipped away through the garden gloom; one by one the guests took themselves to their couches, alone or in the company that pleased them most.

The garden was quiet; dew began to form on the grass. To each of the guests went a servant: "The time has come to leave."

To grumblings and protests the servants made but one reply: "These are our orders. The air-car waits; those who are not on hand must walk their way back to Kouhila."

The guests once more were provided new clothing: an austere costume of blue, black and dark green. They were then guided to an area somewhat south of the Palace where a large air-car waited. Gersen counted: all here except Pruitt and Drusilla. Ethuen, Mario and Tanzel stood nearby. If one were Viole Falushe, it seemed that now he planned to return to the Oikumene with the others.

Gersen went forward, glanced into the pilot's compartment. Here sat Helaunce. The guests were filing into the air-car. Gersen took Navarth aside. "Wait."

"Why?"

"No matter." Tanzel and Ethuen were aboard; now Mario climbed the ladder. Gersen spoke hurriedly. "Go aboard. Make a disturbance. Pound on the bulkhead. Shout. There is an emergency lock between the saloon and the pilot's compartment. Pull this open. Distract the pilot; try not to incite either Mario, Ethuen or Tanzel. They must not be encouraged to interfere."

Navarth looked at him blankly. "What is the use of this?"

"No matter. Do as I say. Where is Drusilla? Where is Jheral Tinzy? Why are they not aboard?"

"Yes...Why are they not aboard? I am truly outraged." Navarth jumped up the ladder, thrusting aside the Druidess Laidig. "Wait!" he called. "We are not all present. Where is Zan Zu from Eridu? We cannot leave without her. I refuse to leave; nothing will remove me."

"Quiet, old fool," growled Torrace daNossa. "You do no good."

Navarth raged back and forth. He struck on the forward bulkhead, pulled on the handle of the communicating door. Finally Helaunce opened the door, went aft to enforce order. "Old man, sit quietly. It is by order that we now leave. Unless you care to walk the long road alone, sit quiet."

"Come then, Navarth," said Lerand Wible. "You achieve nothing. Sit quietly."

"Very well," said Navarth. "I have protested; I have done all I can; I can do no more."

Helaunce returned forward. He backed into the pilot's compartment, closed the door. Gersen, waiting to the side, struck him over the head with a stone. Helaunce staggered, spun around. He saw Gersen through eyes blinded by blood and gave an inarticulate cry. Gersen struck again; Helaunce fell aside.

Gersen settled himself at the controls. Up rose the air-car, up into the light of the rising sun. Gersen searched Helaunce, found two projacs, which he tucked into his own pocket. Slackening speed until the air-car only drifted, he slid open the door, rolled Helaunce out and away.

In the saloon, thought Gersen, Viole Falushe must be wondering as to the peculiar course Helaunce was steering. Gersen sought around the ocean and presently spied a small island some twenty miles from the shore. He circled it, and seeing no sign of habitation landed the air-car.

He jumped to the ground. Going to the saloon port, he pulled it open, jumped inside. "Everybody out. Quick." And he gestured with the projacs.

Wible stuttered, "What does this mean?"

"It means everybody out."

Navarth jumped to his feet. "Come along," he bawled. "Everybody out."

The guests uncertainly filed outside. Mario came to the door. Gersen halted him. "You must remain. Be very careful and do not move, or I will kill you."

Tanzel came by, and Ethuen; both were intercepted, ordered to sit. Finally the saloon was empty but for Gersen, Mario, Tanzel and Ethuen. Outside Navarth excitedly harangued the group. "Make no interference; you will regret it! This is IPCC business; I know it for a fact!"

"Navarth!" Gersen called from the saloon. "Your assistance, please."

Navarth climbed back into the saloon. He searched Mario, Tanzel and Ethuen, while Gersen stood vigilantly by. No weapons, no clues to the identity of Viole Falushe were discovered. To Gersen's direction, Navarth tied the three men to chairs, using various oddments of cord, strips of fabric and thongs. Meanwhile the three excoriated Gersen and demanded the basis for his persecution: Tanzel was the most verbose; Ethuen the most acrimonious; Mario the most enraged. All glared and cursed with equal vigor. Gersen accepted the remarks with equanimity. "I will apologize to two of you later. Those two, aware of their innocence, will cooperate with me. From the third man I expect trouble. I am prepared for it."

Tanzel asked, "In Jehu's name, then: what do you wish of us? Name your third man and have done!"

"Vogel Filschner is his name," said Gersen. "Otherwise known as Viole Falushe."

"Why pick on us? Go seek him at the Palace!"

Gersen grinned. "Not a bad idea." He tested the bonds of the three men, tightened here, reknotted there. "Navarth, you sit here, to the side. Watch these three carefully. One of them took Jheral Tinzy from you."

"Tell me which one."

"Vogel Filschner. You don't recognize him?"

"I wish I could." He pointed to Mario. "This one has his shifty eye." He indicated Tanzel's hands. "This one has a mannerism I remember in Vogel." He turned to inspect Ethuen. "And this one has a store of spite and clearly is unhappy."

"Certainly I'm unhappy!" snapped Ethuen. "Why should I rejoice?"

"Watch them well," said Gersen. "We return to the Palace."

Ignoring the outcries of the marooned guests, he took the air-car aloft. So far so good — but what next? Conceivably his reasoning was awry; conceivably neither Tanzel, nor Mario, nor Ethuen was Viole Falushe. Thinking back over the circumstances of the journey to the Palace, he discarded the notion.

The best method of ingress to the apartments of Viole Falushe was from above; Gersen had no stomach for another climb around the cliff. He landed the air-car beside the stone castle, and went back into the saloon. All was as before. Navarth sat glaring at the three captives, who regarded him with loathing.

Gersen gave Navarth one of the projacs. "If there is difficulty kill all three. I go to look for Drusilla and Jheral Tinzy. You must guard with care!"

Navarth laughed wildly. "Who can trick a mad poet? I know him this instant: I intend to keep the weapon at his throat."

Gersen could not restrain a sense of misgiving. Navarth was not the most stable of guardians. "Remember! If he escapes, we are lost. He may want a glass of water; let him thirst. His bonds may be too tight. He must suffer! Show no mercy if there is interference from outside. Shoot all three."

"With pleasure."

"Very well. Keep your madness in check till I return!"

Gersen went to the door through which three weeks previously the sodden band of pilgrims had entered. The door was locked; he blasted away the hardware and entered.

There was no sound. The dank rooms were empty. Gersen went down the hall, descended by the way the girl in blue velvet had taken him, and finally found the banquet room, now dim, smelling faintly of perfume and wine.

Gersen moved more cautiously. From the banquet room a way led down to the garden. Another must lead to Viole Falushe's apartments.

Gersen checked the walls, and, finally, behind a hanging found a narrow door of heavy wood barred with metal. Once again he burnt his way through.

A spiral staircase led down into the chamber to the back of the circular foyer.

Gersen searched the room. He found a black leather notebook containing exhaustive notes upon the psychology of Jheral Tinzy, and the various methods by which Viole Falushe hoped to win her. It seemed that Viole Falushe wanted more than love: he wanted submission, abject quivering abasement derived from a mingling of love and fear.

So far, reflected Gersen, Viole Falushe had fallen short in his goal. He tossed the portfolio aside. On the wall was a telescreen. Gersen turned a knob. Drusilla Wayles wearing a white robe sat on a bed. She was pale, thin, but apparently unharmed.

Gersen turned the knob. He looked out upon a gloomy area of sand among tall rock pinnacles. To the back were five dark deodars, a little cabin hardly larger than a dollhouse. Sitting on a bench was a girl about fourteen years old: a girl almost identical to Drusilla. She wore a transparent white gown; her face had a peculiarly sweet, peculiarly pensive expression, as if she had only just awakened from a pleasant dream. From the side came a tall non-human creature, walking on thin black-furred legs. It stopped beside the girl, spoke in a thin high-pitched voice. The girl responded without interest.

Gersen turned the knob again, to bring into view a terrace in front of what appeared to be a temple. Inside could be glimpsed the statue of a divinity. On the steps stood another Drusilla, this one sixteen years old, wearing only a kirtle and a copper fillet to confine her hair. Elsewhere were other men and women, similarly dressed. To the side was the suggestion of a shore, with water beyond.

Gersen turned the knob again, again, again. He looked into various environments, various types of rooms and cages. They contained an assortment of boys, girls, youths, maidens, young men and women, sometimes separate, sometimes together. Here were Viole Falushe's experiments, from which he evidently extracted a voyeur's pleasure... Gersen saw no more versions of Drusilla. Urgency prickled at his nerves, stemming from his lack of faith in Navarth; he set off along the hall, and crossing the bridge he entered the laboratory section to the west. Here was the locale of the experiments, in cages and chambers behind one-way mirrors.

Gersen found Retz, the stoop-shouldered technician, sitting in a small office. He looked up, startled at the sight of Gersen. "What do you do here? Are you a guest? The master will be displeased!"

"I am master now." Gersen displayed the projac. "Where is the girl who resembles Jheral Tinzy?"

Retz blinked, half-defiant, half-doubtful. "I can tell you nothing."

Gersen struck him with the gun. "Quick. The girl who came here three weeks ago."

Retz began to whine. "What can I tell you? Viole Falushe will punish me."

"Viole Falushe is a prisoner." Gersen leveled the gun. "Take me to the girl, or I will kill you."

Retz made a despairing sound. "He will do terrible things to me."

"No longer."

Retz waved his arms, walked down the corridor. Suddenly he stopped, turned around. "You say he is your prisoner?"

"He is."

"What do you plan to do with him?"

"Kill him."

"And what of the Palace?"

"We shall see. Take me to the girl."

"Will you leave me here, in charge of the palace?"

"I will kill you unless you make haste."

Disconsolately Retz moved on. Gersen spoke to him. "What has Viole Falushe done to her?"

"Nothing yet."

"What did he plan?"

"An auto-fertilization: a virgin birth, so to speak. In due course she would bear a female child precisely like herself."

"Jheral Tinzy gave birth to her in this way?"

"Exactly."

"And how many others?"

"Six others. Then she killed herself."

"Where are the other five?"

"Ah! As to that I can't say."

Retz was lying, but Gersen allowed the statement to go unchallenged.

Retz paused by a door, looked craftily over his shoulder. "The girl is within. Whatever she reports, you must remember that I am only an underling here; I only obey orders."

"Then you'll obey mine. Open the door." Retz hesitated a final instant, with a glance over Gersen's shoulder down the hall, as if hoping against hope for succor. He sighed, slid back the door. Drusilla, sitting on the bed, looked up with alarm. She saw Gersen; her expression changed from astonishment to joy. She jumped up from the bed, ran to Gersen, sobbed in relief. "I hoped you'd come. They've done such dreadful things to me!"

Retz thought to take advantage of Gersen's distraction and started to slink away. Gersen called him back. "Not so fast. I have use for you." He spoke to Drusilla. "Has Viole Falushe shown himself to you? Will you recognize him?"

"He came to stand in the doorway with the light at his back. He did not want me to see him. He was savage; he hated me. He said I had been faithless. I asked how this was possible since I had promised him nothing. He became absolutely cold. He said that it had been my duty to wait, to maintain my ideals, until he had come. And even then, he said, I had played him false, at Navarth's party and also along the journey."

Gersen said, "One thing is certain then: he is Tanzel or Ethuen or Mario. Which did you like the least?"

"Tanzel."

"Tanzel, eh? Well, Retz here will show us certainly which is Viole Falushe, will you not, Retz?"

"How can I? He has never shown himself to me, except behind the glass of his office."

Unlikely, thought Gersen. Still, not impossible. "Where are the other daughters of Jheral Tinzy?"

"Six there were," muttered Retz. "Viole Falushe killed the two oldest. There is one on Alphanor, this one—" he indicated Drusilla "—was sent to Earth. The youngest is to the east of the Palace, where the mountains meet the sea. The next is priestess to the god Arodin, on the large island directly to the east."

"Retz," said Gersen, "I hold Viole Falushe a captive. I am your new master. Do you understand this?"

Retz nodded sulkily. "If this is how it must be."

"Can you identify Viole Falushe?"

"He is a tall man, he has dark hair; he can be harsh or soft; cruel or easy. Beyond that I do not know."

"These are my orders to you. Liberate these poor captives."

"Impossible!" fluted Retz. "They know no other life than their peculiar environments. The open air, the sun, the sky — they would go mad!"

"This is your task then. As gently and easily as possible, bring them forth. I will return shortly and see how well you have done your job. Further, make known to the folk in the garden that they are no longer slaves, that they are free to go or stay. Mind you, I will pen you in a closet and punish you for your crimes if you do not obey me."

"I will obey," muttered Retz. "I am accustomed to obedience; I know nothing else."

Gersen took Drusilla's arm. "I worry about Navarth. We dare not be gone too long."

But when they returned up through the castle and out to the air-car, circumstances were as before. The three captives were secure and Navarth held the weapon unblinkingly at their heads. His eyes glowed at the sight of Drusilla. "What of Jheral Tinzy?"

"She is dead. But she had daughters. There are others. What has transpired while I was gone?"

"Talk. Blandishments. Persuasion. Threats."

"Of course. Who was most insistent?"

"Tanzel."

Gersen turned Tanzel a cool inspection. Tanzel shrugged. "Do you think I enjoy sitting here trussed like a chicken?"

"One of you is Viole Falushe," said Gersen. "Which? I wonder... Well, we must undo more of the dreadful mischief performed in the name of love."

He took the air-car aloft, cruised slowly east over the mountains. At the ocean's edge, where the crags submerged into the water, a gloomy defile opened upon a narrow gray beach. Behind was a sandy open area perhaps an acre in extent. Gersen lowered the air-car into the shadows and landed. He jumped out. Drusilla IV, the youngest of the group, came slowly forward. From a fissure to the back two non-human nursemaids made angry chattering sounds. The girl asked, "Are you The Man? The Man who is coming to love me?"

Gersen grinned. "I am a man, true enough, but who is The Man?"

Drusilla IV looked vaguely toward the fissure. "*They* have told me of The Man. There is one of me, and one of him, and when I see him I must love him. This is what I have learned."

"But you have never seen this 'man'?"

"No. You are the first 'man' I have ever seen. The first person like myself. You are wonderful!"

"There are many men in the world," said Gersen. "They told you a falsehood. Come aboard, I will show you other men, and a girl like yourself."

Drusilla IV looked around the dreary defile in alarm and bewilderment. "Will you take me from here? I am frightened."

"You need not be," said Gersen. "Come aboard now."

"Of course." She took his hand trustingly and entered the saloon. At the sight of the passengers she halted in astonishment. "I never knew so many people existed!" She examined Mario, Ethuen and Tanzel critically. "I don't like them. They have foolish wicked faces." She turned to Gersen. "I like you. You are the first man I have ever seen. You must be The Man, and I will stay with you forever."

Gersen watched the faces of Mario, Ethuen, Tanzel. This must make poor hearing for Viole Falushe. All sat stony-faced, glaring at Gersen with equal degrees of detestation — Except at the corner of Tanzel's mouth, a tiny muscle twitched.

Gersen took the air-car aloft and flew out toward the largest of the islands; almost immediately he spied the temple looming above a village of cane and frond. Gersen landed the air-car in the square, while villagers watched in amazement and alarm.

From the temple sauntered Drusilla III, a girl confident and self-possessed, exactly identical to the other Drusillas, yet in some sense different, as the other two were different.

Once more Gersen alighted from the air-car. Drusilla III inspected him with candid interest. "Who are you?"

"I come from the mainland," said Gersen. "I come to speak to you."

"You want a rite performed? Go elsewhere. Arodin is impotent. I have beseeched him to send me elsewhere, among other boons. There is no response."

Gersen looked into the temple. "That is his likeness within?"

"Yes. I am priestess to the cult."

"Let us go to look at the image."

"There is nothing to see: a statue sitting on a throne."

Gersen went into the temple. At the far end sat a figure twice as large as life. The head was rudely defaced: nose, ears, chin broken away. Gersen turned to Drusilla III in wonder. "Who damaged the statue?"

"I did."

"Why?"

"I did not like his face. According to the Rote, Arodin must come in the flesh to take me for his bride. I am enjoined to pray to the statue for the earliest nuptials possible. I broke the face, to delay the process. I do not like being a priestess but I am allowed to be nothing else. I hoped that after I defiled the image another priestess might be appointed. This has not occurred. Will you take me away?"

"Yes. Arodin is no god, he is a man." Gersen took Drusilla III into the saloon, pointed out Mario, Ethuen, Tanzel. "Observe the three men. Does one of them resemble the statue of Arodin, before you defaced it?"

One of the men blinked.

"Yes," said Drusilla III. "Yes indeed. There is the face of Arodin." She pointed to Tanzel, the man who had blinked.

Tanzel cried out, "Here, here! What's going on? What are you trying to do?"

"I want to identify Viole Falushe," said Gersen.

"Why pick on me? I'm not Arodin, nor Viole Falushe, nor yet Beelzebub, for that matter. I'm good old Harry Tanzel of London, no more no less, and I'll thank you to take these ropes from my arms."

"In due course," said Gersen. "In due course." He turned to Drusilla III. "You're sure that he is Arodin?"

"Of course. Why is he tied?"

"I suspect him of being a criminal."

Drusilla III laughed, a clear merry sound. "What a dreadful joke! A man like that putting up a statue to himself and calling himself a god! What did he hope to gain?"

"You."

"Me? All this effort for me?"

"He wanted you to love him, to worship him."

Again Drusilla III's laughter rang through the ship. "A great deal of wasted effort."

And Gersen, watching closely, thought to see a pink flush seep across Tanzel's face. "You are ready to leave here?"

"Yes... Who are these other girls, who so resemble me?"

"Your sisters."

"How strange."

"Yes. Viole Falushe — or Arodin, if you prefer — is a strange man."

Gersen took the air-car aloft, set it to cruising slowly on the automatic pilot while he cogitated. Still no absolute proof to the identity of Viole Falushe. A twitch of the mouth, a seep of color, a defaced countenance: interesting but hardly incontrovertible evidence... Essentially he was no closer to the identity of Viole Falushe than when he set out on the journey. He looked back into the saloon. Navarth had become bored with his duties and was watching the girls with a half-expectant half-forlorn expression: perhaps by some miracle they would merge to become his own Jheral Tinzy.

Gersen sifted his courses of action. They were few. If he had access to one or another of the truth drugs, Viole Falushe's identity would emerge swiftly enough... There was no one at the Palace of Love who could recognize Viole Falushe, probably no one at the cities Atar or Kouhila. On Earth Navarth knew Viole Falushe's call-code... Gersen rubbed his chin. "Navarth!"

Navarth came into the pilot's compartment. Gersen indicated the communication system, gave instructions. Navarth grinned from ear to ear.

Gersen went back to the saloon, seated himself near Tanzel. He looked through into the pilot's compartment, nodded to Navarth.

Navarth tapped Viole Falushe's call-code. Gersen bent forward. At the lobe of Tanzel's ear sounded a faint whir — an almost imperceptible vibration. Tanzel jerked, strained at his bonds.

Navarth spoke softly into the forward microphone. "Viole Falushe. Can you hear me? Viole Falushe!"

Tanzel jerked around, to meet Gersen's appraising stare. There could be no more dissembling; Viole Falushe was unmasked. A look of desperation came over his face; he writhed against his bonds.

"Viole Falushe," said Gersen. "The time has come."

"Who are you?" gasped Viole Falushe. "IPCC?"

Gersen made no answer. Navarth came back.

"So this is he. I knew it all the time. He inflicted me with chill. Where is Jheral Tinzy, Vogel?"

Viole Falushe licked his lips. "You two have plotted to kill me."

Gersen and Navarth carried him forward, into the pilot's compartment, closed the door communicating with the saloon.

"Why?" cried Viole Falushe. "Why must you do this to me?"

Navarth turned to Gersen. "Do you need me?"

"No."

"Goodby, Vogel," said Navarth. "You have lived a remarkable life." He went back into the saloon.

Gersen slowed the air-car to a hover. He opened the port. Ten thousand feet below spread the ocean.

"Why? Why? Why?" cried Viole Falushe. "Why do you do this to me?"

Gersen spoke in a dry voice. "You are a monomaniac. I am the same. When I was a child the five Demon Princes brought their ships to Mount Pleasant. Do you recall?"

"Long ago, oh so long ago!"

"They destroyed, they killed, they enslaved. Everything I loved: family, friends, all destroyed. The Demon Princes are my obsession. I have killed two of them. You will be the third. I am not Henry Lucas the journalist. I am Kirth Gersen, and all my life is aimed toward — this." He stepped toward Viole Falushe, who made a terrible wrenching exertion. His bonds snapped; he lurched, flung out his arms and toppled back and out the port. Gersen watched the long figure drifting down toward the ocean, until it passed from sight. Then he closed the port, returned to the saloon. Navarth had already released Mario and Ethuen.

"My apologies to you," said Gersen. "I hope you have not been seriously injured."

Ethuen gave him a look of unspeakable dislike; Mario made a muttering sound in his throat.

"Well, then," said Navarth cheerfully. "What now?"

"We will pick up our friends," said Gersen. "No doubt they are wondering what is to become of them."

"Then what?" growled Ethuen. "How are we to find our way back to Sogdian? We have no spaceship."

Gersen laughed. "Were you deceived? This is Sogdian. That is the sun Miel. How could you not notice?"

"Why should I? A lunatic pilot careened through the cluster for hours."

"A subterfuge. Zog was no lunatic. But he was careless; he performed no acclimatization routine; when he flung open the port there was no difference in pressure or composition. The light was the same intensity; the gravity was the same, the sky was the same color, the clouds the same shape, the flora of the same type."

"I noticed nothing," said Navarth. "But I am no space traveler. I feel no shame. If I ever return to Earth, I shall never depart again."

"First: a stop at the city Kouhila. The folk will be pleased to learn that they need pay no further taxes."

At Atar, Gersen found the Distis Pharaon as he had left it. Mario, Wible and daNossa had spaceboats of their own; the other guests were conveyed back to the Oikumene by the ship which Viole Falushe had ordered for their use. Navarth and the three Drusillas came aboard the Pharaon. Gersen flew them to New Wexford and put them aboard the packet for Earth. "I will send you money," he told Navarth. "It will be for the girls. You must make sure that they are raised properly."

"I have done my best with Zan Zu," said Navarth gruffly. "She is raised. What is amiss with her? The others will need more care."

"Exactly. And when I am next on Earth I will see you."

"Good. We will sit on the deck of my houseboat and drink my fine wine." Navarth turned away. Gersen took a deep breath, went to say goodby to Drusilla Wayles. She came close to him, took his hands. "Why can't I come with you? Wherever you go."

"I can't explain to you. But—no. Not now. I tried it once, to no avail."

"I would be different."

"I know you are. But there might be worse problems. I might not be able to part with you."

"Will I ever see you again?"

"I don't think so."

Drusilla turned away. "Goodby," she said listlessly.

Gersen took a step after her, halted, then swung around and went his way.

Gersen chartered a freight carrier and took it to the Palace of Love. The gardens seemed wild, less well-tended. An indefinable gloom had come over the airy structures.

Retz greeted him with cautious cordiality. "I have been doing your bidding. Slowly, easily, not to disturb or alarm."

He took Gersen on a tour of the special environments; he described the weird and intricate thought-patterns Viole Falushe had imposed upon his young victims. One by one the victims were emerging into the upper air, some astonished, some delighted, some dazzled and frightened and whimpering to return.

The villages in the garden had changed. Many of the Fortunate Folk had departed; others had returned from the backlands with their children. In time the Palace of Love would become a remote farm community.

Gersen could not leave Viole Falushe's books to moulder. He loaded them aboard the freighter and consigned them to the care of Jehan Addels at New Wexford. With a final admonition for Retz, Gersen himself departed, and flew off through the stars of Sirneste Cluster, back toward the Oikumene.

Months later, sitting on the Esplanade at Avente, on Alphanor, Gersen saw a young woman approaching. She wore fashionable garments in the best of taste, she obviously had been raised in an atmosphere of gentility and good manners.

On a sudden impulse Gersen stepped forward. "Please excuse me," he said, "but you resemble someone I know on Earth. Are your parents Earth-folk?"

The girl listened without embarrassment. She shook her head. "This may seem strange, but I do not know my parents. I may be an orphan, or —" she made a rueful little grimace "— something else. My guardians receive money to provide a home for me. Do you know my parents? Tell me, please!"

Gersen thought, what in the world am I up to? Why disturb the girl with the details of her background, or worse, the nightmare she had so narrowly avoided? For here, certainly, was Viole Falushe's urgent business on Alphanor.

Gersen pretended doubt. "I'm mistaken — I think. The resemblance must be a coincidence. You could not possibly be the person I thought you to be."

"I don't believe you," said Drusilla I. "You know, but you won't tell. I wonder why not?"

Gersen grinned. The girl was immensely appealing, with a thousand charms and graces. "Sit here on the bench a moment. I'll read you a ballad or two from the works of the mad poet Navarth. When he wrote them he might have been thinking of you."

Drusilla I seated herself. "An unconventional way to start an acquaintance. But I'm an unconventional person... Well then, read the poetry."

About the Author

Jack Vance was born in 1916 to a well-off California family that, as his childhood ended, fell upon hard times. As a young man he worked at a series of unsatisfying jobs before studying mining engineering, physics, journalism and English at the University of California Berkeley. Leaving school as America was going to war, he found a place as an ordinary seaman in the merchant marine. Later he worked as a rigger, surveyor, ceramicist, and carpenter before his steady production of sf, mystery novels, and short stories established him as a full-time writer.

His output over more than sixty years was prodigious and won him three Hugo Awards, a Nebula Award, a World Fantasy Award for lifetime achievement, as well as an Edgar from the Mystery Writers of America. The Science Fiction and Fantasy Writers of America named him a grandmaster and he was inducted into the Science Fiction Hall of Fame.

His works crossed genre boundaries, from dark fantasies (including the highly influential *Dying Earth* cycle of novels) to interstellar space operas, from heroic fantasy (the *Lyonesse* trilogy) to murder mysteries featuring a sheriff (the Joe Bain novels) in a rural California county. A Vance story often centered on a competent male protagonist thrust into a dangerous, evolving situation on a planet where adventure was his daily fare, or featured a young person setting out on a perilous odyssey over difficult terrain populated by entrenched, scheming enemies.

Late in his life, a world-spanning assemblage of Vance aficionados came together to return his works to their original form, restoring material cut by editors whose chief preoccupation was the page count of a pulp magazine. The result was the complete and authoritative *Vance Integral Edition* in 44 hardcover volumes. Spatterlight Press is now publishing the VIE texts as ebooks, and as print-on-demand paperbacks.

Colophon

This book was printed using Adobe Arno Pro as the primary text font, with NeutraFace used on the cover.

This title was created from the digital archive of the Vance Integral Edition, a series of 44 books produced under the aegis of the author by a worldwide group of his readers. The VIE project gratefully acknowledges the editorial guidance of Norma Vance, as well as the cooperation of the Department of Special Collections at Boston University, whose John Holbrook Vance collection has been an important source of textual evidence.

Special thanks to R.C. Lacovara, Patrick Dusoulier, Koen Vyverman, Paul Rhoads, Chuck King, Gregory Hansen, Suan Yong, and Josh Geller for their invaluable assistance preparing final versions of the source files.

Source: Marc Herant; Digitize: Mark Adams, Richard Chandler, Charles King, Suan Hsi Yong; Diff: Patrick Dusoulier, Alun Hughes, Hans van der Veeke; Tech Proof: Patrick Dusoulier; Text Integrity: Patrick Dusoulier, Alun Hughes, Rob Friefeld, Steve Sherman; Implement: Derek W. Benson, Joel Hedlund; Security: Paul Rhoads; Compose: John A. Schwab; Comp Review: Marcel van Genderen, Charles King, Bob Luckin; Update Verify: Bob Luckin, Paul Rhoads; RTF-Diff: Patrick Dusoulier, Bill Schaub; Textport: Patrick Dusoulier; Proofread: Neil Anderson, Michel Bazin, Mark Bradford, Deborah Cohen, Patrick Dusoulier, Rob Gerrand, Martin Green, Lucie Jones, Robert Melson, Simon Read, Dirk Jan Verlinde

Artwork (maps based on original drawings by Jack and Norma Vance):

Paul Rhoads, Christopher Wood

Book Composition and Typesetting: Joel Anderson

Art Direction and Cover Design: Howard Kistler

Proofing: Christian J. Corley, Steve Sherman

Jacket Blurb: Matt Hughes

Management: John Vance, Koen Vyverman